A STATEMENT

TO SCIENCE FICTION READERS

DAW Books is a new publishing company designed for one specific purpose—to publish science fiction. That is our only directive. DAW Books derives its name from the initials of its publisher and editor, Donald A. Wollheim, who has been in the forefront of science fiction all his life. As a fan, as a writer, as an anthologist, and for the last three decades as the editor whose work has most consistently found favor in the eyes of those who spend their money for science fiction in paperback books.

Donald A. Wollheim is those readers' best guarantee that behind every book bearing his initials is the experience and the work of someone who likes what science fiction readers like, and who will do his best to give it to them.

This is DAW Books . . . the science fiction of today that is most likely to produce the classic fantasy of tomorrow.

DAW Books' contract with its distributor contains a stipulation that no other publisher's contract contains. That is that every DAW Book must be one that has never appeared previously in a paperbound edition. Thus, you can always be assured that, besides being the selection of an expert, the DAW Book you buy will not be something you may have bought once before with a different cover.

DAW equals

DAW Books

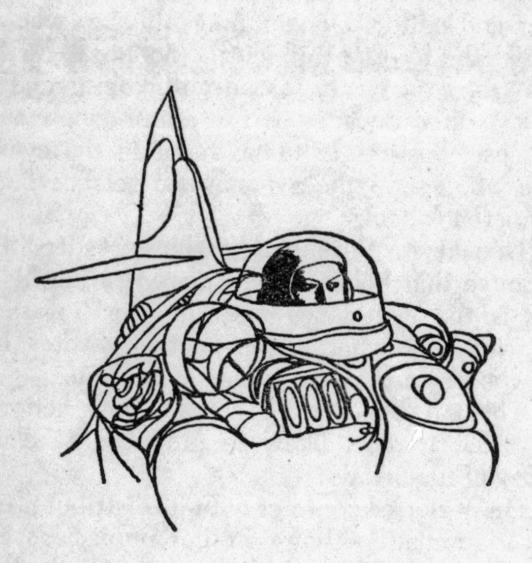

THE MIND BEHIND THE EYE

JOSEPH GREEN

DAW BOOKS, INC.
DONALD A. WOLLHEIM, PUBLISHER
1301 Avenue of the Americas
New York, N. Y. 10019

A DAW Book, by arrangement with the author

A hardbound edition of this novel has been published
in Great Britian under the title of *Gold the Man*,
by Victor Gollancz, Ltd.

Cover art by Josh Kirby.

Second Printing, April, 1972

DAW sf BOOKS

PRINTED IN CANADA

COVER PRINTED IN U.S.A.

chapter 1

GOLD WAS STANDING at his third-floor office window, gazing across the meticulously kept lawn with its mathematically-spaced trees, when the aircar crossed the stone wall surrounding the estate a quarter of a mile away. He saw it for only a brief second, out of the corner of his left eye. It was moving low and fast, heading straight for the house.

Gold was facing north. He turned quickly to the east, and was just in time to catch a brief shimmer of light on silver as a second car passed behind the corner and out of his sight. He swung his gaze back to the peaceful lawn and the misty green tops of the Catskills in the distance, feeling a touch of grim amusement. Only one Earth authority affected that peculiar silvery colour and intruded on a citizen's estate in such an unannounced fashion. Gold was about to be visited by emissaries of the Peacekeeper.

A faint but nagging memory of an object flying into his vision from the left intruded into Gold's conscious mind, at a time when he should be thinking of defending his home. After a moment he realized this was one of those forceful upwellings from his storage banks that seemed to occur at odd times and over which he had little control. He received an associated impression that this was a relatively short scene, and decided to reply rather than exert himself to repress it. Nothing he could do would actually stop the Peacekeeping force.

Gold seated himself in his specially made chair, tilted back, placed his feet on the shining desk-top, and replayed the insistent memory.

Albert was walking with head lowered, breathing the hot muggy air in shallow gasps, his mind virtually blanked out, not actually seeing. And suddenly, impossibly, a man came flying into his vision from the extreme left, a man skittering along like a wind-driven leaf, upright but with feet dragging on the asphalt, body tilted slightly forward, arms loose at his sides. There was a curious, unreal balance to the torso, as though it were held erect only by momentum. He moved further into view, more toward the centre of the eye, and then it was obvious the hurtling form was over sixty feet away. The startling manner in which he had intruded into Albert's field of view had made him seem closer. He was actually flying along the road, a few inches above the hard surface. And then the man's upper body slowly tilted forward. The unbalance grew more and more pronounced, until the trunk was almost horizontal. He hit the pavement in a long sliding dive, skidded several times his length, and lay still.

Only then did Albert hear the soft muffled thump! that had been trying to register on his ear for the past two seconds.

The scene brightened and firmed up; Gold knew where his younger self was and what he had been doing. Albert was fifteen and already a man in height, though far from the six-foot seven and 240 pounds Gold would attain as an adult. He had just run away from the Institute for the fifth time, on this trip getting into a low density area somewhere in South Alabama. It was in the middle of summer, and the long walk from the automated highway, where he had stolen a ride in the back of one of the radio-controlled vans, had left him weak and dizzy. He had been walking down the old-fashioned concrete pavement in the centre of a sleepy little town, intent on buying food with money he had stolen from the Institute, when the accident occurred.

And that was all it had been, a simple accident. A man had been hit by a car, a solid blow just below the hips. The impact had hurled him sideways into Albert's line of sight, propelling him across the road in that abrupt and unnatural manner. In this part of the world there were still personally controlled autos without impact radars or automatic brakes.

An excited crowd began to gather. Albert walked on, and from an air-conditioned booth in the front of the nearest restaurant he watched the traffic monitors appear and gather up the broken form of the victim. After eating he checked into an ancient hotel, took a long nap, and called the hospital; to his immense surprise the man was not dead, and would fully recover.

Gold pulled himself out of the scene after completing the phone call. The rest was vague, imprinted only on his secondary memory and not recoverable in detail. But that had been the start of a grudging respect on the part of his younger self, an admission that *Homo sapiens* possessed at least one quality he could admire. They were a tough species.

Gold put his feet down and activated the TV monitors controlled by a small panel in the massive desk. That short re-run from his permanent memory had taken less than sixty seconds. From the outside cameras facing east and west he saw that the two aircars were just settling to the manicured lawn. The instant they were down five men wearing the spotless white uniforms of the Peacekeeper jumped from each vehicle and scrambled for the nearest doors, leaving the drivers sitting in front of turret-mounted rapid-fire twin darters. Within two minutes from the time the men in white had invaded Gold's property they were storming inside the house.

Belatedly, Gold's private guard force responded to the invasion. A siren wailed and armed men poured out of the small guardhouse just to the south of the main building. As they appeared a loudspeaker on the west side car boomed, "THIS IS A U.N. PEACEKEEPER FORCE! DROP YOUR ARMS AND PUT YOUR HANDS BEHIND YOUR HEAD! REPEAT, DROP YOUR ARMS AND PUT YOUR HANDS BEHIND YOUR HEAD!"

The twin muzzles of the darters had swung to cover the milling men. Gold glanced at the east side—the twenty-eight cameras in the system could be shown selectively on four viewscreens inlaid in the desk-top—and saw that the second silvery car had also landed where its darters could cover the guardhouse. All the men who had hurried outside had no choice but to lay down their arms, or see themselves stretched unconscious on the ground. The Peacekeepers never killed, but being knocked out by one of their darts was an unpleasant experience.

The five men on the west entered through the French doors on the ground floor, brushed two startled maids out of the way, and ran for the stairs. Gold switched cameras to follow their progress. On the second floor a jittery guard carrying a handgun emerged from a door facing the stairwell just as they passed. He stopped, confused and afraid, and Gold's audio picked up the hiss of hand darters. Two tiny projectiles hit the guard's chest and he collapsed, almost instantly unconscious from nerve shock. On the top floor the stairs opened on to a narrow hall, where two armed men sat before a communications console similar to Gold's. They had drawn their handguns but kept them pointed towards the floor, obviously well aware that resistance was not only futile but would result in a charge of obstruction of the peace.

The officer with the Peacekeepers saw the guards' uncertainty and tersely motioned to them to lay down their arms. The men did so with obvious relief; their loyalty to their employer was apparently weak.

"Where is Gold?" demanded the officer, motioning to the four doors opening on to the hall. When the men hesitated he added, "*Answer!* Or be charged with conspiring against the peace!"

One of the men hastily gestured toward the correct room. Gold closed the panel over his monitor screens and put his feet back on the desk. As he looked up his door abruptly opened and the officer stepped inside, coming in at an angle that took him out of the opening. He stopped with his back against the wall, dartgun in hand, looking somewhat foolish.

Gold lowered his feet to the floor and leisurely stood. "It took you almost three minutes from the time you trespassed on my property until you reached this office, Lieutenant," he said coolly. "As a heavy taxpayer I'd like to see a little more efficiency in your operations."

The officer hesitated a second, then holstered his darter. Standing very straight he asked, "Sir, are you Albert Aaron Golderson?"

Gold let his heavy lips form the faintly supercilious smile that he knew irritated most people. He took three light, easy steps and stood towering over the smaller man, staring down into his face. "I am Gold," he said softly.

"Sir, it is my duty to inform you that you have been declared to be in the protective custody of the Peacekeeper." The white-clad officer kept both face and voice carefully expressionless as he rapidly droned through the ritual of arrest, but he could not hide the dislike in the eyes that stared up at Gold.

When the words that safeguarded his rights were all said Gold asked, "Am I permitted to know where you are taking me?"

"Your specific destination when under the protection of the Peacekeeper may not be revealed to you. If you will follow me, please?"

"Why of course, Lieutenant!" Gold said with obviously false heartiness, and trailed the white uniform out of the door and down the stairs. As they stepped outside he placed a large hand on the shorter man's shoulder in an unduly friendly manner. If the crisply correct officer was annoyed by the familiarity he gave no sign of it as he courteously motioned for Gold to enter the aircar ahead of him.

A moment later they were climbing into the cool clear air of the Catskills, newly green with spring. In ten minutes they reached the outer limits of the sprawling Air New York complex, and locked on to the automatic control grid. After another five minutes of straight line flying, broken by abrupt turns into and out of carefully supervised air corridors, they flashed by the massive white spires of the Peacekeeper's Tower and settled on the roof of the old United Nations Building on the East River. His captors ushered him out of the car and into an elevator. Gold was mildly surprised at their destination, but refrained from asking questions. Three minutes later, when the Lieutenant opened an inconspicuous door in a side corridor on the nineteenth floor and motioned him inside, Gold was glad he had not asked.

There were two men waiting in the small office, two of the three most important persons on Earth. Standing facing him was Tharanjit Theta, now serving his second six-year term as Secretary General of the United Nations. The man seated behind the small desk was Carl Frederick von Hessel, the Peacekeeper.

Gold looked around the small office, letting his mouth curl into easy insolence. "And what junior clerk's little hide-away did you commandeer to arrange this important meeting?"

"Please sit down, Mr. Gold," said the frail, grey-haired Indian executive, indicating a chair with one wrinkled dark hand. "We won't waste your time and ours with unnecessary words. We have a proposition to put to you, and we hope most sincerely that you will accept it. I cannot overemphasize how important it is that you do."

"Having me arrested and brought here under duress is a very poor base on which to make a proposition, gentlemen," Gold replied, his voice cold.

Von Hessel pushed back his chair, rose, and said, "Mr. Gold, you are not under arrest." He had a strong clear orator's voice, with only a faint trace of German accent. "For two days I tried to reach you and for two days your secretary denied you were there. But we knew you were. Not many men make themselves unavailable to the Peacekeeper, Mr. Gold. What we must discuss is too urgent to permit further delay and I had to forcefully bring you to us. But you are free to leave when you choose."

"Really?" said Gold, getting to his feet. "In that case I see no point in my lingering here." He turned toward the door. The Secretary General took a step toward him, angry words on his thin brown lips. The Peacekeeper held up a restraining hand. "Let him go," he said calmly.

Gold yanked open the door. The hall was empty. He walked swiftly to the elevator, pressed the "down" button, and stood impatiently waiting. When the doors slid back he stepped inside, held a finger in the air over "lobby," and paused. Nothing happened. He touched the "open" button instead, and walked briskly down the hall to the tiny office. He entered without knocking, to find Theta pacing the floor and wringing his long patrician hands. Von Hessel was again sitting behind the desk, wearing a grim, slightly amused smile.

"Now what can I do for you gentlemen?" asked Gold as he seated himself.

The angry Indian was staring at Gold with a dislike which, unlike the young peacekeeping officer, he made no attempt to hide. "You are an arrogant and presumptuous young man, Mr. Gold," he said at last. "My purpose in being here was only to assure you of the importance of the request von Hessel will make, and that it has my support. I do not share Petrovna's optimistic belief that you will accept the assignment. I bid you good day."

The dignified old man turned and walked out, closing the door firmly behind him. Gold felt a stir of genuine interest. This was the first time Petrovna's name had been mentioned.

"I will be brief, Mr. Gold," said von Hessel, leaning across the small desk. "After twenty-eight years of working in darkness, unable to do more than defend ourselves against each new attempt by the Exterminators, we have a chance to learn why they are trying to destroy us. No news was released on Earth, but we captured one member of the last attacking force, alive. You will recall their ship was on a collision course with the moon when it slowed below faster-than-light speed, and we made an area hit with a lunar orbiting missile while they were trying to change direction. What the public does not know is that one alien survived the explosion, escaping in a one-person planetary lander. He set it down on the moon and our defence people at the U.N. Moonbase took him prisoner. Unfortunately, the circumstances of his capture exposed him to a long period of oxygen deprivation. His brain was irreparably damaged and we were unable to obtain information from him by direct interrogation. Petrovna was flown to the moon shortly after the capture. He had no better luck than the others in restoring the lost mentality, but did suggest an alternative, which was adopted. When his plan was nearly ready it became obvious you are the only person on Earth who can put it into effect. I would guide you wrongly if more was said now. Will you accompany my men to the Moonbase and let Petrovna finish the explanation?"

Gold stared at the German in stony silence. The Peacekeeper met his gaze evenly, quietly waiting. At last Gold said, "You haven't actually told me very much. Is this job you have planned for me dangerous?"

"Indeed so. I would estimate that the odds are against your returning alive. But Petrovna says the time factor limits us to you as the only man able to perform the required functions. We did not bring you here to cause personal annoyance, Mr. Gold. Theta came because I felt seeing both of us would convince you of the urgent importance of this request." A wry smile touched his lips. "I would have arranged for the Coordinator of Defense also if I thought him needed."

Gold found himself accepting the Peacekeeper's words without scepticism. The Coordinator of Defense, an American, was in charge of all armed forces, the third man in the *troika* that ruled Earth.

"I do not want to be melodramatic," von Hessel went on, his voice lower, "but possibly the fate of humanity will rest on your shoulders if you accept this task."

"And what if, like Rand's Atlas, I choose to shrug?" Gold asked softly.

"Shrug?" The German looked bewildered a moment, and then the meaning of Gold's question cleared the semantic barriers. "Oh, a witticism. It would not matter, Mr. Gold. We need information. You will try to get this for us. If you do not—we cannot lose what we never had. Now, will you talk with Petrovna?"

"It seems that I'll be forced to if I want a straight answer," Gold said dryly.

Von Hessel flipped an intercom switch on the desk and spoke a few words in German. Ten minutes later Gold found himself on an SST, heading for Cape Kennedy. Forty-eight hours after leaving New York he was watching the approach of the scarred, barren surface of the moon. It had been an interesting, exciting trip, one of the few his money could not buy. The fact that Pavel Petrovna was waiting below added to a rarely experienced sense of excitement. The world's two genetically altered superbrains were at last to meet. For the first time since early adolescence Gold felt something of the awe and respect a young man should feel on meeting the wise and important leaders of mankind. He had to remind himself that Petrovna was only nine years older than his own twenty-eight. And then he remembered Petrovna had publicly declared that both he himself and Gold were merely normal men with slightly enlarged brains and extensive developmental training, not *Homo superior.* That was a mark against him. Gold had long ago stopped regarding himself as a *Homo sapiens.*

chapter 2

GOLD HAD READ descriptions of Petrovna and seen him on television several times, but he was not adequately prepared for the reality. The Russian's neck, thorax and hips were those of a large man, but the arms and legs were stunted appendages, small, apparently fragile extensions no larger than those of a child. He was almost five feet tall, but the proportions were wrong. The wide chest shaded off abruptly into tiny arms, and even the carefully made tunic he wore could not conceal their size. The short legs supporting him, obviously gnarled and bent as they were, had to be corded with muscle to support their disproportionate load. Most of his length was in his large man's trunk and head. The sleeves and trouser legs were overlarge, to hide the shape of the limbs, but left the little hands and feet free. Both seemed strong for their size, and capable. The impression of fragility was an illusion of size.

Petrovna's most striking feature was his massive head. Here the Russian geneticists had worked with great skill and particularity. Perfectly formed except for the slightly prognathous jaw that he shared with Gold, large in comparison to an ordinary man's but in balance with his wide chest and heavy torso, the head topped the misshapen edifice of his body like a perfect Parthenon above a ruined Acropolis. The features were heavy but clearly drawn, the wide forehead and flat planes of the cheeks lending an ascetic air to a face already lined with thought-wrinkles. The large dark eyes stared up at Gold from beneath prominent browridges, with a look that penetrated and stung. Gold met that piercing gaze with a brief, level stare, and for the first time since his twelfth birthday felt an impulse to lower his eyes. He was looking at someone whom he could honestly respect.

Petrovna took three steps from the lab bench covered with charts he had been scanning. His overlarge body swayed from side to side on the crooked legs like that of a drunken sailor, but he moved fast and well. Gold reluctantly put out his large hand and grasped the small one Petrovna extended. The two took each other's measure for a brief moment, hands still clasped, and then Petrovna dropped his grip and turned toward the table.

"Gold—I understand that you prefer that title and no other—may I introduce my assistant, Marina Syerov." Petrovna had a deep, strong voice that matched the size of his trunk. His international English was crisp and with little accent.

Gold acknowledged the introduction with a brief nod. Marina was a small woman, apparently of Mongolian ancestry, and barely taller than Petrovna. She was famous in her own right, and had been a rapidly rising star in the field of physiology, credited with two important discoveries before leaving graduate school in America, when she gave up an independent career to become Petrovna's assistant.

Unsmiling, Marina extended her hand as a man would, without speaking, and Gold held it a trifle longer than necessary. She lowered her eyes after a brief look at his face, and did not raise them again.

"I understand they told you nothing of our project here," Petrovna said as Marina turned back to her work.

"They told me only that it was terribly important I agree to accept some mysterious assignment. Apparently they feel I can save the world from those nasty little problems our visitors have been tossing at us every other year. I agreed to come because I had no choice but to believe them."

"I think that is overstating the case," said Petrovna carefully, "but it is true that the mission we have for you is extremely important. A look at our captive will do more to explain our situation than any words of mine. If you will follow me? And Marina, will you accompany us, please?"

Petrovna led the way toward the end of the long room opposite the entrance Gold's escort had used. The short Russian moved with ease in the light gravity, and as fast as he could without losing control of his momentum. Gold had found walking on the moon not nearly as difficult as he had imagined, and was already competent at it. He noticed as they strode down a narrow central corridor that the walls on each side were crowded with machinery, all of it in operation and manned by technicians who watched gauges, dials and lights with alert attention. By the time they reached a guarded door at the far end Gold realized the room resembled a utilities annex far more than a laboratory. A maze of pipes, ducts and conduits led from the various pieces of equipment to the wall they faced, twisting back and forth in a vast confusion of serpentine shapes. He recognized much of the machinery. A standard air compressor thudded softly in one corner. A small generator was whining slightly under a no-load condition, obviously ready to supply power instantly in an emergency. A huge air-conditioning unit extended an overhead duct of enormous size that terminated at the wall; to one side was the even larger return duct. Various other items of equipment he did not recognize were performing manifold functions he could not identify. Many of the simpler items he knew, like the generator, seemed to be operating without a load, as though on permanent standby against some extremely important possible failure.

The guard at the door turned his visitor's book around and extended it to Gold. He glanced at Petrovna, waiting for him to wave them through. After a moment Gold picked up the pen and signed. Petrovna meticulously signed in the "authorized by" column. The younger man smiled sourly as the Russian opened the door and gestured him forward.

Gold stepped through, paused, and despite himself felt the breath catch in his throat. His first stunned reaction was a sense of wonder that Earth's rulers had managed to keep this secret locked away on the moon. He had had no word on the capture of an alien until he heard it from von Hessel. Then he realized that the *troika* had kept the secret so well because it was an absolute imperative that they do so. If he was overcome with a sense of awe he had not known himself capable of feeling, the public at large would have collapsed in screaming hysterics.

They were standing in a room even longer than the equipment annex, and with a far higher ceiling. The walls were of worked rock, still bearing scars from the laser beams that had softened them and made it possible to gouge this huge chamber out of the tough igneous material. A series of floodlights ran down both walls, and others hung from the high ceiling on long drop-cords. A sleeping giant lay bathed in their pitiless white glare.

Petrovna had paused, as though knowing the effect it would have on the visitor. Gold glanced quickly at the stunted Russian and saw a faint but understanding smile. He turned back to the huge recumbent body before him, letting his gaze range from the gigantic head, towering above him like a living hill, to the massive thrust of shoulder running across the front of his vision like a cyclopean wall. The door had opened just behind the head. The great body blocked Gold's view of the interior of the cavern, other than what could be seen over the plateau of brown chest. Somehow the giant form gave the impression of extending endlessly into the distance, as though it went on forever.

Gold struggled to regain his sense of perspective. Slowly he realized that this sense of gigantic size was partially an illusion, a result of seeing that which was familiar grown distorted and unacceptably large. The human eye expected to see the human shape in a known size range.

"Your reaction is unexpectedly similar to that of most of our guests, Gold," said Petrovna, his voice edged with irony.

Instead of answering Gold walked past the hairless head to the rising arch of shoulder and placed a hand on the bare flesh. The temperature seemed unusually high, and there was a coarse, grainy feel to the skin.

Gold glanced up. Hanging above him was the huge, bulbous semi-circle of the sleeping giant's ear, misshapen and unusual solely due to size distortion. An odd, distant sigh reached his ear, like the murmur of a gentle breeze moving through thick forest, and he realized he was hearing the giant exhale.

Two technicians in white jumpsuits pushed a small cart to within a few feet of Gold and unhooked what appeared to be an insulated metal plate with an electrical cable attached. One man carefully positioned it on the curve of the shoulder while the other hovered over the cart's controls. As Gold watched, the man holding the device called "Ready!" and the second technician flipped a switch and turned a knob. The cart started humming. Gold turned back to the captive body and saw movement.

"Unexercised muscles degenerate rapidly under light gravity," said Petrovna, who had moved up by Gold. "And of course the lymph system is almost entirely powered by muscular action, as you will remember from your physiology training."

Gold watched the ropey shoulder muscle slowly contract into a hard knot and relax when the current decreased. When it was fully slack the cycle was repeated, growing faster and more rhythmic.

"We have two point-focus stimulators operating at all times," Petrovna said conversationally. "With the exception of the visceral muscles the body has suffered little deterioration."

Gold had partially recovered from the initial shock. "How do you feed him?" he asked curiously. "And what about body wastes? What condition is he in? I understand his brain was ruined by oxygen starvation."

"He is fed intravenously, of course, with a solution which ensures that there is no solid waste. The stomach is completely inactive; one of the problems awaiting us, I am afraid. As for your last question, let's discuss that when we've finished your tour. If you will follow me?"

Petrovna led Gold around the left shoulder, where a light metal ladder led steeply upward. They climbed it easily, Marina bringing up the rear, and Gold saw that a network of catwalks hung suspended in the air just above the body. Petrovna led them across the great shoulder to the centre of the chest, pausing just below the cliff of a chin. Dozens of men and women, most of them wearing the anonymous white jumpsuits of technicians, attended to a variety of duties, most of which were obviously concerned with keeping the Brobdingnagian body alive and healthy.

Petrovna led the way up a shorter ladder to the top of the chin. Gold climbed after him and saw that the catwalk diverged into two sections, one leading to each eye. Petrovna was already standing over the right pupil. Gold moved to join him, letting Marina follow alone.

Petrovna knelt and placed a hand at the bottom edge of the cornea, just under the eyelid. As Gold watched in amazement, the scientist lifted the entire brown circle to a vertical position; it was hinged on the upper end. Petrovna turned to face Gold, stepped backward through the two-foot wide hole, and calmly descended into the eyeball. Just before his face vanished he motioned with his head for Gold to follow.

The younger man knelt, imitated his host's backward scuttle, and found his feet on the rungs of a ladder when he eased them over the edge. Gold descended a few steps, until he touched a solid though rounded floor, and discovered he could not straighten up. The ceiling was too close.

Petrovna was standing a short distance away in the six-foot diameter room, the widest smile Gold had yet seen on his broad face. Behind him the short legs of Marina were descending the ladder. She closed the fake cornea behind her. It was impossibly crowded. The small woman immediately knelt and opened a narrow trap door almost beneath Gold's feet. She asked Petrovna a question in Russian, received an affirmative answer, and descended another ladder, closing the door and providing the two men with more standing room.

Gold still felt disoriented in the cramped area. After a moment he realized that he was accustomed to verticality and linearity in human construction, and this room was almost completely round. The floor on which he stood would become the back wall when the body sat erect. Immediately behind the ladder, which was obviously temporary, was a chair similar to those used by missile launch control officers, equipped with a seatbelt and relief tube. It was mounted on a rail for easy sliding. In front of the chair, and curving around it on three sides, was a large and complex console with a tilted face. A long flexible gooseneck sprang from the console's top and suspended a metal helmet just above the operator's head; it was obviously designed to be worn while in the chair. The console itself was anchored to the bottom half of the eyeball, in such a fashion that a man sitting in the chair would have his eyes only a few inches from the pupil, enabling him to look out. Gold saw the cavern ceiling far overhead. The pupil was made of some form of one-way glass. It had appeared opaque from outside the eye.

As Gold grew more accustomed to the room's roundness he realized that if the giant were sitting erect a man in the console chair would be in a normal operator's position. At present the chair was at the extreme rear of its track and tilted sharply forward. An operator could still grasp and operate all of the console's several hundred controls, though his arms would be reaching upward at a sharp angle.

"Examine the console, Gold, and I think you will see why we need you," said Petrovna.

Gold glanced at the short man, shrugged, and climbed into the chair. He fastened the seat belt, though he ignored the helmet overhead, flexed his fingers over the waiting knobs and switches, and lowered his hands to just above the blank, dead board. Then he pulled his shoulders back in a dramatic pianist's pose and held it a second before bringing the spread digits down in what should have been a crashing chord. Instantly he swung into a silent, prolonged introduction, the big fingers flickering over the uncaring face of the console with incredible speed. He leaned forward slightly, an awkward position with the console almost overhead, and began to move his feet as though pushing pedals. The trained pianist's fingers touched switch after powerless switch, button after button, so rapidly the eye could not follow them. He actually moved nothing.

As abruptly as he had begun Gold stopped, unstrapped, and swung lightly back to Petrovna's side. "Your control system seems unduly complicated," he said carelessly.

A sharp frown had appeared on the Russian's massive brow when Gold started his manic play; it slowly faded. Petrovna smiled slightly and said, "True, but it is as simple as we could design in the time allowed. What you see is the irreducible minimum of individual controls. Many of them must be operated in sequence, or together, to control a particular action by this almost-living body. I had originally planned to man that console myself, but that has now become impossible. Arm reach alone dictates that a large man must be the operator, and of course speed of movement and the generalized ability to operate an extremely complex mechanism are prerequisites. You probably thought this job required your brain. That is only partially true. Your physical size and training as a pianist are equally important."

"Some of the critics said I was a very bad pianist."

"True, you were." There was a hint of a smile on Petrovna's face. "But you achieved your objective, which was to earn enough money by your playing to begin your famous assault on the New York stock market. For our purposes your degree of competence does not matter. Even a poor classical pianist has the trained fingers required for rapid manipulation. And this is not the complete system. If you will follow me?"

The stunted scientist raised the door through which Marina

had disappeared. Gold followed him into a slightly larger square room just behind the eyeball, one crowded with equipment, and saw a second, smaller console mounted on what was now a wall. Most of the machinery was all apparently automatic in function. Unlike the master control console all of this equipment was in operation. Marina had a sideplate off the console and appeared to be making a series of delicate adjustments.

"This is the area where I will work," Petrovna said with a sweep of one small hand. "You will note that the controls I must reach are well within my limited physical capabilities. As you may have surmised, this is the autonomic systems room. The operational console enables an operator to direct the body's external movements. This one activates those internal functions which are a normal accompaniment to physical effort. In addition, all the vital processes which constitute life are monitored and controlled from here. Our living quarters are next."

Petrovna opened still another door beneath their feet, and this time motioned for his guest to precede him. Gold descended a third ladder and found himself in a still small but comfortable room, where most of the furnishings had been ingeniously designed to be usable with the giant in either the horizontal or vertical position. The major appliances were locked to the base of the rear wall, leaving the front and centre open except for some comfort items. The two corners at the rear were occupied by narrow bunks, attached by heavy rings to angled bars in such a fashion both ends could slide freely. Gold saw that the bunks, which had heavy zip-around covers, would move to the horizontal position automatically, whether the giant was lying down or in the vertical position. The food cold storage and warming units had doors that opened from the top at present, but would provide access equally well from the side with the body erect. A small computer, equipped with both viewscreen and printer, occupied the centre of the rear wall. It too was designed to be used in either position.

"This will complete the tour," said Petrovna, opening a final door in what was at present their floor. Gold followed him on to a small platform in what was obviously the heart of the control and life environment systems. This was by far the largest room, occupying more than half the space they had obtained by removing the right hemisphere of the cerebrum. There was no floor here, but both horizontal and vertical catwalks threaded the maze of equipment.

Among the complicated array of machinery, some familiar to Gold but much of it completely strange, he saw an item that seemed incongruous, ludicrous in its simplicity. It was a normal earth-type toilet seat, mounted above a dark opening in a box designed to swivel over the usual ninety degrees.

Petrovna saw the direction of Gold's stare, and frowned slightly. After a moment the younger man asked, "And what do you do with human wastes?"

Petrovna seemed to miss the irony implicit in the presence of the curved seat. "The disposal unit beneath cuts solids into very fine particles, puts them through an acid bath to neutralize the bacteria, through a passivation process which removes the acid, and then slowly feeds them into the bloodstream."

Gold raised his eyebrows slightly. "The small amount of waste you and I will inject into his bloodstream is of little consequence," Petrovna said briskly. "The normal flushing and purifying processes in the blood will remove it." He saw from Gold's grin that the subject seemed funny to his companion and said testily, "Gold, there is nothing laughable about a workable solution to a problem. Since we may be in here several months, we must dispose of our wastes without poisoning our host or causing obstruction problems in the smaller capillaries."

Gold changed the subject by asking where the system obtained its power. Petrovna pointed to the wall, where Gold recognized the shape of an apparently normal electrical generator. "We have a simple paddlewheel device suspended in one of the larger veins. The pressure is quite adequate, and we gear up to the required speed. There is an auxiliary battery system, but hopefully it will not be needed."

"Doesn't that slow blood circulation?"

"Not to any measurable extent. A small power drainage such as this is hardly noticeable."

"And the air we're breathing? And the comfortable temperature in here, though I noticed the giant's skin seemed hotter than ours?"

"The environmental control system takes oxygen from the host's blood and distributes it through these rooms. Carbon dioxide and water vapour are returned the same way. Incidentally, a by-product is the fresh water you and I will be drinking. As for the temperature, these rooms are air-conditioned in a fairly standard manner. Once again, the blood supply is capable of absorbing the heat removed from here with only minor effects on the body. The higher external skin heat you noticed is one of the more interesting differences between their metabolism and our own. The temperature in the centre of the trunk, head and limbs is much lower than that of the skin. There is a heat progression from the centre outward, and the epidermis is a fairly efficient radiator. But let's get into the functional differences between the two species at a later time."

"I'd like to know how this fellow exists at all, since I remember being told giants were impossible," Gold said dryly.

"Several of the physiologists here are busily rewriting the textbooks now," Petrovna said, again with that faint grin that indicated a strong sense of humour lurked beneath the professionally studied calm. "Unfortunately, they can't publish at this time. These giants exist despite our theories because they are not simply humans grown ninety-two metres tall, but a totally different species. The resemblance to ourselves is more apparent than real, as you will learn when you study a chemical analysis of their bones. But the law of nature that compels form to follow function works with this species as well as our own, and apparently we function very much alike. That is why we were able to trace the neural pathways and design our control consoles."

"So that you and I could crawl in here, like two worms in the brain of a sick dog, and go out to spy on the enemy," said Gold musingly, several formerly cryptic remarks by various U.N. officials now being clear.

"Your simile is not too apt," Petrovna's voice was cool. "Worms, or any other parasites, do not control their host. You and I will be in complete charge at all times, I assure you."

"Let's get out of here," said Gold suddenly, turning to the ladder.

The deformed Russian gave him a sharp glance, but turned and followed him back through the series of rooms. Gold noticed as he passed the autonomic console that Marina had already left.

When they reached the exterior catwalk Petrovna carefully lowered the hinged cornea back into place, fastening it with the almost invisible latch inset in the eyeball just under the lid. Gold took several deep breaths, and realized that the sudden yearning for fresh air that had overcome him had been entirely psychological. The air inside had been perfectly good.

Petrovna, without comment, led the way toward the feet, moving along the spread of interconnecting catwalks with the ease of familiarity. When they were almost to the navel Gold turned and looked back. He was disappointed. The chin towered higher than himself, hiding most of the face behind its high promontory. The nose stood out sharp and clear, rising like twin cave mouths opening into caverns of pink flesh.

Petrovna had paused over the juncture of thigh and trunk. Gold joined him, gazing outward at the huge penis, lying flaccidly on the sunken belly. The equally large scrotum, a heavily wrinkled bag holding two testicles, hung down between slightly parted thighs. There was no hair in the pubic area, and he realized he had seen none elsewhere on the body. Evidently the species was hairless.

Petrovna was doing little lecturing, letting the obvious facts speak for themselves. They passed fairly rapidly down the length of a muscular thigh, over a rocky hump of knee, and on down the calf to the foot, which towered up into the cavern. Gold saw that it was larger even than justified by the size differential, indicating that as the weight of the body increased the feet had grown to match.

The awe and sense of strangeness had started to wear off, and Gold was able to begin placing individual features in perspective. The muscles seemed unusually large and firm. The skin was a dark brown, coarse in appearance, with many veins and arteries standing out just below the surface. He could see the slow pulsing of blood, moving through its endless miles of circular tunnels. The heartbeat, Gold suddenly realized, was inaudible. Somehow he had expected to hear a great heavy thump! with each visible movement of blood through the giant arteries.

As they descended the catwalk to ground level Gold saw with interest that one crew was doing nothing more than scrubbing the coarse skin with stiff brushes. A rain of thin, almost translucent fragments was being caught by waiting vacuum cleaners.

Back in the equipment room they found Marina again working at the table from which Petrovna had called her. The short Russian led Gold back into the main body of the station, where a brief walk brought them to his office suite.

"General Cloke requested that you call him as soon as

you returned, sir," Petrovna's pretty secretary informed him as they entered.

Petrovna scowled slightly, nodded, and led Gold to his inner office. "General Cloke is a very good fighting man, but I am afraid he does not understand the scientific necessities here," he said as he seated himself behind a wide desk. "Now what would you like to know about our giant friend?"

At one time Gold had been mildly interested in physiology, and had a better background than Petrovna probably suspected. He drew on this knowledge to ask several questions about the methods Petrovna had used to attach the control console to the body's efferent neurones, and learned that the feat had been possible because the individual fibres were far larger than those of a human. He also learned that a network of afferent nerves brought a constant stream of sensory data into one portion of the computer, where it was synthesized and transmitted to the helmet attached to the console. When the operator wore the helmet, which was precisely fitted to his skull, he could receive the basic input of all the giant's senses except the most complex, sight. The helmet had been an afterthought, and no one knew how well it would work.

The door opened without ceremony while Petrovna was in the middle of an involved explanation, and a grizzled, white-haired man wearing the green uniform of the United Nations Armed Forces came barging in. There were two stars on his shoulders. Behind him Gold heard the protesting "But sir!" of the pretty secretary.

The general shut the door, nodded curtly to Gold, and marched to the scientist's desk. "Damn it Petrovna, I wish you would have the courtesy to return a call," he said crossly. "We must come to an understanding about the amount of time your people are keeping the defensive fire pattern computer tied up. Right now we are sitting ducks for a determined assault by our large-sized friends. Don't you realize—"

"George!" Petrovna interrupted him, his voice conciliatory. "Why should the giants suddenly attack in force after a lapse of twenty-eight years? There has been no direct assault on an Earth base since the Mars colony was taken in 1981—and we can be fairly sure that one occurred only because they needed some living specimens for study. They intend to eliminate us in one easy operation, not by small fights. Calm yourself. Have you met Gold? Gold, this is our base commander, Major General Cloke."

The general took a brisk step toward him and Gold reluctantly rose to shake hands. He disliked physical contact with another male. The British officer was a man of indeterminate years, despite his rugged features and white hair.

"Heard a great deal about you, Gold. None of it true, I hope?"

"Probably all of it," Gold replied.

"That so? Even the bit about the 365 most beautiful women in the world who could be had for money, one each night for a year while you were stacking up a cool billion in stocks during the daytime? Well, well. Had my doubts about that one."

"All perfectly true," Gold said coldly.

"Well, I assume there were no pregnancies or we'd have heard about it," the U.N. officer went on briskly. "Doesn't matter, really. Think of all the fun you had trying."

"I—" Gold started to speak, but closed his mouth. There was little point in trying to explain.

General Cloke glanced up quizzically. "Oh, I see. All in the cause of science, eh? But I understood that the American chaps took sperm directly from your testicles and tried to fertilize an ovum artificially, with no success. Now if they couldn't accomplish the job with the latest techniques and the most modern equipment, how could you possibly get a girl pregnant the old-fashioned way?"

"Human conception is not really that well understood, George," Petrovna cautiously entered the conversation. "The field has received little study since the invaders launched that first biological attack in 1989 and tied up Earth's scientific talent in defence-related work. There are certain intangible factors—"

"I slept with those girls because I wanted to share sex with some of the most attractive women on Earth for a solid year," Gold calmly interrupted the scientist.

"Possibly," Petrovna agreed, "but for some reason each girl was brought to you thirteen or fourteen days after the beginning of her period, the time of maximum fertility. It is also a fact that it has been two years since the 365th girl, not a single one became pregnant, and you have been impotent since that time."

Gold whirled toward the Russian, who had risen to stand behind his desk. "How in hell did you know that?" he demanded angrily.

"Oh, come now," the general's tone was patronizing. "Surely, Mr. Gold, you realize a man of your importance would never be left unguarded by the United States, and of course by the Peacekeeper. Your every move since you forced your way out of the Genetics Institute when you attained your majority has been as carefully watched as when you were a ward there. I've seen some of the reports. And frankly, nothing I've heard and seen inclines me to think you're the man for this job."

"He's the *only* man for it, George," Petrovna said more loudly, some controlled anger beginning to show. "Now will you please leave and let me get back to explaining our plan to Gold?"

"All righty," the general said, rising, "but I think you're making a mistake. This young pup is rather on the rotten side, and I haven't the faintest notion he'll take us up on your fantastic idea. His record has been one of complete self-indulgence since he surprised his American mentors by walking out on them." He turned and stared directly up into Gold's face. "I doubt that this man has the capacity, the will, the guts, or even the inclination to work for his fellows. I most assuredly don't think he's willing to risk his precious life." The general swung around and strode out with a final, "And untie my damn computer, will you?"

chapter 3

PETRONVA SAT DOWN again as the door closed behind the general's stiffly erect back. Behind a desk he appeared almost normal, and was obviously aware of it.

"I'll make this as brief as possible," said the Russian scientist, leaning back in his chair. "As you must have surmised, we intend to allow the Exterminators to 'rescue' their missing comrade. The method chosen is comparatively simple. We plan to put this animated body back aboard and fly their planetary lander to Mars; it has already been prepared for the trip. We will activate the distress signal they left behind in the caverns and wait for the next attack. Our expectation is that the enemy ship will stop for us. After that it will be a matter of learning all we possibly can.

We may find that in their culture a brain-damaged person is killed on the spot . . . perhaps by ritually cracking the skull!" Petrovna smiled at his own grim humour. "Hopefully, we will survive and manage to get aboard their ship, at least for a few minutes. We will learn all that we can in whatever amount of time we spend in their company. The worst that can happen is that we will die without relaying any useful information to Earth. The best we could hope for, and this seems highly improbable, would be to capture the ship and its crew."

Gold listened in growing amazement. The plan sounded highly quixotic and dangerous, but within the framework Petrovna had outlined it also seemed plausible. Earth's scientific station on Mars had been easily taken in the only physical assault the enemy had attempted, when they first appeared in 1981. They had occupied the red planet for eight years, until Earth developed interplanetary missiles with ninety megaton warheads and launched a determined attack during the Earth-Mars opposition of 1989. The enemy had successfully defended their conquered territory by destroying or deflecting every missile . . . but they abandoned the planet and apparently left the solar system shortly thereafter. Debris gathered from space had enabled Earth's technologists to verify that the enemy interceptors were simply more sophisticated missiles. No "super-weapons" such as giant laser beams or force fields had been used. It seemed obvious that the interceptors had been aboard the alien ships, and the invaders were incapable of manufacturing more while away from the home planet.

Earth's victory had been a pyrrhic one. They could not re-occupy Mars for the same reasons the aliens could not continue to defend it. The logistics problems involved in manning complex weapon systems so far from home were too costly for the benefits gained. The moonbase was retained only because it could be protected by missiles launched and maintained from Earth.

The aliens had made a direct attack against Earth at the time of departure, but it had not been very effective. They had swept close to the outer defence perimeter and released a single rocket toward North America, then easily outdistanced the early primitive interceptors sent after them. That single missile had contained a deadly virus. The biological weapon they had developed caused a few deaths, but was only mildly contagious and died out naturally in a short time.

The first expedition to reach Mars and enter the huge natural caverns, which the giants had enlarged for their own use, found a few buried humans but no live ones. Most of the base personnel had been captured and taken away when the aliens retreated, undoubtedly to serve as guinea pigs in the production of more biological weapons. The most logical reason for retreat, other than possible fear of a second attack, was that the enemy had not brought along enough laboratory equipment to construct the complex and highly selective biological mechanism they wished to release against Earth. The most noticeable characteristic of the alien virus had been its specificity; it killed only humans.

The passage of time had proven the logical supposition the correct one. The enemy had returned seven more times over the next eighteen years, one of their huge spaceships appearing from nowhere and sweeping past Earth at a speed far in excess of even the best defence missiles. Each ship released one or more small, highly manoeuvrable penetration devices, which utilized the approach speed of the mother ship and a complex closing pattern to evade both Earth's outer defence net and the last-ditch overhead interceptors. Each probe released a new virus or bacteria into the atmosphere; all were highly selective, and the chosen target was man.

Until the lucky accident of the last attack twenty months before, when the alien ship had apparently dropped out of faster-than-light travel off course and heading directly for the moon, Earth's thousand-billion dollar defence network had been completely helpless. Several thousand-million dollars in missiles had been wasted in futile attempts to intercept the probes and mother ship, and pursue the latter when it curved away and apparently accelerated until it exceeded the speed of radar and broke contact. All had been totally useless.

Gold brought his mind back to the present. "What makes you think an attack is imminent?" he asked curiously.

"The fact that the time between attempts gets shorter at an easily plotted rate. We estimate the next one as due in approximately two months. A simulator is ready, and a training course almost complete. Intensive practice should shorten the time required on the actual console to a few days. And if you are wondering why we have not utilized the onboard computer more fully and designed better associated-series actions in logical progressions, the answer again is lack of time. The best we could do was retain those functions that are semi-automatic once started, such as a series of conditioned reflexes we call walking. The process must begin by stimulation from the console, and the speed must be regulated, but once in motion the body will walk, including automatic balancing."

"Why do you feel that you absolutely must have me? Why not a trained test pilot?"

"Quite possibly one could meet the physical requirements, though these are quite demanding. We doubt that a normal man could learn the complex routines involved in the time we have. No one knows precisely how much of the added potential built into your brain has been developed, since your teachers are now certain you deliberately scored high or low on every test since the age of four, but we *are* certain you are the world's best quick-study. Your performance on the New York stock exchange, where you amassed a great fortune in one year, proved that. The financial world is an extremely complex institution. We feel that the task of mastering the console will require both your trained fingers and all your learning ability."

"And what will you do if I refuse?"

"After we realized the limitation under which we were working, we designed the console specifically for you. The sensor helmet will fit your head precisely after the hair is removed. We did not consider the possibility that you might refuse to serve."

"A typical communist attitude, Petrovna. The individual must sacrifice himself for the good of the mob."

"There are two other equally valid reasons, Gold. First, the genuine challenge it affords you. Second, the preservation of your own life. I realize it is useless to appeal to you in the name of your fellow men—you think those four extra ounces of association neurones you and I possess raise you above common humanity—but you can hardly deny that you suffer from the same primitive desire to go on living as the rest of us. And these giants intend to eliminate mankind as a life form, down to the last baby in the last crib."

"Why do you think they are so intent on killing us off?" Gold asked the scientist. This was a subject on which everyone had an opinion.

"The highly specific nature of all the organisms released against us makes it seem likely they want our planet, unchanged other than by our removal."

"With the humans gone it might become a nice piece of

real estate," said Gold, making no effort to hide his contempt. "Incidentally, what happened to all those people infected during the various attacks, including the doctors and nurses who cared for them? I believe you were in charge of negating all biological attacks except the first one."

Petrovna's massive head turned away, and for a moment the piercing black eyes seemed to grow dim and lustreless. "I think you know," he answered quietly.

"So the mob is willing to sacrifice large groups as well as individuals," Gold said musingly.

Petrovna raised his head. "A typical American attitude, Gold, derived from your over-emphasis on the individual and unwillingness to accept the fact man is a social animal," he snapped, almost crossly. "If you had been raised in a communist society you would not have become the extremely selfish and anti-social person American tradition has made you."

Gold laughed, but there was no mirth in the sound. "And if you had been designed by American geneticists, Petrovna, perhaps they would have done a better job on your arms and legs."

The Russian visibly stiffened, and his face turned white. After a moment he slowly leaned back again and relaxed. When he met Gold's gaze his face was curiously impassive, as though in spite of Western training he had retained the oriental impassivity of an older Russia. "I deserved that," he said slowly, and then with returning vigour, "let's not get lost in semantics, or make ourselves hate each other. If you accept this assignment we have an extremely difficult job to do, one that will require the closest possible co-operation. I apologize for my unwarranted statement. Now I will have someone escort you to your quarters. We would like to have your decision as soon as possible."

As his last words faded into Gold's unreceptive silence the speaker on the wall behind Petrovna burst out in the short, savage wails of a siren screaming "*Attack Imminent.*"

The siren died away and was replaced by a masculine voice, excited but under control. "Dr. Petrovna! Dr. Petrovna, report to the annex at once, please! The captive is stirring. Repeat, the captive is stirring!"

The scientist, obviously startled, almost ran for the door. At the last minute he remembered his guest and motioned for Gold to follow. They found Marina at the same large table where they had left her, clutching a sheaf of recording graphs. Her face was as agitated as those of the surrounding technicians, nervously working with their equipment throughout the long room.

"I was going to discuss this with you as soon as you had a free moment," the short woman said hurriedly. Her voice was thin and a little high. "The readings indicate a small but measurable increase in activity over the past several hours, in almost all bodily systems. The chart on the anaesthetic feeder indicates a normal dosage throughout the same period." She paused, waiting expectantly.

Petrovna's face seemed to blank out, as though all faculties had been directed solely to an internal function. Gold recognized the equivalent of his own ability to withdraw so completely into memory that he could recall even physical sensations. But Petrovna was apparently thinking, not remembering. It was over in seconds. He snapped a quick question at Marina, and she hastily consulted one of the graphs and gave him a figure. The scientist nodded in satisfaction. "Yes yes, that confirms it. One becomes so buried in complexities the simple tends to be overlooked. The body has built up a partial immunity to our anaesthetic. We must increase the dosage."

"We can't," said Marina, her voice worried. "He's already broken our ground control wiring. We would have to get inside to the autonomic console."

There was a tremendous thump! at the opposite end of the long room. The thick rock wall suddenly cracked.

"Your patient seems to be taking the place apart," Gold said pleasantly to Petrovna.

The stunted Russian glanced at the damaged wall. "Yes, we will have to return him to unconsciousness quickly or he may injure himself," he muttered, more to himself than Gold or Marina.

The door leading to the main base area opened and admitted General Cloke and two armed security guards. He walked rapidly to Petrovna, though his eyes were on the gaping crack in the rear wall. Several white-clad technicians had also clustered before the scientist, awaiting instructions.

"And what brought this on, Petrovna?" the general asked, his voice harsh. "I thought you had our large friend under control."

The scientist swiftly explained why he thought the giant had suddenly become active. The base commander listened attentively, and said, "Then perhaps we'd better destroy the big fellow. With the end wall cracked we'd have an air-out if he smashes through the roof."

"Don't be absurd, George," Petrovna gave him a disgusted look. "Our large friend is made of the same soft flesh as you and I. He could not possibly break the roof."

"And how do you propose to calm him down?" the general asked coolly.

"For now we will have to administer a large dose of anaesthetic externally," Petrovna said with a frown. "With a little adaptation we should be able to use the blood sampler as a hypodermic." He turned and snapped rapid orders to some of the waiting men. Almost immediately purposeful activity replaced confusion, the technicians working rapidly at a variety of tasks under the expert direction of Petrovna and Marina. Gold and the military personnel found themselves gradually edged to one side, out of the way.

There was another jarring impact of a giant hand against the cracked wall. The whole room shook slightly. The four idle men turned in time to see a flash of brown skin through what was now an opening they could crawl through.

"And just who is going to bell the cat?" asked General Cloke of no one in particular.

"That's a job for men of action, I would think," said Gold, glancing at the two security guards. They returned his stare with blank faces that still managed to convey an impression of dislike.

"I expect you're right. As soon as they get their equipment together my lads and I will tackle it."

"You will not lay a finger on my patient!" snapped Petrovna, suddenly appearing at General Cloke's elbow. "The injection will be administered by the medical staff and myself."

The equipment the technicians were assembling had taken its final shape. A hollow stainless steel lance over three feet long had been connected by several feet of clear plastic hose to a cart-mounted pump. A large open-topped tank on the cart contained the anaesthetic. Gold saw a technician start the motor and open a hand-valve. A jet of fluid shot out of the needle's tip before the man could control the flow.

"Good! Let's go," said Petrovna, and grasped the needle himself. Another man lifted the trailing hose, and two more started rolling the cart down the room.

"Just a moment!" General Cloke called sharply. "Petrovna, surely you aren't going to risk your life here. I'm certain these lads can handle the job without your personal help."

The cart stopped. "He's right, sir," one of the men in white said quickly.

Petrovna hesitated, then grudgingly yielded. "Very well, I'll remain at the door. Take the needle, Hans. Claude, take his place at the valve."

In seconds the cart was moving again, Petrovna and Marina at the rear. Gold and the three military men were only a few steps behind. The technicians busy at the equipment on both sides turned to stare at them, but only briefly; they were too busy trying to compensate for the damage their patient had caused.

The door into the second chamber was of the heavy air-lock type, and the second blow had warped the steel frame. The lead technician struggled vainly to open it. After a moment Gold pushed him aside, seized the heavy ring in both hands, and braced himself with one foot against the wall. He put all his strength into one great heave, and had the satisfaction of feeling the door move slightly. One more pull and it opened. The four men with the cart hurried through and dodged to the right, along the wall. Petrovna followed them, but stopped just past the door. Gold, after a quick glance at the twitching giant, moved inside and to the left.

The position of the immense body had changed dramatically. The catwalks were gone, scattered in disarray over the cavern floor. Their former occupants, the technicians on duty, were huddled against the walls. The left hand was now curled across the great chest, knuckles scraped and bleeding. The head was turned toward them, cavernous mouth open, features twisted in pain. Muscles were rippling and twitching in restless spasms, as though spurred by a hundred exercise technicians. The dormant brain was struggling toward wakefulness.

Marina slipped through the door and started toward Petrovna, but he imperiously motioned for her to return to the other room. Almost sullenly she retreated, but remained standing just within the equipment annex.

The giant head turned toward the opposite wall, pulling the neck muscles taut on the left side. At a signal from Petrovna the men pushed the cart forward, to the juncture of neck and shoulder. The technician called Hans searched for a moment on the apparently featureless expanse of skin, then called for the man carrying the hose to help with the needle. The two gripped the shaft firmly, poised the sharp point, and abruptly and forcefully pushed it through the resisting skin. When it had penetrated almost a foot Hans yelled "Now!" The man on the cart opened the control valve, and the hose swelled with a rush of fluid.

The skin twitched convulsively as the point entered. Abruptly the head rolled toward the cart, almost crushing the technicians at the needle before they could dodge beneath the rising curve of the shoulder. The bloody hand on the chest moved toward the source of irritation. The needle popped out when the skin twitched a second time, spurting a jet of fluid before the man on the cart could close the valve.

Petrovna started forward with a sharp exclamation, short legs churning. *Then the huge brown hand moved down the shoulder in an unco-ordinated, scrambling crawl, reached the floor, and suddenly loomed ahead of Petrovna like a wall of brown boulders. Before the startled scientist could retreat one twitching finger smashed into him. The impact lifted his short form clear of the floor and hurled him toward the rock wall a few feet away. He hit head-first, the sound of impact a sickeningly soft thud in a room suddenly deathly quiet. Petrovna fell to the floor. Gold saw the large torso shudder twice, and then he was still.*

Marina darted through the open door and along the wall to the Russian. Two of the technicians who had retreated under the curving shoulder broke and ran for safety, moving at a sharp angle that would take them away from the groping hand. Hans, still holding the needle, stayed with the cart. The two fleeing men reached the wall and ran along it toward the door. Behind them the brown hand lifted from the cavern floor and returned to the chest, while the head twisted until the giant was again facing the opposite wall. The entire body was twitching and stirring more vigorously than before.

"Come on!" snapped General Cloke, and his two guards followed him across the open space to the cart at a run. Gold started after them, hesitated, then returned to the safety of the wall.

"Can we find that same vein lower down?" the general asked Hans. The shoulder had shifted until the original point of entry was above their heads.

The technician nodded. "Yes, but we'll have to go a little deeper. He's probably going to twitch again when we hit him, but if we're low enough we may be able to hold it in."

The general motioned for one of his men to pull the cart closer and operate the controls. The other guard, without being told, seized the hose and cleared it of kinks. Hans left his post long enough to murmur some brief instructions to the man on the cart. He opened the correct valve, and filled the hose until a small amount ran out of the tip of the needle.

Hans and the general poised the sharp point above the selected spot, and at a sharp "Go!" from the officer they shoved hard on the shaft. It penetrated the skin immediately and drove into the flesh, but slowed as it went deeper. The two men redoubled their efforts, bracing their feet and pushing hard against the shaft and rounded end. The mountainous shoulder jerked spasmodically and a mindless, mournful groan of animal pain went reverberating throughout the long cavern.

Hans seemed to recognize a difference in resistance when the needle was in almost half its length, and yelled at the soldier on the cart to open the valve. The hose swelled under a surge of pressure. The shoulder lifted and moved several feet, hitting both men and knocking them to the ground. The cart was just far enough away not to be crushed when the wall of brown flesh descended again, and the needle held. A low, rumbling sigh broke from the open mouth as the head turned back toward the door. The twitching eased as the last of the fluid left the cart's tank. Hans, back at the needle, motioned for the guard to turn off the pump. After a moment he seized the end of the shaft, withdrawing it without help. A small torrent of very thick blood followed, but quickly diminished to a trickle.

The giant's breath began to lengthen and deepen, returning to a long, steady sighing that seemed his normal pattern while unconscious.

Gold suddenly remembered Petrovna, and started along the wall toward him. Marina had been joined by several men, all huddling around the short, broad form on the floor. When Gold reached them he saw why they were simply kneeling there. Part of the oversized brain that the Russian geneticists had laboured twenty years to build lay nakedly exposed, oozing outside its enlarged and weakened container of protective bone. Petrovna was irrevocably dead.

Marina finally stood erect, turning away from the body. There were no tears on her face, and her eyes were glazed. Gold saw that she was in severe shock.

Hans brushed by Gold and took Marina's arm. "I'll take care of her, I'm a doctor," he threw over his shoulder to the base commander, who was right behind him. Gold saw the general's eyebrows lift, and shared his surprise. Petrovna had employed high-calibre people as technicians.

The doctor led Marina away. Cloke spared them a brief glance, then turned and took charge. With a few crisp orders he had the technicians scurrying about to locate more anaesthetic. Within ten minutes the catwalks leading to the right eye had been restored, and a technician was crawling inside to renew the autonomic console's supply and increase the automatic dosage. Other men were preparing the rigs which would return the body to its original position.

When order had been restored the white-haired officer turned to Gold, waiting quietly by the door. All the general's foppishness and exaggerated British mannerisms were gone. "Gold, I don't know at this point precisely what this tragedy does to our project. I'm calling a conference as soon as Marina has recovered enough to attend. I request that you join us, and we'll attempt to prepare an alternate plan before we inform the U.N. politicians of Petrovna's death."

Gold nodded, and the general assigned one of the guards to show him to his assigned quarters. Once in the small but comfortably furnished room Gold stretched out on the bunk, placed his hands behind his head, and stared at the bare rock wall. Very slowly he began to confront the actuality of the death of Petrovna.

chapter 4

A MEMORY OF another time when he had lain on a similar narrow bed and confronted the reality of death intruded into Gold's conscious mind. This was not one of those forceful upwellings that had to be repressed if he had no time for a replay, but an immediately identifiable memory little different from any other in his permanent banks. But running it would at least get his conscious attention away from the present, which was unbearable.

Gold let the scene emerge and firm up.

Albert lay on his back on the extra-long bed that was already too short for him, head cradled comfortably in his arms, eyes closed, the small speaker in his ear almost hidden against the pillow. A white wire that blended with the government-issue sheets dipped under the pillow and out of the head of the bed to a wall socket, where the single male plug on its end entered the ground hole at a sharp angle. There it made contact with an extra wire that threaded its way through the building's maze of conduits to a light fixture in a small conference room two storeys below. The five remaining members of the huge team that had been organized to produce an enlarged brain, and develop and train its owner, met there twice a week. The Institute's primary function for the past decade had been to convince the entire population of Earth that it was everyone's duty and obligation to support the war effort; the Director begrudged every penny spent on Albert Aaron Golderson.

Albert lay quietly following the conversation, without real interest. The microphone he had installed above the light fixture had been the best he could steal, but one of the two women, Carlotta Jones, had a low, husky voice that did not project well. These late meetings were seldom very productive. All the educated people on Earth, loosely referred to as the technocrats, had long been on a ten-hour day six-day week. What leisure time they had was usually devoted to the pleasures still available that made life worthwhile. When the team met at the end of a long day they wasted little time in conversation. Albert had decided to listen in on this meeting to see if they would comment on Petrovna's recent performance as head of the Russian team that had produced an antidote for the aliens' second biological attack. The Russian genius was only twenty-three, and his appointment to a task where failure might literally mean the death of all mankind had been denounced in every country but Russia. But Petrovna had not failed, and Albert was anxious to learn what his teachers thought of his rival *Homo superior's* feat.

"I don't really understand it," Wigman Boyles, the physiologist, was saying as full audio memory returned. "He seems to be undergoing the normal physiological and psychological changes associated with puberty, and yet all the sperm samples I have examined are completely inert. I can only conclude that we have erred, and our Albert is as sterile as Petrovna."

"May I ask how you obtained your samples?" asked Carlotta's soft voice. She was an intense, black-haired psychologist of just past thirty, whose husband was a high-ranking physicist in the defence forces.

"Certainly. I asked the boy to masturbate into a passivated test tube for me," replied Boyles coolly. "Short of an operation there is no other practical way to obtain samples."

"Isn't that likely to induce regular masturbation?" asked Carlotta.

"Probably, except that you can be reasonably certain he's already started. It's perfectly normal behaviour, and I imagine he's been doing it for the past year or more."

"I wouldn't be too certain of that," broke in a new voice, which Albert recognized as Edward Martin's. The young psychologist had started with the original team as a graduate student and was now the chief of this last small remnant. "Remember that his puberty changeover lasted two years, and though he started at about the normal age of twelve this stretched-out development is distinctly unusual. I would guess that he has been able to ejaculate for less than a year."

"The point is immaterial," replied Boyles. "At ejaculation all human and animal species are capable of inducing fertilization. Albert Golderson is not. This ties in quite well with what little I've heard from our secretive Russian colleagues on the development of Petrovna as a boy. Apparently our work has duplicated theirs even more closely than we expected. But at least we didn't repeat their worst mistakes, thanks to Pawel and his cohorts."

Pawel Jampolski said something in acknowledgement which Albert did not catch. Pawel was the one geneticist who remained out of a team of over twenty who had successfully borrowed genes from a donor chromosome and added them to a prime to produce an enlarged brain. His primary responsibility to the project was long finished, but he remained a member of the team and took notes on the results for a book he hoped to publish one day on his work. So far the notes, which Albert had sneaked into his apartment and read, were highly self-congratulatory on Albert's physical characteristics and condemnatory of the young genius' behaviour. The latter failure Pawel blamed on the team's two psychologists, Carlotta and Ed Martin.

Anita Savez, the fifth member of the group and a confirmed spinster at thirty-four, broke in with, "Is all this actually relevant? I was under the impression we were meeting to decide what to do about his peeping activities."

"I don't want to shock you, Anita," Martin answered, his voice dry, "but peeping is a normal activity engaged in by all boys his age, and nothing to be alarmed about. Let's not forget that while he may be a potential mental giant like Petrovna, at the moment he's still a normal fourteen-year-old boy. Send the maintenance crew in to plug that hole he drilled in the ceiling of the ladies' restroom and forget it. Let's move on to the next item. Any luck deciphering that last dream Albert recorded for you, Carlotta?"

"Yes, enough to think he was being reasonably honest with me. He wants to be rid of those nightmares as much as we want him cured of them. I'm sorry to say that the heavy birth trauma is still there, and apparently ineradicable."

There was a brief silence, and Albert realized they were thinking back to the tragedy that had ushered him into the world. He had read lurid accounts of his birth, by authors normally more concerned with science than sensationalism. The basic facts were a matter of record. His mother had been carefully selected from a healthy and physically large Swedish family with a history of high intelligence. His father, an American of Swedish extraction, was a brilliant physician with an equally imposing family tree. To simplify matters the chosen parents had agreed to legally marry, and had lived together for several months before the geneticists took them into the lab to start the long series of treatments they hoped would produce a child with four extra ounces of forebrain. And it was then that the Goldersons told the experimenters that the scientifically selected mates had varied from the prescribed path . . . they had learned to love each other.

After weeks of final preparations a sperm with several chromosomes lengthened by the addition of selected genes had been carefully implanted in a similarly modified egg. Test tube conception was a well-established technique, but the geneticists could not know how well the gene manipulation had worked until the foetus was several months old. The fertilized egg had been returned to the mother's fallopian tubes, to descend to the uterus in the normal manner. When the egg burrowed into the uterine wall and pregnancy was assured, the scientific community involved had breathed a collective sigh of relief. And then a large part of the world had awaited Gold's birth with fervid interest, since the Russian's eight-year-old boy wonder, Petrovna, had been only a partial success.

Gold's birth, when it came, was almost ignored. The Exterminators attacked the Mars station two weeks before the event, and there was no room in the headlines for any news except the imminent destruction of Earth.

The birth of the Goldersons' baby had been planned as a Caesarian, to avoid the normal birth trauma and the possibility of damage to the brain through pressure on the enlarged skull. But Nancy Golderson, tired of close confinement in the Institute and the careful supervision of an entire staff of doctors, had rebelled when her baby was seven months along and insisted on being allowed a trip into New York. The infant was fully formed, completely healthy, and apparently normal. A friend of hers had a minor part in a new play, and she wanted to attend the opening night performance. In the end she received reluctant permission from the project director, with the stipulation that her physician husband would accompany her with a well-stuffed doctor's kit.

As Francis Golderson told it later, he and his wife had enjoyed a good dinner and the show, which was excellent, and started home. Traffic was light, and they spent the hour from New York to the edge of the Catskills discussing the subject preoccupying the world at the moment, the meaning of the unexpected attack on the Mars station by unknown invaders. The ramifications and implications staggered the imagination. If the attackers were from another solar system, which seemed almost certain, then interstellar travel was a proven fact and faster-than-light speeds a high probability. And another ancient question, whether or not other intelligent life existed in the galaxy, had been emphatically answered in a very unpleasant way.

Golderson turned on to the narrow road leading up into the foothills and the little town supported by the Institute. These scenes were not in Albert's original memory; he had deliberately created them in his mind, working from the several descriptions available. But Albert could replay them almost as well as a true record, and decided to do so once more while waiting for his training team to mention Petrovna again.

Someone in a low sportscar started around the Goldersons, attempting to pass them on a short straight stretch. The driver overestimated the power of his small car and was still even with them when an oncoming vehicle appeared around the next bend. Instead of falling back the sportscar attempted to pull ahead and squeeze in. Golderson applied his brakes, trying to make room, but it was too late. The other driver, desperate, turned in too quickly. The tail of his car hit the Goldersons' left front fender. The impact turned the nose of their heavy automobile off the road, while throwing the lighter car into a skid. It slid half around and turned over, rolling directly into the oncoming car.

Francis Golderson caught only a brief glimpse of the two other cars as they slid off the highway, locked together in a deathly embrace. His own vehicle was bouncing down a steep slope, half-sliding on coarse gravel as he fought with brake and steering wheel to bring it under control. He almost succeeded, but then a front wheel hit a deep depression, spinning the car half around, and forward momentum and the sharp grade flipped it over. The heavy sedan rolled twice, smashed into a boulder almost as large as itself, and shuddered to a stop.

Francis Golderson was tossed violently about, but the seat belt and harness held him firmly in place, and he did not lose consciousness. When he recovered enough to turn to his wife he saw that she too had remained locked in her seat, and was apparently unhurt . . . and then she opened her eyes, started to smile, and a bloody froth bubbled over her lips.

The car had come to rest almost on its right side, supported by the boulder. He was partially suspended in the air above his wife by the seat harness, but was able to reach her for a hurried examination. The impact had ripped a jagged hole in the thin double-walled door, and one of the long pointed metal strips had penetrated her side. It was still there, held in place by her weight. His groping fingers found the base of the point; it was almost two inches wide. The sharp end was near her heart, and the right lung had to be mangled beyond repair.

The wound was dangerous, but not necessarily fatal. As he drew back Nancy looked at him through shock-dulled eyes, and more red froth appeared on her lips when she said, "Francis! The baby . . . it's coming!"

A hundred yards ahead the two tangled cars were burning brightly. There was no possibility anyone had survived. The road in both directions was clear of lights. There was little chance another car would travel this road before dawn.

Golderson dug his medical kit out of the twisted back seat, snipped and cut away his wife's maternity smock where the splinter had penetrated her side, and started trying to examine the wound without moving her.

"Francis!" she gasped urgently. "Francis, you've got to

deliver the baby! We only have a few minutes. These pains . . . I think I skipped most of the labour."

She took a deep breath, and he heard a strangled bubbling deep in the torn lung, and felt the flesh he was touching pull against the ragged metal embedded within her.

"No! I'll give you a shot, try to hold back the labour pains until I can get you free and close up that gash. The contractions will kill you if that baby comes now!"

"Can't stop it, too late for medicine—oh!" Another pain followed so swiftly on the heels of the first that he knew birth was imminent; she was right. Nancy threw her arms around his neck and held him tightly, ignoring the next pain. Her voice was unexpectedly firm when she said, "I'll be all right. Deliver the baby, and then see what you can do for me. Francis, the baby must live! Why he might . . . might . . . oh!"

He remained bent over her for a moment, one hand on her abdomen above the moving baby and the other on the blood-slick flesh where the jagged metal wedge was swiftly taking her life. He thought about their genetically advanced child, apparently physically perfect, and knew she had been trying to say he might be the harbinger of a new race, the first true *Homo superior*. And he had to live.

It was awkward and clumsy work, delivering a child while hanging in the air above a woman who writhed and twisted in pain, but the baby came with merciful speed. He was a diagnostician, not an obstetrician, but it seemed to Golderson that cervical dilation must have occurred with unusual rapidity. He knew, at the end of the final long contraction that thrust his son's head into view, that his wife would live only minutes longer. Despite her best efforts to keep the impaled side still, the wide metal spike had penetrated deeper, twisting and tearing the already ravaged tissues. The bloody froth on her lips was now a continuous bubbling wetness.

The baby slid into Golderson's hands. He removed the mucous plug and spanked it firmly. The tiny mouth opened immediately to vent a thin squall, and the small body came vigorously alive, kicking and squirming. He cut and tied the umbilical cord, wrapped the wet form in his coat, and laid it carefully in the back seat. He finished delivering the afterbirth, and checked for serious vaginal bleeding; there was none. He examined the enlarged cut in her side . . . and then he kissed her once, on the forehead, and held her head and shoulders cradled in his arms. At last the bubbling stopped, and she smiled at him, faintly, as if in approval. There was a look of awareness and understanding on her face. She did not attempt to speak again, and the chin dropped and the mouth became slack and loose when she died.

Francis Golderson hung in the safety harness above his wife's body until a feeble crying from the back seat reminded him of his son. He picked up the baby and opened the coat. In the bright moonlight flooding the car he could see that the blood and fluid had dried. The doctor's eye noticed what the husband had been too preoccupied to see before, that there were several large black marks on the infant's soft head, and the small body was bruised in many places. The baby had taken several rough blows in the crack-up. One of the bruises on the enlarged skull was severe enough to indicate that the government's several billion dollar investment had almost been lost. Only the hydraulic shock absorbing system in the mother's womb had prevented the fragile bone from cracking.

He covered the baby again and clawed his way out through the remnants of a window, taking several minor cuts in the process. It was not a cold night but the air was brisk, and he had no way to protect the baby. He wrapped it in several folds of the coat and laid it against the large rock. It took him several minutes to remove the body of his wife from the tangled wreckage. He straightened her maternity dress and covered her with the torn garment as best he could. There was nothing he could do to change the fact she was a bloody, horribly ugly corpse.

Francis Golderson picked up the infant, held him against his chest for warmth, and started climbing the steep slope to the highway. At dawn he reached the Institute, walked into the building's clinic, handed the baby to the astonished nurse on night duty, and said, "Feed my son." And then he collapsed.

The scene faded out, and Albert returned to the present. He lay quietly for a moment, thinking about what he had just reviewed, and realized that when he created that imagined sequence he had unconsciously taken the viewpoint of his father. No one but Francis Golderson could have known how he felt when he sacrificed his wife's chance to live to save a baby not wholly of their making. But it had been what she wanted, and she had died smiling.

The replay had taken less than two minutes, and the voice of Ed Martin was saying, "Isn't it possible that due to his increased capacity to absorb data Albert was more sensitive than normal even at birth, and so more easily scarred mentally by the physical stresses present? We've had a difficult time with him since he became old enough to reason, and I'm inclined to blame that persistent birth trauma. Remember that the Russians had no similar difficulties with Petrovna."

"I think we're paying entirely too much attention to the birth and not enough to the environment we provided afterwards," Carlotta Jones said firmly. "You must remember that Petrovna was raised by his parents in a perfectly normal fashion, including even suckling at his mother's breasts. He had a father and an almost normal life, except for the same intense transactional education we have tried to provide for Albert. It seems to me that our ward's wildness and irresponsible behaviour may well be a result of having us for abstract authority figures when he should have had normal loving parents instead."

"I've always wondered why Francis Golderson committed suicide while the baby was so young," Pawel Jampolski said in a musing voice.

Albert, lying quietly on his bed, felt his breathing stop. All the official accounts stated that his father had died from a virulent laboratory infection when his son was almost a year old. It had always seemed a typical accident, and suddenly he knew why accounts of it had bothered him slightly. The infection had obviously gone deliberately unreported until it was too late for treatment.

Suddenly a vision of his mother's dying body, impaled on the killing spike, welled irresistibly upward and appeared on Albert's inner screen. He saw his own baby head emerge under his father's hands, the large skull covered with the dark marks of severe bruises. And as though a camera had jumped to the next scene he saw his father a year later, lying collapsed across a bench in the laboratory, black splotches covering his gaunt Nordic features. And then the baby head reappeared, superimposing itself on the face of the father, and the dark marks on the faces of father and son matched, merged, and became one.

For the first time Albert felt that he finally knew his father, and could understand the sorrow and brooding anguish that had driven a brilliant physician to suicide. Suddenly he experienced an acute and overwhelming sense of loss, as though the tragedy had just occurred. He confronted the reality of death, and the grief he felt was almost unbearable.

After a timeless interval, a period without limit, without definition, the mental pain eased slightly. Albert still lay immobile on the narrow bed, no longer listening to the conference, letting the feeling of unacceptable hurt slowly subside. And then a flash of insight, so strong and certain it could not be disbelieved, lit the internal horizon of his mind like a lightning bolt . . . *His father had committed suicide because of him!*

However unjust, however unfair the accusation might be, Francis Golderson had held the son responsible for the mother's death. And he had loved his wife, not the mutated baby that was more the child of America's scientific community than his own true son.

The hurt came again, as bad as before, but now it was the pain of rejection as much as loss. Albert lay quietly enduring it, and then slowly began to fight back. The total tragedy of his birth had been no fault of his. There was no justifiable reason why he should feel responsible for the death of his parents.

After a time he became aware that the conference had ended. Slowly he reached behind the bed and pulled the plug out of the wall socket. Evidently the fact that Petrovna had saved the human race by producing an antidote to the Exterminators' mutated diphtheria bacillus meant nothing to them. And the discussion he had missed meant equally little to him. In the end he knew that Ed Martin would come into his room one night with plastic models and biology books filled with illustrations in bold colours, asking for questions to which he could provide answers. His mentors would tell him the complete and total truth about the sex act, as they had on all other subjects, and in the end he would feel again as if his mind had been filled with semi-useless knowledge. They would do this because they had no better substitute for reality. And he knew equally well that he would listen, and smile, and absorb the gist of what they told him, in case he was questioned about it later. And the next time he ran away—which would be soon—he would steal enough money to buy the services of a prostitute, and experience the truth for himself. Masturbation, at first so pleasurable, was already turning into a dull and lonely exercise.

chapter 5

THE EMERGENCY CONFERENCE began less than twenty-four hours after Petrovna's death. Marina was the last to arrive. When she seated herself General Cloke rapped lightly for attention and said, "Let's start with a report from Dr. Barnstein on the condition of our large friend. Doctor?"

Gold did not know most of the men gathered around a long table in the general's office, but Dr. Barnstein was the technicians' supervisor called Hans who had played an important role in subduing the waking giant. He leaned forward and said, "The patient seems back to normal. The abrasions on the fingers have been treated and appear to be healing. The new variable dosage controller we installed in the autonomic console is working properly and should prevent another unplanned activation."

The doctor sat down and General Cloke went briskly around the table, requesting reports from supervisors in charge of the giant's support systems and other base activities. One of the latter interested Gold; the giant's small lifeboat had been modified for human control and was ready for flight.

The general smoothly skipped over Gold. Marina was last. "Do you feel able to return to work?" he asked the small woman.

"Yes," said Marina, her voice low but firm. She did not raise her eyes from the table.

"Then we'll proceed with formulating our alternate plan," the base commander went on. "Dr. Barnstein, are you capable of replacing Petrovna on the autonomic console?"

"I know enough to operate the console," Hans said carefully, "but my understanding of the modifications made to the internal physiology of our captive is weak, and one mistake can kill him. I doubt that anyone other than Petrovna understands the system he designed well enough to man that console."

He sat down in an ominous silence. Marina broke it by saying, "No, I can operate it." Her thin voice and small size made her seem an impertinent child speaking out in a meeting of adults.

"I was afraid of that," General Cloke said with a brief smile.

"The body will undergo major changes when it resumes charge of its own functions," Marina went on quietly. "Only someone who thoroughly understands the total hybrid system can adapt it from external to internal controls. And a large percentage of the changes Petrovna made were never documented; he could not spare the time. I am afraid I must be Mr. Gold's partner if he accepts the assignment."

All eyes at the table swung to Gold. He kept his gaze on the slightly florid face of the base commander and asked, in a voice heavy with irony, "Do you really expect a 'rotten young pup' to take on a job that will probably get him killed?"

General Cloke met his stare without flinching. "Don't be ridiculous, Gold. That bit where I played the part of the heavy was intended to assure a 'yes' answer from you. Petrovna felt the acting was unnecessary, but the psych boys insisted on it and he finally went along. And no, I don't actually consider you a 'rotten pup,' though I think it's perfectly true that your emotional development hardly matches the physical and intellectual. I apologize for my part in playing that small trick on you. Now we must do what we can to salvage something from the tremendous effort involved here."

Gold felt slightly stunned by the bland acknowledgement that even Petrovna had joined in a small deceit to manipulate the emotions of the younger *Homo superior*. For a moment he considered walking out, although he had made up his mind before the meeting to do what he could to fulfill Petrovna's scheme. And then he decided one more bit of trickery hardly mattered, shrugged, and said, "I accept."

There was no discernible change in the Britisher's face, but Gold felt a tenseness flow out of the room. The general's answer was a brief, "Good." He launched into a series of details on getting the giant back into his lifeboat, and Gold was soon bored. After a few minutes the base commander noticed his restlessness and interrupted a windy report to suggest that Marina take Gold to the simulator and start his training programme.

Marina led Gold to a small lab, where a console identical to the one in the giant's eye waited in a tangle of wiring and associated machinery. A large curved screen stood where the transparent cornea would be above the real console. Several men were working at various tasks in the small room.

Marina introduced Gold to Teddy Parkinson, who had assisted Petrovna in designing the console and was the author of the training document. Parkinson was a lean Nordic almost as tall as Gold, with a ready smile and an indefatigable attachment to his work. He shook hands affably, and in five minutes had Gold strapped into the operator's chair, his large fingers moving hesitantly from knob to knob under the guidance of the programme book. Marina quietly left.

It took only a few minutes for Gold to realize the true complexity of operating the great body. Individual movements were easily started, but controlling the extremely complicated series of interrelated actions necessary to accomplish even simple tasks was unbelievably difficult. Five knobs had to be turned, each to a separate point, for the action of raising an arm, extending it, and opening the fingers. Grasping an object was not a simple matter of reversing some of the same knobs, since a different set of efferent nerves controlled finger closing action. Two of the original five knobs had to be returned to neutral and two more activated. And at that, he learned, the computer that relayed each of his commands was actually enlarging and expanding his control by a factor of over eight to one. There were very few single nerves connected to individual controls on the console.

Memorizing the first series of programmes was a slow process. Gold moved carefully through each routine, imprinting the various knobs and their positions on his permanent memory. Each knob controlled not only a portion of an action, but the speed at which it progressed, and once a movement had been completed each control had to be returned to neutral or the affected muscles would remain in constant tension. Gold looked ahead to the more complex tasks awaiting him, such as getting the body erect and walking it into the alien's lifeboat, and wondered if they were physically possible. As Petrovna had said, this was going to be one of the few tasks he had attempted that afforded him a genuine challenge.

Grimly, Gold concentrated on his work.

"Do you think you are ready, Gold?" the high voice of Marina asked in his left earphone.

"I took a nap before coming to work," he answered with

studied carelessness. "Any more training and I'd be past my peak."

"The roll-out will begin in a few minutes. I suggest a preliminary run through of the cart removal movements in the 'power off' mode."

"Nope," Gold answered cheerfully. "I'm accustomed to seeing the little lights blinking on my board. It would throw me off stride if I turned a knob and nothing happened."

There was a brief silence before Marina said, "Very well. I am going to increase the heartbeat rate as a precaution in case of emergency."

"No emergencies in the programme," replied Gold.

The silence that met his sally held more than a hint of frostiness. He grinned sourly at the multi-faceted control board and let his fingers stray back and forth over the hundreds of knobs and switches. His view through the one-way fake cornea showed only the ceiling, but he knew that many technicians were scurrying around the great body, in the final steps of lifting the giant's limbs and placing them on specially designed powered vehicles. There was little for him to do until they were in the open and he could activate the dormant muscles.

"We're almost ready, Gold," the deeper voice of Hans Barnstein said in his right ear. "Did it jar you when we set the head on its platform?"

"I don't think our host bit off more than a yard of his tongue," Gold answered.

"You're a lying bastard," Hans said affably. "I doubt you even felt it." He was one of the few men in the crew who seemed to like Gold, and a member of the even smaller number that found him acceptable company off the job.

"How long before we start to move, Dr. Barnstein?" the cool voice of Marina broke in.

"About five minutes. The boys on the carts are finishing their pre-roll checks now."

The great body was resting comfortably on twelve self-powered vehicles whose tops had been formed to the contours of the area they supported. When the giant had been brought inside, twenty months before, the base personnel had used what equipment they had on hand, resulting in many bruises. The damage would have been worse, despite the moon's low gravity, except for two interesting facts Gold had learned after starting his training course. Each individual cell in the alien's body was several times larger than the equivalent human one, and the tissue as a whole was of a much lighter, more flexible, yet far stronger construction. It was commonly agreed by base physiological experts that this meant the giants' home planet was considerably larger than Earth, but with a lower gravity . . . a notion that met with no favour among the few astronomers still manning the 120-inch telescope which the moonbase had been originally designed to support.

"Ready to roll," a new voice announced on the external channel.

"Roll 'em then," Hans said briskly.

The twelve drivers applied power to their wheels, but the command had been too abrupt for some of them. The giant body shuddered, lurched forward, rocked back in place, and then slowly edged ahead. There were several garbled exchanges on the external channel as too many people attempted to use it, and then Hans and the other supervisors regained some measure of control and began coordinating the speed of all vehicles. Gold saw the rock ceiling moving backward at a barely perceptible rate.

The prisoner had been brought into the long room head first, and was exiting feet first. The speed of movement increased as the twelve operators gained proficiency, and within five minutes Gold saw the formed rock edge of the swinging door pass above his head. They were in the airlock that had been lengthened to admit the almost 300-foot long body. The emergency enlargement had taken two weeks during which they had pumped air into the planetary lander. For some reason the life-boat's oxygen supply had been low and the alien was breathing from his spacesuit tank, itself almost empty, when he landed. Gold's growing respect for General Cloke had risen again when he learned the apparently foppish base commander had made the decision to provide the obviously dying giant with air. Unfortunately, by the time the technical problems involved were worked out the suit oxygen had been exhausted and the alien brain severely damaged. The moonbase personnel had succeeded in keeping the giant alive, but at the cost of all intelligence. Petrovna had been called in to restore it, but not even he could do the impossible. And now Gold was here, and attempting to do the almost impossible.

Gold flipped his mike switch to the internal channel and said, "Marina, I hope you people understand this boy's tight underwear as well as you claim."

"There is no danger," Marina said evenly. "This close-fitting spacesuit is radically different from the pressurized type you are accustomed to, but it is equally effective. The thousands of tiny air ducts incorporated in the material itself work as well as the larger ones in our suits, I assure you."

The studied calmness of her tone masked irritation and dislike. Gold turned partially around in his console chair and glanced downward. The doors between compartments had been removed. When the fake eyeball was centred in its socket he could see through the opening to Marina's console, where she sat with her back to him in the second compartment. She was busily at work.

The tangle of voices on the external channel was overridden by Hans. "Stand by; the door's starting to move."

Gold heard a whistling hiss as air started fleeing into the external vacuum. He was hearing the sound through the console's sensory helmet, which was connected to external sound receptors located in the right ear and left nostril of the host. The close-fitting faceplate of the giant's suit contained its own receptors that relayed external sounds to the air inside.

It took only minutes for the shrill whining to die away. The giant body had been taking air from its own backpack for some time. After a moment Hans said, "Gold, we're about ready to move again."

"Waiting on you, Doc."

"Good. Drivers, this time we will start on my countdown. And try to stay together a little better, please." Hans droned through a brief five-four-three-two-one-go!, and the forward movement resumed. This time it was both smoother and faster, and it was only a few minutes before the outer door was passing above Gold's eyes. The light faded as the head exited into shadow, out the sheer side of one of the centre mountains in the mighty crater Copernicus. Gold found himself looking up at the stars.

It was only another minute before Hans called the procession to a halt. "Ready for the sit-up whenever you are, Gold," he added. "Just don't squash any of us when you place those hands, please."

"I hear ya' tawkin'," Gold replied noncommittally, though he was grinning to himself. Exchanging pleasantries did not come easily; he had had little practice.

The programme called for Gold to raise the great arms one at a time, freeing them from the trucks supporting each elbow, move them backward as far as they would go, and place the hands flat on the surface before he attempted to sit erect. The trucks supporting the great buttocks were designed to withstand the full weight of the body.

Gold had rehearsed this initial programme a thousand times. He operated the first eight controls involved, and had the satisfaction of feeling the mighty arms lift, slowly extend, and move back. When the broad hands came to rest he swiftly restored three of the knobs to neutral, turned off two switches, and twisted the single knob controlling the forward tilt of the head. He felt a tremor of motion as the neck muscles tightened and increased the current; the compartment in which he sat slowly rose and tilted toward the horizontal. It had not quite attained it when the muscles reached their limit and the forward motion stopped. Gold found himself looking across the great depression at the massive grandeur of the northern wall, rearing skyward in an indescribable jumble of craggy prominences. He had landed at night and missed this awe-inspiring landscape.

Gold locked the neck in its forward position and returned to the arms, this time exerting a downward pressure on the wide-spread forearms. The trunk moved slowly upward, bending at the hips. There was an unplanned shifting and trembling in the head, and for a moment he thought he had neglected some part of the programme despite his intensive training. And then he realized it was a nervous shaking in the long unused muscles, a reaction beyond his control.

"Speed up the erection!" Marina said sharply on the internal channel.

Evidently something was not going according to plan. Gold fed more power to the arm muscles and saw the horizon swing sickeningly as the torso lifted at greater speed. A moment later he was leaning forward in his chair, held in place by the seat-belt, as the trunk neared the vertical position and the head tilted sharply downward. He moved knobs back to neutral and turned off switches as fast as his fingers could fly. The forward motion stopped just after the torso swayed past centre. Gold left enough tension on the arms for the palms, now flat on the crater's surface, to hold the trunk erect. Then he raised the head until his compartment was level again. To his surprise Gold realized he was sweating profusely. He had been actively operating their giant host for less than three minutes.

"I believe you should lift those arms long enough to swing them as far as you can to the rear, to relieve the strain on the torso," the voice of Hans said in Gold's ear. "The back muscles appear almost ready to spasm."

Gold followed the suggestion, and felt a slight settling in the body that indicated it was in a more relaxed position. This had not been on the programme, but it seemed a sensible step.

"Let's give the heart a rest before we start the side tilts and truck removal," Marina requested. "I received unexpectedly high strain indications while the torso was rising."

"You're the doctor," Gold replied, and relaxed. After three minutes Marina informed him the heart action was back to normal. Gold twisted the torso and raised the right hip, then the left. The heavy duty vehicles moved out and joined the others against the mountain.

Gold moved to a new area on his control board. He drew the left leg upward and placed the foot flat on the ground, just in front of the buttock. He repeated the previous roll made to free the truck under the right buttock, and saw with surprise that the right arm lifted clear of the ground and swung forward in an automatic balancing motion. Gold assumed charge of the moving limb and placed the palm flat on the rock surface, activated the left leg muscles, and felt the great buttocks clear the ground as the torso tilted forward. Then the body was on both knees and the head was swinging downward. Gold swiftly compensated and brought it erect again, realizing as he did so that the host had somehow exerted his own sense of balance and was crouching in apparent comfort on his hands and knees.

Gold found his hands flying over the familiar console with a speed that matched the best runs he had made on the simulator. He tilted the torso back until the body was sitting on its haunches, extended the left leg, and stood erect. There was a dizzying sense of speed as the terrain flowed before his eyes, and then Marina was saying urgently, "The heart! It's failing! Can you move to the wall and lean against it? Quickly! I'm pumping in adrenalin and stepping up the pacemaker voltage."

The body was facing the slanting rock wall in which the airlock door was embedded. Hoping the innate sense of balance that seemed so strong would continue to operate, Gold moved the switches that activated the walking muscles. The body took two easy steps, reached the wall, and leaned against it just as Gold was returning the switches to neutral. And then he saw that the right arm had moved again without his direction, this time shifting away from what was apparently a jagged protrusion in the rough surface.

The earphones were quiet for a few minutes while the

body rested, and then Marina said, "The pulse rate has gone down and the adrenalin level in the blood is dropping. Recovery seems to be quite rapid. I apologize for overestimating the strength of this body."

"Do you think he can make it to the lifeboat?" Gold asked.

"Yes, but not yet. Are you maintaining this posture, or is the body's own balance system working?"

"A little of both."

Four minutes later Marina reported that according to her indicators the host was almost back to normal. It was time to move. Gold checked his own board one last time, saw nothing wrong, and took the final step that would determine success or failure. He pulled the slumping shoulders erect again and let the body find its own balance. Then, his fingers a blur of motion across uncounted switches and knobs, he turned the body and started it walking toward the planetary lander a half-mile away.

Walking and guiding their host provided some surprises. The body's own sense of balance took over completely. The legs responded to steering commands immediately and to the correct degree. Once the optimum speed was determined Gold had only to watch ahead and guide the tremendously long feet away from major obstacles. But the speed of motion from that height was bewildering; it was much like driving a car with the seat and controls 300 feet above the rest of the unit.

The door to the lander was open, and Gold moved the body inside its tight-fitting single compartment without difficulty. He utilized the giant's strength to close and lock the swinging panel, having difficulty only with the finger motions. After that the body was to become a passenger. Auxiliary controls had been rigged into a small console in the top of the nose, where two experienced pilots would actually operate the vehicle. In overall dimensions the lander was only half again the passenger's height and barely wide enough to admit the broad shoulders. It was powered by a small fission device using direct explosive impact for propulsion, and represented only a minor improvement over similar vehicles built on a smaller scale on Earth. It was obviously not the power source used by the huge interstellar ships.

Gold used the giant's hands to connect the lander's oxygen supply to the skin-tight spacesuit, saving the gas in the back-pack tank for emergencies. After a moment the pilot's voice came over the external channel with a brief report. "All systems functional. Ready for lift-off whenever you are."

Gold checked briefly with Marina and Hans, and reported, "We're waiting on you, Cap."

"Very good. If you'll move the arms forward I'll lock you in place."

Gold moved the arms as bidden, and protective pads came out of recessed niches and pressed against the wide hips, locking the host gently but firmly upright. There was no other shock-absorbing system on the one-man craft. It was designed to land under the direct control of its occupant, and slowly enough not to endanger life.

Gold felt the first faint vibration as individual uranium molecules merged in explosive fury, and a moment later the lifeboat gently lifted from the surface. The craft gained speed, curving away from the surface of the moon. The pilot had operated it several times previously and knew his business. Within five minutes Earth's satellite was a swiftly receding golden ball behind them.

Mars was less than fifty million miles away, and the small ship had enough fuel to cover the distance in two days of constant acceleration and deceleration. After the first four hours of flight it was obvious even to Gold's inexperienced eyes that they were building up an enormous velocity. When he became bored he placed his console under the control of the computer, unstrapped himself from the chair, and stepped through the rear door into Marina's chamber, stooping to avoid the low overhead. Their rate of acceleration was maintaining gravity at slightly better than earth-normal. Marina glanced up from her smaller console without speaking. It was obvious from the almost motionless dials on her unit, and her lack of activity, that the autonomic processes were also working well.

"I must admit that this hair-brained scheme is off to a good start," Gold ventured, somewhat uncertainly.

Marina turned and gave him a calm, cool stare. "Petrovna planned well; his projects always succeeded."

She antagonized Gold immediately. He stared down at the withdrawn oriental features in quizzical mockery. "Perhaps, but he died by the finger of an idiot that didn't even know what it was doing. He died quickly and uselessly, and he will never know if his master plan was a tremendous wasted effort or a success."

Marina turned quickly to her console, but not in time to

nide the hurt. After a moment she said, "No one can know in advance if the giants share our cultural patterns enough to be willing to rescue a lost comrade. The part of the plan which Petrovna had under his direct control has been proven." Her thin voice was icily controlled, but hot anger lay just beneath the surface.

Gold found himself staring at the coarse black hair on the back of her round head. He turned and strolled into the living quarters without answering, drank some water from the cooling unit, and idly inspected the quarters he and Marina would share for an indefinite period. They seemed far more adequate and livable with the giant in the upright position. He was hungry, and after a few minutes of hunting managed to find some immediately edible food. After eating he used the waste disposal in the equipment room and returned to his console.

As he passed Marina she stopped him with a worried, "Gold, I'm afraid we have a problem developing. The peristaltic rushes in the intestines are proceeding more swiftly than I had expected. At this rate the rectum will fill in a few hours and the body will need to defecate."

Gold threw his head back and laughed. Marina tilted her chair to stare up at him, her face expressionless. When he stopped she said quietly, "I fail to see the humour in the situation."

"You wouldn't," Gold agreed, still grinning. "Tell me; doesn't it strike you as ridiculous that we can be controlling the actions of a billion-dollar machine made of flesh, flying an alien spaceship to a planet fifty million miles away, and the one problem we can't solve is that our host needs to take a crap?"

Marina's face remained set and cold. "The alien spacesuit contains a relief tube for urine. There are no provisions for disposal of solid wastes. The suit must be worn until we reach Mars." She said it as though lecturing to a child.

"Then why did you start him back on solid food before leaving the Moon?" Gold asked, in what he felt was a reasonable tone.

"We felt it best to activate the digestive system while we had the equipment in the lab to support us. Are you aware that reviving organs that have been dormant for twenty months is a major operation?"

"Our large friend may not have any choice about crapping without the support of lab equipment," Gold replied, grinning.

"Yes, he does," Marina said as she turned back to her console. "I'm going to see if I can inhibit the gastrolic reflex and lock off the first anal sphincter. He's going to arrive constipated but clean!"

The landing on Mars was uneventful. The pilot brought the lifeboat down within easy walking distance of the largest cavern. The airlock was open, waiting for them, and Gold manoeuvred the body inside with little difficulty. A crew from Moonbase was waiting to dismantle the temporary controls installed in the alien lifeboat. When they were through there would be no evidence it had been tampered with. The four ships that had brought the Earthmen, and with whom the two pilots would return, were parked over a low rounded hill, at the second and smaller cavern.

The technicians were efficient and fast. Within ten minutes Gold had the body lying down inside the single huge room the giants had made by enlarging the original series of caverns, and trained men were busily removing the tight-fitting spacesuit. He attempted to help them with the body's hands and fingers, but his control of delicate manipulation was poor at best, and in the end he stretched the arms out and let the Earthmen complete the disrobement. When the giant was stripped to his even tighter inner garment Marina called Gold and told him with reserved earnestness what they must do next.

Gold managed the complicated ritual of getting the body to its feet with comparative ease. Their host seemed to take all actions necessary to maintain his balance with even less help than before. Within three minutes Gold had the Brobdingnagian buttocks sitting on a waste disposal box not too dissimilar to the one in their own equipment room. Marina had succeeded; their host had landed still clean.

The body needed rest, and so did its passengers. After a long break Gold returned to the console to begin a planned series of exercises, and for the next several days seldom left his chair except for short periods of exhausted sleep. Marina started warming and bringing him his meals. At the end of the second day he had mastered enough finger control to place food in the mouth without dropping it, and could put the body through most of the simpler actions a normal human performed, though the movements were slow. Once he almost stepped on a soldier when making a turn without sufficient warning, and another time he bruised the right knuckles by an accidental encounter with a rock wall. The bruises indicated that the sensory helmet, till then apparently useless, was beginning to function. Gold felt a diffused but definite sense of pain.

The function of the helmet was to relay sensory impressions from the host's skin to the equivalent receiving area of Gold's brain. The helmet itself was only the end of a complicated system of relays and amplifiers, with the broadcasting elements so arranged that a radio impulse was transmitted by point focusing to the chosen neural area in Gold's cortex. He had been warned that this part of the system was very much experimental, and might require a long adjustment period. It would be an extremely useful device if it functioned, though. Without a sense of touch it would be impossible to become proficient at manipulating the fingers.

At the end of three days Gold and Marina had a short enforced intimacy. The tool that had been especially designed to remove the stubby growth of hair on his head proved awkward for self use, and she had to complete the job for him. They agreed that in the future she would maintain his scalp in the pristine state of baldness required to keep the sensory cap fitting properly.

On the fourth day Gold fumbled and the host took a full-length fall. As they were going down, far too swiftly for him to do anything with his controls, he felt certain the venture was going to end then and there. They were falling toward a solid rock wall, and both head and passengers were seconds away from destruction. And then Gold learned to appreciate the brilliance of Petrovna. The arms moved of their own accord, both hands slamming into the rock face before the bare skull followed.

When the pandemonium subsided and the skull was examined by the attending technicians, they found the impact had caused nothing worse than a severe bruise. Gold discussed the incident with Marina, and learned what he should have already suspected. Petrovna had made no hook-ups that interefered with the functions performed by reflex action in the spinal column. When a bodily emergency occurred the brain was temporarily shorted out and the connections between afferent and efferent nerves in the spinal column ruled. Part of Petrovna's genius had consisted of knowing when to leave well enough alone.

After a week of preparations the crew from Moonbase was ready to return home. The distress signal had been in operation for two days, and according to the best estimates the giants' next attack would occur within two weeks. Gold said good-bye to the colonel in charge of the expeditionary force with mixed feelings. With the sole exception of Marina he was about to attain a fantasy he had often dreamed of as a boy, a world of his own. But he had never expected to feel regret at seeing the last Earthman depart, nor possession to be under these peculiar circumstances.

The Exterminators arrived one day early.

chapter 6

THE EXTERMINATORS LAUNCHED their tenth biological attack against Earth from a new approach angle, having obviously changed course behind the sun while curving around it and slowing to below FTL speed. They were within four million miles when detected, and their course took them closer than three. The huge interstellar ship registered on the defence forces radar screens for less than four minutes, from pick-up to loss after acceleration to FTL. The capsule they released had an initial velocity of over 100,000 miles a second. It performed the usual evasive manoeuvres, started braking while still several thousand miles away, and was coming down over Australia when a useless barrage of missiles left the atmosphere above North America and Russia to intercept it and chase the receding mother ship. The capsule reached the upper air layers and released its new strain of bacteria, to be wind-blown over much of the down-under continent. Petrovna's successors inherited the responsibility of saving all humanity from death, as the stunted Russian had saved them some eight times previously. Only the first attack, at the time the Exterminators abandoned the Mars Station, had died out naturally.

Gold and Marina heard the news on their external headphone channel, which had been tied in to the station's powerful radio and large antenna. They would have no way of knowing if the gamble had succeeded until the huge vessel appeared overhead, or enough time elapsed to be certain it had gone. The imponderables were incalculable. There was nothing to do but sit and wait.

One factor, at least, was in their favour. The new approach the Exterminators had used would bring them close to Mars on their way out of the solar system.

Five minutes went by, and then ten. At the end of half an hour Gold asked, "What do you think?"

"It looks bad, but let's not give up yet," Marina said carefully. "Perhaps it's taking them several minutes to make a decision."

Gold searched his memory banks for knowledge he had had to store to pass physics courses, and realized after two partial playbacks that the major problem would be decreasing the velocity of the ship before turning back. It was definitely too soon to write off the mission as a failure.

It was over an hour after the Exterminators' ship had vanished from Earth's radar before it landed outside the cavern on Mars.

Gold had the body sitting against an inner wall, facing the airlock door. The plan called for them to make the giant behave as though he were brain-damaged and acting primarily from instinct and training. There was little else they could reasonably do, and if the giants' cultural conditioning did not require them to return injured brothers to the home planet the venture would fail at the first contact.

The inner airlock door opened and two great clothed figures stepped inside. Their spacesuits were identical to that worn by the body, and they moved with fluid ease. In motion they seemed even larger than the host, whom Gold had seen only in repose. They walked quickly across the room and bent over the motionless figure on the floor. Gold kept the body's face slack and vacant by holding the mouth partially open.

One of the two visitors placed his face directly in front of the host's, gazing intently into the eyes. Gold found himself staring up through the transparent cornea into a great frowning countenance, where perception and intelligence combined into an expression he had yet to see on their captive.

The giant straightened up and turned to his companion. There was a rapid radio exchange, and then the first man began looking around the room. He spotted the discarded spacesuit and went after it. The two of them pulled the body away from the wall and laid it flat on the floor. Gold tried frantically to flip switches and turn knobs fast enough to compensate for the muscular movements, then realized that was the hard way and returned all his controls to neutral. The two men made allowances for slack muscles and kept the body from falling as they moved it about.

In five minutes the visitors had the suit on and functioning, and were attempting to get the host to his feet. This time Gold helped them, and with one man supporting each arm they moved out of the airlock and toward the spherical ship, which seemed to tower for miles into the thin Martian air. They boarded so rapidly the vessel's interior was only a blur to Gold. The host was strapped into a chair, which immediately tilted back and locked in place. In less than thirty minutes from the time it had landed the interstellar ship was climbing swiftly into space.

Gold was pressed back into his console chair by the G forces of rapid acceleration. He managed to turn his head when he remembered Marina's position, and glanced at her through the doorway. She had swivelled her chair around and was facing him. In that position she could endure the stress as well as he, but could not reach her console controls.

Gold found himself staring at a blank, featureless metal ceiling over a hundred feet above his eyes. He made himself as comfortable as possible and waited out the time. At the end of two hours the acceleration eased and then died away. A moment later, the chair in which the host sat was tilted back to the horizontal, and Gold found himself staring around at what was obviously a spaceship's control room. Three of the giants sat at consoles not too dissimilar to his own, though much less complicated. One was standing by the host's side, examining him solicitously, and a fifth was moving toward the rear of the compartment. Gold saw by the odd, jerky way the man was walking that he was held to the floor by magnetic shoes. Evidently these people had no artificial gravity.

The room was filled with such a maze of equipment that it had no discernible pattern to Gold. He ignored it for the moment, concentrating on what the giant standing by him was attempting to do. It soon became obvious. Their host's faceplate was removed, and a moment later the backpack. Gold kept the body passive as the man swiftly peeled off the rest of the spacesuit. New shoes of the magnetic type appeared and were slipped on the extra-long feet. Gold saw that the others were also stripping down to the close-fitting undergarment. The spacesuits were stored away in a compartment. All the giants had the same dark brown skin, lack of hair, and heavy musculature as the host.

The rest break was brief. After a few minutes of stretching and moving about the fifth man returned and claimed his seat. The one who was apparently assigned to the host tilted the chair back to the rest angle, and a moment later the force of acceleration was pinning them down again.

"This is an excellent angle for prolonged exposure to G forces," the voice of Marina came over his earphone. "The heart has a natural tendency to beat slightly faster, and there is a slight but definite percentage increase in blood flow to the brain."

Gold slowly turned his head—sudden movements could be painful—and saw that Marina was sitting facing her console, one arm resisting the strong forward pull while she carefully checked dials and gauges.

"You'd better turn around. That position will become painful," Gold said sharply.

Marina did not answer, but after a moment she settled back in her chair, letting the safety belt restrain her, and slowly worked it around until she was facing him again. "I wanted to be certain there were no physiological problems inherent in this long stress situation," she said calmly.

Gold carefully worked his gaze back to his own console, and checked his hundreds of signals. All were normal. There was nothing to do but wait.

The rate of acceleration never varied, but the second period lasted four hours. When it ended there was a moment of weightlessness, and then Gold felt a gentle tugging of gravity, accompanied by an odd horizontal pull. The semi-spherical ship was rotating on its long axis.

"Gold, do you have any indication of our direction?" Marina asked. She sounded worried.

"Not the foggiest," Gold answered cheerfully. "This control room is completely enclosed. I caught a glimpse of a viewscreen on one of the pilot consoles, but the star patterns meant nothing to me."

The conversation was interrupted by two giants, who unstrapped the body and assisted it to its feet. Gold cooperated by letting the autonomic system supply balance and leg motion. A few steps brought them to the medical facilities, and the two men helped the host lie down on a couch. Gold found himself in the uncomfortable position of having his chair at the extreme rear of its track while he leaned forward and reached upward to touch the controls. It was an awkward arrangement, although made physically easy by the light gravity. He tightened the neck muscles and raised the great head. After a moment someone took the hint and slipped a support beneath it. Gold let the neck muscles relax, and found himself tilted at only thirty degrees from the vertical.

The man who had removed the spacesuit leaned over the host. Gold was suddenly blinded by a flood of light through the cornea, and twisted the knob that would close the eyelid; it was being held open. He began to move the host's neck muscles, causing the head to twist from side to side, and succeeded in freeing the eye. The lid closed under the impulse he was already feeding it, and Gold hastily returned the neck controls to neutral. The left eye had closed also, and he opened it by itself. The light had gone away. Gold cautiously cracked the right eyelid again, and found himself looking at a great bony ridge of forehead. The giant examining the host, obviously the crew's medical specialist, had taken the hint and was looking at the other eye.

After a moment the man straightened and returned his equipment to a holding device on the wall. He donned a pair of very thick opaque glasses and started passing what appeared to be a small hand mike slowly back and forth in front of the neck and chest. Gold saw that a thin wire connected the sensor to the glasses. He had no idea what the instrument was telling the examiner.

The giant used two other instruments whose purpose was equally lost on Gold, and then left the room. He turned and told Marina about the examination. She looked worn and tired, as though the constant strain of the past several hours of acceleration were telling heavily on her. When he finished he saw that she was staring at him with a questioning look that seemed vaguely familiar.

A fragment of memory intruded into Gold's conscious mind, annoying him slightly. After a moment he realized this was another of those insistent upwellings from his permanent memory, triggered into being by some strong reaction Maina's expression had aroused. He could replay at will almost any scene which he had noticed with strong conscious attention, including the individual words of a book's page that he had photographically scanned. His guardians had never understood why he had taken to the piano in his eighth year, and spent long hours practising during the rest of his stay at the Institute. Young Albert had not bothered to explain that he was playing mechanically, while his real attention was centred on an internal mental process. And he had never become a good pianist. People had flocked to see and hear Gold after he left the Institute because he was a genetically evolved freak, not a great player. For Gold's purposes it hadn't mattered; as Petrovna had pointed out, he had obtained the capital which enabled him to make his successful assault on Wall Street.

Gold knew that he could exert himself and dismiss the intruding memory, but he was curious about it being triggered by Marina's face. His partner had turned back to her work, question unasked, and he let the thrusting image from the memory banks appear for a moment. When he recognized it he hastily looked again at his console, checking the entire face; all controls were in neutral. Gold relaxed in his chair and concentrated on the insistent scene. He realized this would be the first time he had deliberately recreated this sequence in its entirety, though vagrant parts of it had returned before. It was not a pleasant memory.

The woman's face took on form and substance. She was only part Oriental, and it was more the expression than the features that had stirred Gold's memory. She obviously had several racial strains in her ancestry; one of them had turned her skin a rich brown.

The face diminished in size as the area around her came into focus. The woman was standing in front of a door, holding out one hand. The curious expression faded as Albert removed a money clip from the pocket and peeled off thirty dollars. She took the bills and slipped them into her blouse, stepping away from the door. As Albert started inside she said, "That pays the bill, Whiteboy, but if you wanna hot time you better tell Littlebit you gone leave 'er a good tip. I dunno why you picked that youngin' anyway. One'nah our grown wimmen 'ud be better for a boy like you."

Albert closed the door in her face without answering, not wanting to admit that he had chosen the one called Littlebit precisely because she looked small, young, and inexperienced. He had just turned fifteen, and she seemed hardly older. Littlebit was apparently new at her vocation; his own awkwardness and lack of knowledge might not be so obvious to her.

Littlebit, who had preceded Albert, was already in bed. She was a short, slim girl with an adolescent leanness in hip and shoulder. The faded grey cover sheet was pulled up to her waist; the exposed breasts were small. Her skin was a dark tan, and she had coarse black hair that fell straight to narrow shoulders. Albert saw that her features were even and smooth without being pretty. Downstairs she had seemed to have a quality of shyness and lurking innocence that indicated she would uphold her end of any bargain, but this was all new to her.

Albert looked around the narrow, dingy room, desperately wishing he was back in his comfortable quarters at the Institute. This was the sixth time he had run away, and the first when he had left with a specific aim. It was also his shortest trip. He had hidden in the back of a delivery truck and ridden it to Manhattan, hopping out at a stoplight just past the Washington Bridge. The entire northern end of the island was now one vast slum, and he had located a house of prostitution by simply offering a young boy a dollar to point out the nearest. Once inside he had known enough of the normal routine to examine the girls lounging in the parlour and make his choice. At that time of the afternoon he had been the only customer, and most of the girls had been loafing, not soliciting business.

The girl on the bed was staring questioningly at Albert, a slightly mocking smile on the young face. She had one hand on the sheet, ready to throw it back and admit him. *And then suddenly the girl's face and the dingy room seemed to recede, spinning out of sight, and another face loomed before his eyes, growing tangible, firming . . .* something from deep in his childhood was rushing forward, blocking out the reply, and *abruptly Gold yanked himself out, back and away, and opened his eyes,* to find himself sitting in front of his console. There was sweat on his forehead. With a feeling of surprise he realized that for the first time he had encountered a memory that his conscious mind did not want to recall. The odd part of this was that he was quite certain there had been no playback at the time he had entered the room and stood staring at the girl. This unrecognized stranger pushing up from deep within his subconscious had been triggered by the replay process itself, and specifically by the sight of Littlebit's face with its mocking half-smile.

Gold turned for a quick look at Marina. She was busily writing in her notebook. He spun around again and relaxed, letting his mind plunge back into the scene he had just left, back to the point where the girl waiting in bed had seemed to trigger the older memory. He tried to stop the flow and bring the girl's features into sharper focus, seeing again the quizzical, half-scornful expression on her young face. That was the key into the more distant past. *And after a moment Littlebit's face blurred, shifted, and then appeared again, subtly altered. She had turned into a photograph.*

Albert blinked his eyes, and refocused them. He was holding a small folder, one made of a thick stack of black-and-white photographs. The top picture was of a young Negro girl lying on a bed with a sheet pulled up around her neck, staring toward the camera with mocking inquisitiveness. He turned to the second photograph. It showed the girl with the sheet pushed down to her waist. Her large breasts swung forward as she leaned on one arm, chest thrust outward and one hand behind her head in an assumed siren's pose. Her eyes were still fixed on the camera.

In the third picture the young woman had retained the pose but kicked the sheet away. The camera angle had changed slightly and now took in the entire body. Albert stared with absorbed interest; this was the first time he had seen any adult with all clothes off.

In the fourth picture the girl had rolled over on her back. The camera had moved closer and above, to focus on the full-length figure. The mocking smile on her face had deepened, become more challenging. She continued to reveal more and more of her body until the eighth frame, when there was an abrupt, unexplained intrusion by a male figure. The girl had retreated to the head of the bed and gotten to her knees, holding the sheet around herself in apparent fright. As the series continued the person who had appeared from nowhere, a wide-shouldered, powerfully built nude man with a very white skin, ripped the sheet from the girl's hands and laid her forcefully on the bed. The next two pictures showed the two clinging tightly together, the girl's fright completely gone, their mouths pressed together.

"Whut you doin' here, boy!"

There was menace and anger in the tone. As Albert spun around, guiltily closing the folder without having seen the last few photographs, the man in the doorway sprang at him. One hand snatched away the pictures and the other caught the boy across the face with a slap that knocked him sideways to the floor. For a moment he hovered on the verge of unconsciousness, and then rough hands picked him up and shook him violently. Through eyes swimming in tears of pain he saw a middle-aged, red-faced man he recognized as one of the janitors, hand drawn back for another slap. It came, rocking his head from side to side, but this time the grip of the other hand held him erect. Abruptly he was propelled across the floor, out of the door, and tossed on his face into the corridor, skidding down the cold slick tile until he banged up against a side wall. Then he did lose his senses, but only for a moment. When he recovered the florid, angry face was bending over him, and the janitor was saying, "Listen, boy, I dunno whose littl' bastard you are, but don't you never come pokin' around my room again! Now you just forgit you saw them pictures and don't tell nobody I slapped you or I'll fix you good! You hear?"

Albert, numb with fright and pain, could only nod with desperate earnestness. His mouth was filling with blood from a cut inside his cheek, where the first slap had smashed the flesh against the teeth, and he still felt light-headed. And then he saw a subtle change come over the face of the man bending over him. The adult studied the cringing boy for a moment, then abruptly turned and went to his room.

When the door closed behind the janitor Albert lay still, too frightened to move. When the quiet endured he scrambled to his feet and fled down the corridor as fast as he could run, taking the stairs at the end rather than wait for the elevator. Minutes later he was lying across his bed, still trembling with fright and receding pain. He was forced to stumble to the bathroom and empty his mouth of blood, and while there he bathed his face. The bleeding finally stopped. He returned to the bed and fell at once into an exhausted slumber.

Albert was awakened by a firm knock at the door. Still half asleep he called, "Come in," and before he could retract the permission one of his teachers had entered. She gasped in fright when she saw his swollen face.

"I slipped," Albert said immediately, his voice thin but firm. "I slipped in the bathroom and fell and hit my face on the tub. I'm all right now though."

"My heavens, Albert! Your face—I'll have to call the doctor! Why your precious brain could have been . . . now you just wait right here! I'll be back in a minute."

She turned and fled, forgetting there was a phone in the room. And then the scene started blurring before Albert's eyes. He suddenly found himself back in the dirty room, staring at the young prostitute again.

Gold pulled himself out of the later memory, opening his eyes to the reality of the cornea and the wall of the interstellar ship's dispensary. The feelings of pain and terror he had just re-experienced were so vivid some traces lingered on, and he sat quietly until they died away. Then he went back over the replay, examining details that bothered him. The most obvious one was the odd look that had appeared on the southern white technot's face while he was bending over the boy he had just beaten. The adult Gold could recognize it as compassion, and regret. The man had examined Albert that extra moment to be certain he was not seriously hurt.

The technot could not have realized that he had just endangered the brain the entire Institute had originally been built to serve. Certainly he would not have known that his concern came far too late, that the damage he had inflicted was not physical in nature.

The Institute's purpose had changed when Albert was less than two years old. The original huge team had been reduced to five people, and the building's new business was convincing all humanity to serve the war effort. At that time the invaders—they were not called the Exterminators until they launched the first biological attack in 1989—were holding Mars, and the reorganized and strengthened United Nations was building a fleet of interplanetary missiles. Some seven years of world-wide effort had gone into that mighty force, and it had partially served its function; though all Earth missiles were destroyed, the aliens gave up their base in the solar system after the battle. But the total concentration on war had brought a degree of regimentation that would not have been acceptable to democratic countries before, and the loss of many programmes that might otherwise have prospered. Gold was one of them.

The traumatic experience with the janitor had occurred when Gold was barely five, and the team was still concentrating on giving him the tools with which to learn. They had started trying to pound actual knowledge into his curly blond head shortly afterward. To that point he had progressed at approximately the same speed as Petrovna, though it was unlikely Petrovna had shared the child's habit of spying on adults and searching their rooms when they were out.

When the accumulation of facts began it was accompanied by an intensification of training, and young Albert had rebelled. If a test bored him he deliberately performed it incorrectly, leading to highly erratic scores. He was already beginning to feel what he would later assume was the dominant attitude of his mentors—that he was an object to be manipulated. At that early age the feeling was not clearly defined, but it bred a confused and resentful attitude that caused him to question his tutor's insistence that he learn. He could not verbally express his resentment, and had kept it to himself. The small feeling of power that came from keeping secrets had become a habit with the child.

Littlebit's dark face had reappeared and passed before Gold's eye twice while he was thinking. He decided to finish the second sequence.

The thin young face solidified, became real. The scene firmed up, and she was still lying on the bed, staring at him, an expression of contempt on her face. Littlebit seemed to dislike his hesitancy; after a minute, very deliberately, she tossed the sheet back and moved both arms and legs wide apart. Her genitalia were plainly visible.

Albert stared at her in troubled wonder, then lifted his gaze to the single window. Bright afternoon sunlight fought its way through a dirty pane and peeped past slatted blinds, making golden bars on the floor. The walls were stained and old. The room had an ancient, musty stench, partially hidden under an overlying smell of disinfectant. The air was still and dead, and it was already uncomfortably warm. Albert felt a sheen of perspiration on his forehead, and a stickiness under his arms. At the moment he wanted nothing more than to be out of there and back in his clean, cool rooms at the Institute, free from the insolence and growing contempt on the young girl's face.

"Listen, white boy," she spoke slowly and deliberately, "you want it, come git it. We don' give no refunds."

Albert spun around and reached for the door. With one hand on the knob he changed his mind and turned back, frantically stripping off his clothes. In blind desperation, knowing that if he stopped all was lost, he piled clothes on the chair and then almost hurled himself at the waiting girl. His mind was in a whirling, chaotic confusion; he could almost sense his brain recording the visual image of the room and its occupant, the smell of the overwashed sheets when he reached them, the feel of sweat on his body. He landed too heavily on Littlebit, and saw quick anger on her face. He had no true consciousness of what he was doing, but felt that he was not able to perform the act. He tried to reach the girl's lips, and she turned her face away. Slim arms locked around his neck, pulling his head down on her shoulder. She began to writhe her hips. After several futile tries, with no conscious effort on his part, with no true awareness of whether or not he was capable of performing, he suddenly found that he was moving almost in unison with the girl, that she was holding him with one hand, guiding his thrusts, and that somehow he had actually started to penetrate her.

There was no time to feel satisfaction, or wonder if this was all the sensation provided by sex. He was suddenly aware of the unmistakable feeling of having passed the point where he could hold back. And then a series of shuddering convulsions seemed to emanate at the base of his spine and move over his entire body in peristaltic waves of inevitable, irresistible force. He collapsed on her thin chest, breathing in heavy gasps, and it was done.

After a moment, impatiently, she pushed him off and wriggled from beneath, sitting up on the side of the bed. Albert lay on his stomach, numb and dazed, staring at Littlebit. She met his gaze levelly, and the look of contempt had faded, though there was still no trace of warmth or affection on her cold face.

When Albert continued to lie on the bed, not moving, she said, "Listen, you wanna go again, it's another ten dollars. You oughta' gi' me ten mo' anyway, considerin' you a cherry." When he still made no move she added, "An' if you don't, git outta here. I don' like you white boys too much no how. Always sneakin' up here from downtown 'cause the black stuff's cheaper."

Her words jarred Albert into reluctant action. He sat erect, staring down at his lap in stunned wonder. After a moment the girl rose to her feet and walked to a washbasin, where she wet a cloth and tossed it to him. "Clean yosef' up and git outta here."

Slowly Albert did as she ordered, regaining his self control as he dressed. When ready to leave he opened the moneyclip and extracted its contents. He had a little over forty dollars of what he had stolen from the Institute's petty cash drawer. The girl watched him counting, the disdain on her face struggling with obvious greed. She said nothing, but stood there waiting as he turned to go.

Albert paused in the door, pulled a five from the roll, and tossed the rest to Littlebit. The money hit the girl between her small breasts and fell to the floor. She made no move to pick it up. He hastily closed the door and almost ran for the street.

On the sidewalk in front of the ancient brownstone, indistinguishable from a hundred of its crumbling neighbours on both sides, Albert paused to orient himself. Then he headed south, knowing that he must walk for several miles to reach a street served by a busline. Neither subways nor buses now ran north of Central Park.

The streets were not crowded, but many middle-aged and older residents sat on their stoops to escape the heat inside. They stared at Albert as he passed with lack-lustre eyes. Many small businesses were open along the jumbled street, but there was a curious lethargy, an uncaring attitude about both the shop owners and their few patrons. These were the technots, the dispossessed people who had nothing to look forward to except another day's aimless wandering through their ghetto, or ten hours of mindless mechanical labour in one of the few unskilled jobs still available. The revolutionary social changes that had swept the country in the sixties had been followed by determined governmental action in the seventies. But then the vast technological resources of the country, which were slowly being mobilized against the internal problems of poverty and ignorance, were suddenly diverted back to making war when the aliens struck in 1981.

Gold realized that the scene before Albert's eyes was dim, and the thoughts as much his as those of his younger self. He pulled completely out of the playback; Albert had walked until he caught a bus downtown, and another back to the Institute. There was nothing else of sufficient interest to have impressed itself on his permanent memory.

Gold spun around, and saw that Marina's chair was empty. Her console status lights were solid rows of green. He checked his own dials, and saw that nothing had moved during the few minutes he had been withdrawn. He was aware of a gnawing sense of hunger, and realized it had been several hours since he had eaten. Gold unstrapped himself and headed for the living quarters. If the giant's friends returned they would be able to move the limp body around to suit themselves.

Marina was evidently in the equipment room. Gold busied himself preparing a snack from their ample store, his mind still preoccupied with the past. He was thinking not so much of Littlebit as the huge technot class she represented, those who had seen all their gains disappear between 1981 and 2000. The attack by aliens had had a unifying effect world wide—Russia and the United States were now the firmest of allies—but it had heightened the internal problems of many countries. All of Earth's resources had been needed to provide the powerful missiles that were launched against Mars while at the same time building a network of defensive interceptors and exploring every super-weapon concept that seemed remotely feasible. The United States, like the other technologically advanced nations, had had to discontinue internal social improvements. In countries more advanced in integration this had caused few problems, but the world's major industrial power, as a grim and prophetic book published in 1968 had warned could happen, became two societies, separate and unequal. The American Negroes formed the bulk of the technot class, but it also included many whites from rural areas, Latin Americans, and dropouts from the dominant middle-class white culture.

No one knew who had coined the term technocrats for the educated and trained people who manned the war machine, but the word technot had been a natural follow-on for the deprived class.

There had been a series of small civil wars in the early nineties, when it became clear that the nation was moving backward in its social programmes. But wars by a poor minority against a rich majority had little effect. They had been put down with all necessary force, and the end result had been many technot lives lost and tremendous property damage, mostly in the ghetto areas. As usual, the poor had suffered most.

Each country had its own unique problems. Many of the smaller nations in Africa and Asia had disintegrated back into hostile tribes, ignored by the rest of the world unless their material resources were needed . . . in which case they were taken.

After the abortive wars the United States government had herded the poor and ignorant into big city ghettoes and established a pass system; no technot left his area without permission. A few held jobs in the white community and moved back and forth between the two societies. Others distributed the free food that was provided by America's mechanized farms, and administered what other goods and services were available. The technots were left to eat, talk, read if they could, and watch television . . . which was also free. The old Harlem, now grown to cover almost half of Manhattan Island, became a typical isolated community, racial prejudices almost forgotten by a new class integrated in economic misery. These communities were growing like cancers in every major city in the United States. It took much less effort to feed, clothe and provide television to twenty million lost human beings than to educate and train them for useful occupations in a highly complex technological society. Some forgotten President had promised that the great social programmes which had started to eliminate poverty would be resumed when the world was again safe. There was little the technot class could do but wait.

Back at the Institute Albert had received the usual sane, sensible lecture on why he should not endanger his very valuable life on mere adolescent whims. As Martin made his reasoned, deliberate points Albert had wondered how the scientist could fail to realize he was winning every battle with his young charge, but losing the war.

As a concession to the difficulties his mentors could put in his way Albert made his next trip to New York at night, at a time when he was supposed to be in his room studying. It was child's play to steal money and a vehicle. Passing as a technot was somewhat more difficult. He changed his appearance by standing in front of a mirror, squinting slightly, and pulling his thick lips down in a permanent scowl, achieving a look of deep stupidity. The impression was helped by his prognathous jaw. He cultivated a hesitant, slurred way of speaking, imitating many of the speech mannerisms used by Littlebit.

Gold remembered that first trip into town quite well. Albert had never driven a car. There were few vehicles on the road even in New York—gasoline was severely rationed—and he survived long enough to learn. He parked in a garage south of Central Park and walked into Harlem. For four hours he did little more than prowl the streets, shoulders slouched, stub of a cigarette in his mouth, his bright blond hair hidden under a soft cap. When he grew tired he went home, only to repeat the trip two nights later. On the third excursion he started patronizing some of the small stores, and within a month became well enough known in the area he frequented to have acquired an identity. The walls of the Institute had shielded him from this grim, purposeless world, so different from the antiseptic, ordered environment in which he lived that he found it endlessly fascinating.

He did not visit another prostitute during the entire year he spent becoming acquainted with the forgotten denizens of Harlem.

chapter 7

GOLD CHECKED THE exterior scene; all was quiet and the lights had dimmed as though for a rest period. He was ragingly hungry. Marina had left her station, but he decided to take a chance and prepare a sandwich. The living quarters were empty but Marina entered from the equipment room as Gold finished his food. She seated herself in the computer chair and said immediately, "Gold, I think we should discuss our future course. It seems apparent that our first priority, capturing this vessel and holding it for boarding parties from Earth, is impractical. Priority Two, gathering information and relaying it back by radio, is obviously impossible. We are therefore left with Priority Three, which requires us to accompany the Exterminators to their home planet, gather all possible data, and return to Earth as best we can. You will recall that the major suggestions given us under Priority Three were to learn the language, accumulate all possible data on both the giants and their home environment, and determine the reason for this unprovoked effort at human genocide. Do you have any ideas on how to accomplish these objectives?"

Gold shrugged. "Why not follow such a well-planned procedure to the letter? I presume our computer's been stuffed with info on how to learn a language. Have it print out a few books and I'll start absorbing the basics."

"Very well. I'll attend to the books while you get some sleep. I think we are going to be left alone while the crew rests after that period of strain under constant acceleration."

Gold suddenly realized how tired he really was. He agreed with alacrity, and within three minutes was drifting off to sleep, lulled by the soft clicking of the computer printing out pages. He awoke some indefinite time later, to find Marina shaking him. The lines of fatigue around her eyes were deep and drawn.

"All quiet," she said briefly. "I collated and stapled your books." She turned toward the other bed, undoing the fasteners on her standard white coveralls as she walked. Gold, still lethargic with sleep, lay watching with bemused eyes as she stripped down to a soft protective undergarment that covered her short form from neck to ankles. It was a light shade of green, and the colour contrasted oddly with her dark skin and rich black hair. With an audible sigh of relief she stretched out, pulled the zippered cover up around her neck, and fell asleep almost immediately.

Gold carried the five books Marina had chosen to his console chair. As was his custom with quick-study projects he ran through the material at a speed that would imprint it only on his short-term memory, and then relaxed and let the analytic portion of his subconscious—which he had learned to use without understanding it—compare and condense the new inputs. After a few minutes the knowledge that one of the five was grossly inadequate slowly filtered into his consciousness. He smiled when he realized it was a well-known and accepted book used in many college courses. Gold discarded it, along with duplications and inadequacies in the others, and was left with the equivalent of two full books. He closed his eyes and concentrated on replaying the portions he needed to retain, scanning them at a pace slow enough to ensure their being imprinted on his permanent memory. There was still an integration phase to undergo before the new knowledge could be fully absorbed, during which it would be compared to, evaluated against, and eventually become part of the matrix of his total education. This was another subconscious process over which he had little control. He did not have to await this final synthesis before starting to learn the new language.

Gold was pulled out of his reverie by the sound of approaching footsteps. Hastily he strapped himself in and slipped on his sensor helmet. When he looked up the man he had assumed to be a medical specialist was staring intently into his face, from only a few yards away. After a moment he spoke, the deep voice carrying a questioning tone common to many human languages. Gold hesitated, thinking rapidly, then touched a small control he had not yet utilized, located at the extreme left end of his console. He turned it slowly for half its range, and though he could not see the effect he did note the look of acute interest on the giant's face.

Gold had made the corners of the host's mouth move upward.

The attending giant leaned forward, placed one hand on the host's shoulder in a companionable gesture, and said three sharp words. Gold stored them away with the others he had already memorized, and briefly increased the size of the smile before returning the features to their usual neutral expression. When the giant spoke again Gold pulled the forehead down in a frown of concentration. It was time for the host to become something more than a vegetable; the medical man must be convinced the damaged brain could learn again.

Abruptly the visitor pulled a sliding panel out of a wall socket, seated himself on it, and slowly and clearly enunciated a series of what were obviously test words. Gold activated his single control to the larynx and caused the host to utter a deep, muttering groan.

The other giant accepted the mournful sound as encouraging. He rose and stepped to a grille in the wall that was evidently an intership communicator, and spoke briefly. The grille answered, and after a moment the giant returned to his seat, lifted his left hand, and pointed all five fingers at his chest. "Ru-A-Lin," he said gravely.

Gold, at a loss, did not respond. After a moment the giant repeated the word and gesture, and then pointed all fingers at the host's chest and said, "Soam-A-Tane."

And now Gold knew the body's official name.

The tests and one way conversation went on for an hour. It was apparent Ru-A-Lin was attempting to determine the degree of damage to his patient's brain. Gold responded throughout as best he could. At a minimum he was acquiring vocabulary. He had no way of knowing if he had convinced the medic that the host's injured brain could be reeducated and salvaged.

Gold returned the body to a resting position on the bunk and went in search of Marina. She was still asleep. He made himself comfortable and began the process of recall and study that he had used so effectively while playing the piano as a boy. Four hours later Marina stirred, attempted to sit up, and then remembered where she was and zipped down the safety cover. When she seemed fully awake Gold brought her up to date, including his expectation that Ru-A-Lin would be returning for more sessions.

Marina prepared food for them both as Gold talked, and though it was hastily done he discovered that his companion had a skill he did not possess. She was an excellent cook.

After the meal Marina ran some routine checks and updated her records. Gold returned to his studies. They ate two more meals and slept through one more quiet period before Ru-A-Lin returned to put the host through another session. This time Gold used his limited control of the host's larynx and facial expression more frequently. Marina was at her console during the second round, and after an hour she informed Gold the host needed to eliminate. Gold guided it to the disposal unit and seated the great bulk, a manoeuvre he performed with comparative ease. He saw the puzzled, somewhat abstracted look on Ru-A-Lin's face, and realized the action did not match the idiot level at which the body otherwise functioned. It seemed obvious that, as with humans, the excretory functions were among the first to fade from conscious control when the brain suffered extensive damage.

Ru-A-Lin watched the entire operation—there was no wall around the disposal unit—and took notes with what was apparently an electrostatic pen and slate set. Gold saw that there was no physical transfer between the stylus and thick pad, but a dark mark appeared where the point touched the flat surface. When the smooth, opaque pad was covered the giant pressed a button on the bottom and the writing disappeared; the content had obviously been transferred.

When the session was over and Ru-A-Lin had gone, Gold turned to Marina. "What are the chances of modifying this control on the larynx to build up a speaking ability?"

Marina pondered a moment before saying, "Almost none. Speech is a complex interaction of larynx control, moving air, shape of the mouth, tongue position, and so on. Almost impossible to duplicate in the lab, much less here."

"Then we'll establish communication by writing." Gold told her what he had seen of the electronic notebook, and its unusual ability to store information.

Marina nodded thoughtfully. "Apparently it's simply an advanced version of our own computer's ability to read data written on its faceplate. Probably the input is transmitted to the ship's equivalent of a computer, not stored in the pad. As for learning to write rather than speak, we have no way of knowing if this is in conformance with their culture or will stand out as an oddity."

"Then we'll just have to take a chance, won't we."

"I presume so," Marina replied, with the coolness that seldom left her voice. She turned back to her console.

The days settled into a routine of eating, sleeping, and learning. The medic seemed willing to concentrate on teaching his patient vocabulary. Gold found that the host was to be fed twice each alternate shift, two hours after the second sixteen-hour period started and two before it ended. The non-eating shift was a rest-sleep period for all but a watchman, and he and Marina took turns and managed a full night's rest for both.

On the eighth day of lessons Gold felt ready to try his hand at writing. Ru-A-Lin had given him a physical examination, taking frequent notes. When it was over Gold hesitantly picked up the stylus and made some scribbles across the pad's blue surface. Ru-A-Lin watched him, highly interested, and Gold diligently drew nonsense figures before running out of room and cleaning the board. Then he drew a man's figure, and printed beneath it the symbol Ru-A-Lin had used on each set of notes. According to his growing understanding of the language this was the written version of his name.

The host handed the pad to Ru-A-Lin. He examined it and looked up, his face unusually animated. "Soam-A-Tane!"

Gold's assumption had been correct, and he had at least a partial understanding of the written language. It tied in quite well with the fundamental laws of language and speech he had absorbed from the four good books. Evidently humanoids, regardless of size, were forced to operate within a fairly narrow range of possible means of verbal and written expression.

Gold settled down into some of the hardest work of his life. He discovered early that there was a strong correlation between the written and spoken word. He soon learned that the language possessed sixty phonemes, each usually with four phones. The basic structure was quite similar to that of several Indo-European languages. The primary difference he could see was that the giants' longer vocal cords gave them a verbal apparatus capable of finer distinctions, as well as the obvious quality of deep voice. The finer control had apparently led to a more complex verbal language.

Within six study periods Gold had learned the basics of the spoken tongue, at least enough to understand some of the questions Ru-A-Lin kept asking. Marina followed his progress with strong interest, but otherwise maintained her cool reserve. After a few more shifts Gold was tentatively writing on the pad, with the encouragement of Ru-A-Lin. He made no further effort to use the body's larynx. This seemed acceptable to his mentor, who concentrated on the writing lessons. Ru-A-Lin started coming in twice a day, and extended the sessions to four hours. The medic seemed convinced that his patient was slowly recovering his normal faculties.

Six weeks after the lessons started Gold attempted his first actual conversation with the giant. He wrote questions, his control of the heavy fingers rough but firm, and Ru-A-Lin both wrote and spoke his answers.

//I am Soam-A-Tane, question?//

Ru-A-Lin quickly wrote out his answer, then read it aloud; "You are Soam-A-Tane."

//You are Ru-A-Lin, question?//

Again a hastily written and spoken answer, "I am Ru-A-Lin."

//We are *Hilt-Sil,* question?//

"We are *Hilt-Sil.*"

//I have lost my memory, question?//

"Yes, but you are slowly recovering it."

//One day I will remember, question?//

"One day you will remember everything." Ru-A-Lin's voice did not sound too positive.

//We are going home, question?//

"Affirmative."

//I have a wife and children, question?//

"Yes, and they have been waiting for you since your ship failed to return."

The exchange was torturously slow. Gold's control of the stylus would never match that of a normal adult, although the body had received intensive practice in writing and the faculty was still partially under the control of the autonomic nervous system. Gold had only to start shaping the correct symbol and the fingers would finish it.

The session lasted for the usual four hours. When Ru-A-Lin left, Gold found that he was drenched with sweat, despite the constant cool temperature in the compartment. He placed his controls in neutral and spun around to face Marina, who had relaxed at her own console and was looking at him through the door. He briefly brought her up to date on what he had learned, including the fact that in four more shifts they would start decelerating to land on the home planet . . . which he still had not located in the galaxy. His mate would be notified when they dropped below FTL—evidently there was no way for an electromagnetic wave to exceed the speed of light, making physical delivery the fastest communication system between stars—and he would be placed in her care until Ru-A-Lin could make his trip reports and finish restoring his patient's memory and full mental powers.

"This Ru-A-Lin seems to be the equivalent of a combination doctor-psych officer on one of our submarines," Gold finished. "He's concerned with mental as well as physical health. I'm trying to make him think Soam-A-Tane's brain is responding to therapy so well that surgery won't be necessary."

Marina nodded without smiling. "You are doing well, Gold," she admitted, grudging admiration in her thin voice. "Your choice as console operator was one of the few times I disagreed with Petrovna. I thought he was wrong, but as usual it was myself."

Gold flashed her a mocking grin. "Petrovna? Wrong?"

He saw anger tense the muscles in her face. She turned her back on him, and he whirled around to his own console. A moment later her cool, controlled voice came over the earphone; "The body needs rest now. I suggest we move to the bunk for a minimum of four hours."

Gold mentally shrugged, and did as she said. When the body was comfortable he left to catch a nap himself, feeling in need of one. Marina acknowledged his passing with brief instructions on how to prepare food for them both.

The few remaining days before deceleration passed quickly. According to the counter on Marina's console they had been in space over seven Earth weeks. She worked out a rough estimate of the distance they had travelled by calculating their attained speed—the acceleration rate was known from several consistent readings by Earth radars, and her console had recorded the time under G-stress—and multiplying it against the time in coast. Then she added the expected distance they would move while decelerating, and adjusted the final figure downward to allow for not travelling in a straight line. Marina was reasonably certain their course had been altered during the first rest period, and that this was a consistent habit to prevent Earth getting a direct fix on the alien's planet There was no other logical explanation for the fact all ships left on courses a few de grees apart but within the radius of a very large circle toward the galaxy's centre. According to her figures they would have travelled approximately 700 light years, which would place the giants' planet near the outer edge of the Orion arm, bordering on the great 10,000 light year gulf between their spiral and the inner arm, Sagittarius.

If the Exterminators wanted to eliminate *Homo sapiens* in order to claim his planet, the generally accepted opinion, they had apparently passed several thousand solar systems on the way to their goal. Which indicated that planets with Earth's particular attributes were rare, as had been frequently postulated.

Ru-A-Lin continued to visit Gold almost up to the first period of deceleration. The other members of the five-man crew wandered in and out at intervals; Gold had learned their names but little else. Ru-A-Lin evidently had the fewest routine flight duties and was free to devote most of his time to Soam-A-Tane. Gold had swiftly learned that the giant was a patient man, evidently kind by nature, doggedly determined to do his best for an injured comrade, and timely almost to the second. The study programme he had evolved would have been excellent for a damaged brain seeking to recover buried memories, but was less than ideal for Gold, learning from the beginning.

There was a quiet, methodical, rather slow sureness about the actions of all the crew that made Gold wonder if their basic nature was not somewhat phlegmatic and calm. He saw little of the emotional conflict that would have been obvious in a crew of Earthmen confined in close quarters for a period of months.

One of Ru-A-Lin's attempts to restore the host's memory had consisted of leading him around the spaceship and identifying objects. When Gold was able to do little more than memorize the names without understanding form or function, the effort was abandoned.

Due to the long sessions with Ru-A-Lin Gold found himself becoming very proficient on the console. He also discovered that he was making finer sensual discriminations from the sensations beamed into his brain by the point-focus helmet. What had formerly seemed the most rudimentary indications of heat-cold-pressure-moisture became identifiable as warm food, the resistance of the stylus in the clumsy fingers, and even muscular fatigue. The relayed sensations never attained the sharpness and clarity of his own, but they were accurate enough to greatly aid in controlling the host. Petrovna had designed far better than he knew with his experimental receptor cap.

Marina spent much less time than Gold at her console; it was primarily automatic in operation, though frequent adjustments were desirable. She prepared their meals and performed all the routine maintenance work required for both their own comfort and that of the host. There was a set coolness in her attitude, a deliberate emotionless quality in her voice, that convinced Gold she heartily disliked him. Nor did he find Marina attractive. On the few occasions he saw her partially undressed the sight did not disturb him. Nor did Marina seem embarrassed if she saw him on the toilet or undressed. She seemed unaware of sex distinctions.

Ru-A-Lin appeared to strap the host in, and the deceleration started shortly afterward. This time the newness had worn off, and the hours spent resisting the steady pressure were a dull monotony of light torment. The break between deceleration periods was a welcome relief, but passed all too quickly. At the end of the second period Gold found himself as fatigued as if he had been engaged in hard physical labour.

When Ru-A-Lin returned to unstrap the body Gold learned they were about to enter an orbit around the home planet. A few minutes later there was a gentle bump as another ship, obviously a shuttle, attached itself to the starship. Gold found one of his earlier thoughts confirmed. The larger ship was not designed for landing on planets. It had been possible on Mars only because of the light gravity and extremely thin atmosphere.

Gold was able to assist Ru-A-Lin in enclosing the host in his spacesuit, and the job was soon accomplished. The giant psychdoctor led the way to the airlock, and Gold saw that the control room was deserted except for two new faces. Apparently a maintenance crew had piloted the shuttle up and would stay with the orbiting interstellar ship. His guess was confirmed when he saw the other four crewmen, and no one else, in the shuttle. Most of the men had a look of mild elation on their faces, and the highest sense of excitement he had yet seen. Some of them seemed almost gay when they broke loose from the larger ship and dropped swiftly toward the planet below.

The shuttle was equipped with large areas of polarized

glass. By turning the host's head to compensate for the nose that blocked his view to the left, Gold saw that they had arrived just after dawn; a sun that seemed far larger and more yellow than old Sol was advancing slowly from a distant horizon. There were only scattered clouds below, and the air seemed unusually clear compared to that of Earth. The horizons appeared to move backward on both sides as they descended.

As they reached the upper edges of the atmosphere light shields moved into place over the windows. There was a teleview screen in front of the pilot, but the view was straight ahead only. Gold's brief survey of the surface had indicated the planet was similar to Earth, except for a light yellow tinge in the atmosphere.

The landing was performed in what seemed to Gold a less than proficient manner, as though the pilot was not an expert with this machine. He never faltered or made a real mistake, but his actions were almost unduly slow and measured. The shuttle handled and landed like an aircar, and when its wheels touched down the contact was jarring. Gold noticed that his sense of weight had gradually returned, increasing until it seemed only a little less than normal. The curve of the land as they made their approach indicated the planet was roughly twice the size of Earth. So the biologists on the moon had won their argument with the astronomers. It *was* possible for a planet much larger than Earth to possess a slightly lower surface gravity. And in turn this made the physiology of the giants more believable, even though their size was still irreconcilable with current Earth theories.

As the shuttle coasted to a stop the screens over the windows were lifted again.

chapter 8

GOLD HAD NOT really known what to expect, but the scene outside would have been at the bottom of any ordered list. They were sitting near the edge of a grass-covered meadow that ended abruptly in trees and shrubbery, green but with a faint touch of red. Most of the vegetation seemed gigantic by Earth's scale, but was otherwise normal. The total effect added up to a little-used landing field in a rural area, hardly the complex facilities he would have expected of a spacefaring species. To one side, almost hidden in a grove of the huge trees, was an open-front building similar to an airplane hangar. Inside were two more shuttles like their own. There was no other sign of habitation.

Ru-A-Lin appeared to unstrap Soam-A-Tane, and for the next several minutes Gold was too busy for further observation. Once outside he was able to walk the host in a fairly well co-ordinated fashion. Ru-A-Lin led him away from the rest of the crew, who had been met by several new giants and were walking with them toward the hangar.

"Your wife, Leet-A, should be arriving shortly," said the medic. "I have warned her that you are not fully recovered mentally from the effects of being stranded."

They stopped at the edge of the field to wait. It was only two or three minutes before a flyer arrived, but it landed just outside the building. A female got out and ran toward one of the giants, who strode rapidly to meet her. For a first meeting after a long separation their greeting was restrained, by human standards, but the woman did run into the man's arms for a tight hug and a long kiss. Evidently their manner of showing affection was quite similar to that of the majority of people on Earth.

Gold saw that the woman had hair, a long, dark-yellow mane of it that hung to her waist. She was dressed in a form-fitting tunic that left the muscular arms and legs bare, and except for the *Hilt-Sil* comparative heaviness and shortness of form, was an attractive female.

Gold saw several men who had emerged from the building looking toward them, and realized they were discussing the unexpected return of Soam-A-Tane with the space voyagers. Evidently Ru-A-Lin had not wanted his patient to mix with people who did not understand his condition.

The wife and husband soon left, and as they entered the flyer Gold saw that it was actually a very small vehicle compared to its passengers. Obviously individual air transport was the primary form of travel for the *Hilt-Sil.* Two more craft landed shortly afterward, and then another. Finally a fourth floated to the ground in front of them. Gold saw that it was little more than a flying box with rudimentary streamlining and no wings. A woman emerged and spoke briefly to Ru-A-Lin. Gold understood enough of the medic's reply to realize she was being informed the brain had been damaged but was slowly recovering. He also caught part of Ru-A-Lin's instructions to take good physical care of him, and that the compassionate medic would be along later to continue the therapy.

The woman nodded, and helped Ru-A-Lin fasten the host in a small but comfortable seat. She closed the door, strapped herself in, and a moment later the flyer lifted off.

As usual when there was a great deal of external activity, Gold had not been able to take it all in. His view through the eye was limited on the left, and the console demanded most of his attention. Simply manoeuvring the body, and performing the hundred actions needed to complete any complicated motion, kept him very busy. He was now good enough to make the host do reasonably complex activities, but the process required all his conscious attention.

Now that the host was still again Gold turned the head and looked at the woman on his left. He saw that she in turn had been looking at Soam-A-Tane, a deeply troubled expression on her face. Leet-A's hair was similar to that of the first female he had seen, but confined in a narrow braid that fell to her hips. It was a rich, russet gold in colour. She seemed as tanned as the males he had seen, and for a *Hilt-Sil* was quite slim. She was only slightly shorter and sturdier in general form than Marina.

As Gold stared at Leet-A she suddenly reached and impulsively clasped the host above the elbow, in such a fashion their two forearms came together. Gold felt the warmth of her skin through the sensor helmet, another indication that he was learning to pick up relatively weak sensual signals. Her skin seemed smooth without being soft. She held the contact tightly for a moment, looking into his eyes; the look of distress on her face grew stronger. Gold, uncertain of the proper response, did nothing. After a moment two huge globules of water welled from the corners of Leet-A's eyes and ran in small streamlets down her brown cheeks. They were followed by more, but there were no sobs or other sounds of anguish. After a moment, very slowly, she turned away, broke the physical contact, and wiped her eyes with the back of a hand.

Gold had decided in advance to play the reunion as numb and unresponsive as possible. Somehow he sensed that the woman sitting beside the host was suffering more than was outwardly evident, and his resolve weakened. After a moment he made the body rumble deep in its throat, the only sound he could manage, and reached with the right arm to clasp her above the elbow. With a cry of happiness that told him he had guessed correctly Leet-A moved her elbow and brought their forearms in contact again. The tears started flowing once more, but now Gold could tell they were signs of joy. This was confirmed a moment later when she leaned forward and planted the great soft lips on those of the host, so quickly Gold was shocked into paralysis for a few seconds. He hastily moved the correct controls to draw the mouth into the only expression he could manage, a half-smile. Through the sensor helmet he felt her lips press tighter against the body's in response. The caress held for a moment, and then the woman broke the contact and resumed her place at the controls.

Gold returned his attention to the ground below. They were flying over what seemed primarily woods, broken by frequent areas of cultivation. But even the tilled soil did not have the regular spacing of ploughed rows on Earth, and he had seen many individual trees standing in otherwise clear fields. There were also frequent areas of grass, but little animal life large enough to be seen from the air.

A few minutes later the aircar descended, slowing with a deceleration that pulled Soam-A-Tane hard against his straps and Gold tight against the seatbelt in his console chair. They drifted gently to a stop on the grass; evidently these people had no use for concrete.

They had landed in front of a grove of the towering trees. Gold saw something odd in their midst and studied it, trying to understand. To his amazement he saw that every tree was growing into, through, and about a structural form that could only be a type of house.

As his eyes began to pick out more details he saw that the home of Soam-A-Tane and Leet-A was so built into and a part of the grove that it was difficult to distinguish between the trees and the dwelling. Many areas were partially open, shielded from the rain only by sloping roofs. Others were obviously sealed with movable walls, usually oval in shape. Only the central hull seemed completely enclosed. It was both the most rustic and most beautiful house Gold had ever seen.

Leet-A had already got out. She came around to his side, opened the door, and unstrapped the host. Gold manoeuvred the body out and upright, and turned to see two wildly running young giants rushing toward him, a girl who would reach to Soam-A-Tane's waist and a boy slightly taller. He spread his arms and bent to gather in his children.

The two young ones snuggled into the host's arms with glad cries and affectionate pawing. There was a sudden blurring on the exterior of the plastic panel through which Gold saw this world of giants, a film of moisture he recognized as flowing tears . . . the host was crying.

The implications of this sudden surge of raw emotion, of which he would not have thought the body capable, jarred Gold. Evidently the left cerebrum was more active than anyone had suspected, and was functioning at more than the autonomic level. Apparently strong memories were still available in that remaining centre of intelligence, and they were capable of causing semi-voluntary actions not subject to Gold's immediate control. And yet, the impulse for movement had acted through him. Soam-A-Tane had knelt and clasped his children because Gold's busy fingers had moved the right controls. It had become obvious during the first activation that the giant body still controlled more of its own functions than had been anticipated by the human designers. Now Gold found himself wondering if the charade he was playing with Ru-A-Lin was backed by reality, and the remaining hemisphere of the damaged brain was now indeed slowly recovering.

Gold saw that Leet-A had moved toward him and was looking critically at the tears on her husband's cheeks, a tremulous smile on her lips. He carefully lowered the children to the ground and took each by the hand as they turned toward the house. His human eyes had grown accustomed to the huge scale, and he realized that the trees around which the building spread its multi-faceted exterior were actually short in comparison to a *Hilt-Sil,* barely four times an adult's height. The grass on which they walked seemed only a few times larger in stem and blade size than the coarser grasses of Earth. The grain crop he could see growing in a field to their right stood less than thirty feet high, though the heads were heavy with seed. He received a general impression that the *Hilt-Sil* were larger in proportion to their vegetation than any animal on Earth.

Gold's eyes turned back to the odd house. Apparently the many cornices and slanting surfaces that formed the roof were made by fastening the tree trunks together with large timbers. The walls were suspended from this roof, rather than supporting it. The shape of the exterior was determined by the position of the individual trees within the grove; there were at least twenty vertical surfaces set at angles to any given centreline. Evidently not a single tree had been cut to make room, and those supporting the house appeared green and healthy. Their growth must have somehow been arrested, or the structure would not have been stable for very long.

The walls were painted many shades of green. There were no windows, or glass of any sort, but many openings led into the house at ground level and higher. As they approached the main entryway Gold saw one resemblance to Earth-type buildings. There was a solid hardwood floor extending the full length of the area under roof.

Gold stopped at the door and turned the host for a long look at the countryside. He saw several more groves of trees, two in the distance apparently with houses like this one. Between them and on all sides, as far as he could see, cultivated fields alternated with trees and grass. Most of the trees were in groups, and there was very little dense undergrowth. The entire countryside had a clean, tended look, and Gold suddenly realized the distinction between cultivated food-growing areas and "woods" was a construct of his own mind. The whole area was cultivated, part for food and the rest for natural beauty. He was standing in the middle of a huge park. That thought was followed by one that almost physically jarred him. From the air the country had seemed remarkably uniform in basic layout. He had failed to spot houses because of their unique construction as part of the total scene, and what had seemed deserted woods and farmland was actually identical to the area before him. The entire *planet* was one gigantic park!

Lee-A stepped inside and gently tugged at the host's arm. Gold reluctantly followed, while the stunning knowledge of how wrong he had been sank in. Subconsciously he had been expecting cities, factories, and technological marvels perhaps new to human experience. Instead he had found a species that apparently lived evenly scattered over their planet's habitable area, with a life style that did not require grouping for productivity. But that meant . . . Gold's mind reeled at the thought, but it had to be true. They were even *more* advanced than he had expected! The only reconciliation between interstellar travel and this benign rusticity was that they had moved *past* mass production, into some unguessed system of need fulfilment not yet dreamed of on Earth.

The implications were staggering. This might be a form of civilization so completely alien to all that humans considered inevitable in technological progress that Gold had no basis for comparison. According to what Earth had learned of the Exterminators' technology it was only a few measurable steps above the human, at least in those areas where they had alien artifacts for comparison. This tied in with what Gold had seen of their rudimentary space port facilities, obviously temporary buildings that had not been designed to blend with the environment. These people were extremely advanced on their own planet, but comparatively primitive in space.

As the host stepped inside the entryway after Leet-A, Gold felt a mild tingling transmitted through the sensory cap, followed by an immediate change in temperature. The apparently open area was guarded by an electrical field of some sort, and the air inside was artificially cooled.

The interior was a surprise. Most structures appeared to be made of wood. Cupboards and compartments were everywhere, attached to the various tree trunks, hanging on the interior walls, or sitting on the floor. There were no wall partitions, but it was obvious from the arrangement of furnishings that certain areas were used for specific activities. There were manufactured articles in abundance. A grid of metallic wires hung just below the ceiling and spread over the entire area, in a fairly even distribution. They were glowing faintly and Gold realized they would brighten as the outer light dimmed. One corner formed by an odd arrangement of tree trunks was apparently a laboratory, filled with equipment strange to Gold. Many other items throughout the house were obviously powered, though Gold could see no connecting wires. They probably operated on broadcast power.

The dominant item of furniture was a great black cube, almost as tall as the host, that stood roughly in the centre of the enclosed area. The vertical face fronting the entryway was animated, two hairless male *Hilt-Sil* of half normal size standing and talking in front of a round door. Gold saw that the cube was a playing or recording device, similar to a television set except that there was no glass face and the images were three-dimensional. As he watched the two men turned and entered the door. The scene faded, to be replaced by one of the interior of an interstellar ship. The two males were now sitting at the controls.

There were several chairs scattered around the four sides

of the cube, in careless disorder. The two men were talking again, though Gold could not understand the words. And then Leet-A led him around the cube to the right, and to Gold's amazement the voices were suddenly chopped off as abruptly as if he had lost his hearing. Seconds later he heard a female voice and glanced at the second face of the cube, to see a scene so strange his mind could not absorb it. A woman's face was superimposed over the unacceptable image, and the words he was hearing matched the movement on her lips. Evidently each animated face on the cube broadcast both sound and picture, and somehow walls of silence in the room separated the different programmes.

Leet-A led him on past the cube, and the female voice vanished as they passed another invisible partition. The third face was blank, and he saw that it was actually concave instead of flat. The image somehow appeared in the space between the extended sides. The curving surface was a lustrous black in colour, and appeared moist.

Leet-A stopped in what was apparently the eating area. There was no table or other central eating facility, but four large chairs were equipped with flat attached panels. She positioned the host in front of one and gently pressed on the shoulders. Gold sat him down with an unplanned thump. Leet-A looked alarmed at her husband's lack of co-ordination.

The children moved away, looking back over their shoulders with puzzled, unhappy expressions. Leet-A said something to them and they nodded obediently and returned to the entryway cube face, where they picked up the pads and styli they had evidently dropped to run to their father. The boy stepped to the face of the cube, touched some hidden control, waited, touched it again, and returned to his chair. After a moment both children began writing.

Leet-A opened cabinets and removed foodstuffs. She prepared a meal for the family, moving with the slow sureness Gold had come to consider a *Hilt-Sil* characteristic. He studied her equipment. One unit which had appeared to be made of wood was actually of quartz or some similar mineral, and had metal rings on the inside which seemed to heat without changing their colour. Another deceptively similar item turned out to be a cooler, which held mostly liquids. There was no meat in sight.

The food was soon ready. For a moment Leet-A acted uncertain, then placed dishes and utensils in front of Soam-A-Tane and watched him. Gold fed the host, spilling a little because both food and instruments were different from those on the ship but avoiding major disasters. The children had returned and occupied two other feeding chairs, but spent more time watching their father than eating. Leet-A watched him also, and cleaned up his small spills immediately.

The wild joy the children had felt on seeing their father had vanished. They went outside after the meal, and Gold saw them playing with two strange children. They soon moved out of sight.

Leet-A cleared away the remnants of the meal, packing the scraps in a basket of pressed vegetable fibre obviously designed to decompose in the ground. Gold had a familiar feeling that a few years later they would eat the remnants in a new form. And he felt that another of his tentative conclusions had been confirmed. Though the *Hilt-Sil* still had the omnivore's dentition they had long ago lost their taste for meat.

Leet-A paused for a moment after finishing, staring at Soam-A-Tane. Then she gathered up several items he recognized as gardening tools, and a small bag from the laboratory. The last thing she picked up was a sunhat. One hand went to the long red braid and stripped it off. She placed it in a nearby cabinet drawer. The change in her apperance was startling, much of her femininity vanishing. Gold concluded that this was cultural bias, but for him it was true. With something of chagrin he realized he should have anticipated that the long hair would be a wig; the female faces he had seen were as hairless as the males. The hairpieces were evidently a custom tracing back to the time when hair had been a mark of beauty. Leet-A brought another sunhat and carefully tied it on Soam-A-Tane's bald head. She took one hand and led the host out of the door, Gold physically very busy with the controls but finding that they required little more conscious thought than needed to walk himself. Leet-A headed for the nearest open field, and carefully inspected the grain growing there as they travelled through it to the next grove of trees. Once in the shade she seated him at the base of a rough trunk and turned back to the field. A thick low hedge separated the woods from the growing grain. Leet-A pruned and clipped back the hedge for several yards, then opened the bag she had brought and extracted several faded twigs covered with scores of small buds. Working slowly and carefully she started grafting each twig to a carefully prepared branch of the hedge.

The work was as repetitious as most farmwork and Gold soon grew bored, but he dare not leave the console. He turned and glanced at Marina, who had not spoken for hours. She was slumped forward, fast asleep. It had been over thirty hours since they had rested, far too many of them in the fatiguing grip of deceleration. For some reason he was extremely tired but not sleepy. As he stared idly at Marina the intense blackness of her hair suddenly jarred his memory and he saw the face of another brunette, the only woman he had ever genuinely cared for. He had long ago realized that he was incapable of deciding if what he had felt was love or a mixture of gratitude and sexual attraction. She had been a substitute mother, a tutor and a friend; she had also been his woman. If he had not loved her then it was quite certain that he had not loved anyone since. And yet she too had failed him.

To rest as best he could without falling asleep Gold decided to replay the scene where Carlotta Jones had suddenly and drastically changed the nature of what she was teaching him. It was one of the happiest nights of his life, and he had played it so often it was like running through a familiar movie. He ran the memory before his inner eye at the slowest possible speed, with all the tactile and olfactory sensations he could recall. There had been few nights like it in his life.

chapter 9

ALBERT UNLOCKED THE car door and reached for the gearshift. As his hand touched the knob a husky voice said, "Isn't it about time you told us of these frequent excursions of yours, Albert?"

He froze for an instant, then turned slowly toward the back seat. It was dark night, and Carlotta Jones' face was only a white oval in the dimness, her black hair lost in the shadows. As he stared a lighter suddenly flared and she touched the flame to a cigarette held in the full-lipped mouth. Albert smelled the acridly sweet distinctive odour of marijuana.

Albert moved the gearshift to neutral and released the brake. "I don't see why my trips should concern you, Mrs Jones."

"Everything you do concerns me, Albert." She took a deep drag on the illegal cigarette, ignoring the coldness implicit in his use of her last name. "What we can't understand is why you go so often to the ghetto. You don't indulge in drugs, liquor or women while you're there."

"How do *you* know what I do?" Albert asked sharply

"We've kept a strict watch over your movements, and at least three trips have been photographed in detail. I repeat, what's so fascinating about the technots?"

Albert seated himself in front and rested his arms and chin on the back of the seat. "I'm trying to learn about life through experience, the one commodity you haven't provided me. Do you also know about the young whore I shared sex with on my first trip a year ago?"

Carlotta was taking another drag on her cigarette. She held the smoke this time, absorbing it. Her voice was even when she finally said, "No, we didn't. We *have* noticed you were often solicited by prostitutes, and turned them all down. We thought it was probably due to your virginity and the shyness you try so hard to hide. Now I see we were way off base. You had already 'shared' with a prostitute and found that particular 'experience' distasteful."

"You could say that." Albert's voice was non-committal. "Anyway, what do you want? I'm going whether you like it or not, you know."

Carlotta abruptly reached overhead and flipped the ceiling light-switch on and off. In the brief illumination Albert saw that she was dressed in mannish pants and a loose blue pullover sweater. Her long black hair was hidden beneath a heavy cap and there was no lipstick or other obvious make-up on her face. "I intend to go with you, if you'll let me," she said calmly. "Ed Martin thinks we've been concentrating too hard on tutoring and not providing you with enough companionship. I would like to be your friend as well as teacher . . . not that I think we've taught you much for the past two years! I want to share whatever it is you're finding in Harlem."

"And then you'll prepare a nice long detailed report on it?"

There was another brief silence, and then her soft troubled voice said, "I will, Albert; I *have* to! We can't seem to make you accept the fact that you're just too valuable to risk yourself this way, but at least we can try to learn what it is that's eating at you. Oh, we have security men in the area wherever you go, but if a nearby drug addict suddenly went at you with a knife . . . but that's not the only type of risk, and probably not the worst. We're aware that we've failed miserably in trying to raise you as a normal, emotionally healthy young adult, but we still have hopes of saving you from this compulsion to waste your abilities. Will you let me come?"

Albert was not particularly surprised to find that he had got away with these twice-weekly trips to Harlem only for the first few times, and had since been guarded by the autocratically benevolent arm of the Institute. In turn, he spied on his mentors at every opportunity, and he had not yet been detected.

"Yes, you can tag along, Carlotta," he said wearily, conceding to the applied pressure. "I don't think you'll learn what you want to know, though."

She opened the rear door, slid out, and got back into the front seat. The overhead light did not come on; Albert had long ago disconnected both automatic door switches. As she buckled her seat harness he braced himself and gave a powerful shove against the frame, with the door open. The car eased forward, picking up speed as he put his back into it. He jumped inside and closed the door with very little sound by pulling it into place with great pressure, slowly exerted. Carlotta had closed hers with a normal slamming noise, but he received a certain perverse pleasure from following his usual routine. They probably had a dozen infra-red films showing the door slowly closing.

The car coasted to the road, turned on to it, and was immediately headed downhill on a mild grade. With the skill of much practice Albert guided the auto for a quarter of a mile in the darkness, until it passed around the first turn that hid the Institute. Then he turned on the lights and started the engine.

Carlotta finished her cigarette and tossed away the stub. "When did you acquire the habit?" Albert asked.

"In college. I know it's illegal, but like a lot of other minor pleasures, no one really gives a damn any more. We types who find it relaxing indulge in privacy."

Albert shrugged massive young shoulders, already hard to fit though he was not quite sixteen. "The technots in

Harlem don't bother to hunt privacy. Are you aware that both synthetic marijuana and LSD are furnished in great quantities, along with their food? When they get bored with television they can always take a trip inside their heads for entertainment. I've always wondered how your self-righteous government justified supplying illegal drugs to twenty million people.

"Our beloved leaders don't give a damn what the technots do. It's different with us; a technician can't concentrate on designing complicated circuits when he's high. Do you want a stick?"

"No thanks, I've tried hallucinogens and the light stuff isn't very effective. I can get as much 'kick' in my head without it."

"Really?" Carlotta sounded interested. "Will you tell me about it? And I don't mean in the way you turn in faked test scores just to keep the team happy. Tell me what you *really* do."

"The first part of your statement is a request," Albert said slowly. "The second part takes it for granted that the request will be honoured."

Carlotta accepted the rejection in silence. The car swept down the mountain at the maximum safe speed. In less than an hour they were crossing the George Washington bridge, and minutes later stopped on a crooked back street where Albert had rented space in a private garage. A short walk took them to the basement of a crumbling old apartment building, where a dice game was just getting underway. The sponsor was a swarthy Navaho Albert knew slightly called One-Eyed Jack; all the Amerindians had been moved from their reservations to the ghettoes a decade ago.

The big Indian looked up as Albert and Carlotta entered, flashing the blond youth a buck-toothed smile. "Hey there, here comes some real easy money! Join the crowd, Goldboy. We need som'a that go'ment issue you always carrin' aroun'."

Albert waved negligently, spoke to two or three men he knew, and took the place to the right of One-Eyed Jack. When the older man lost possession on his first roll, and the play passed to Albert, the Amerindian rocked back on his heels and looked up at Carlotta, standing just behind her escort. "Where you find this hot-lookin' walkin' lay, pinky-toes? This too much grown woman for you. Now you an' me, baby," he spoke directly to Carlotta, "we could really beat a mattress together."

"I like 'em young and tender," the psychologist said coldly, placing a possessive hand on the kneeling Albert's shoulder. "Old bastards like you I can do without."

"Hey, she got fight too!" One-Eyed Jack yelled delightedly, getting to his feet. "Say, I bet you *are* a hot-box baby! I got ten dollars for you any time. I gi' you five jus' for a stand-up job against the wall!"

Albert looked up from the dice. "She's with me, Jack. Knock it off."

"Oh, you want it all ya'self, huh. You have'ta watch these women when they gi' past thirty, Goldboy; they so hot they screw a young kid like you out'a ya' nex' fi' years growth! Say, I jus' thought. You two ain't *married*, ar' ya'? I didn't mean to get smart wi' yer wife, now."

"Naw, just good friends," Albert said as he turned back to the dice. "She'll be leavin' with nobody but me, though, so keep your hands to yourself."

The big man squatted down again, watching the play but still casting appreciative looks at Carlotta. "Hokay, boy; I still think you got ya'self somethin' there, though. Jus' hope you kin handle it, 'cause I don' think you as big down below as you look up above." He laughed uproariously and slapped down money to cover the new bet as Gold lost the dice. The next player in line, a heavy-set young man with Appalachia written over his red face, picked up the small cubes and rubbed them vigorously between his palms, crooning a doleful plea for luck. The eight other men in the circle had already looked Carlotta over and returned to their game. Albert was known and liked; none would try for her unless she made the first move.

There was a half-hour of quiet play before the dice returned to Albert, who was slightly ahead. Several of the players did not know how to bet the odds on points and consistently lost except when they held the dice. Albert lost on his first throw, which cut him back to about even. The men had become intent on the rolling cubes and paid little attention to Carlotta, who was wandering around the dank, dingy basement.

The red-faced Appalachian made two straight passes on seven, threw a nine for his point on the third, and rattled the dice for an extra long time before trying for it. As the white cubes left his hand the man on his right, a husky old Negro, suddenly clamped powerful fingers across the player's wrist. The younger man scrambled to his feet, trying to jerk free, but his attacker seized the clenched fist with his other hand and managed to pry the fingers apart. An identical pair fell to the floor, and rolled less than a foot before stopping on three and four; both the previous passes had been three-four combinations.

The cheating player finally wrenched his hand free and stood confronting the suddenly silent group, breathing heavily. "Well,! well! well!" said the game sponsor after a moment, his voice low and almost unpleasant. "So you slipped a loaded pair on us, Alfie, and even they let'cha down and you rolled a nine. Then you wanted to get back to the regular ones 'cause you knew the loaded babies would crap you out in a hurry. And would you look at that?" One-Eyed Jack pointed to the playing area, where a six and three lay unnoticed. "There's your nine, right on the money. An' you got a smooth hand, Alfie; good thing ol' Willy there's got sharp eyes. Take 'im boys!"

The suddenness of the order caught the players by surprise, but Willy grabbed Alfie's arm before the red-faced younger man could move. Albert knew the rules of conduct in such a situation as well as anyone, and they called for him to seize Alfie's other arm and hold him while the men beat the cheater into insensibility or death. Albert did not move, and after a moment's struggle Alfie managed to shake off Willy's grip and back away. One hand darted into a hip pocket and produced a knife. There was a charp *click!* as the spring-loaded blade slipped into place. Alfie waved it menacingly as the players advanced on him. "First one 'at lays a han' on me gits it!"

Most of the players drew weapons, but apparently none had a pistol. Alfie stopped, aware that he was backing into a corner. Desperation and a terrible fear drained his red face to a sallow whiteness. "All right, you can have it all back," he said suddenly, retreating again. "Jus' let me out'ta here!"

One-Eyed Jack, who was in the lead, chuckled softly. "That ain't quite good enough, Alfie. You know what it takes to buy your way out'ta this."

Carlotta had moved to one side and was watching with breathless interest. One white hand crept to her throat. She looked equally fascinated and repelled. There were no mixed emotions in Albert. His stomach was already queasy, and he knew he would be sick, as had happened before, when the beating started.

The men continued to advance on Alfie, who was waving his knife threateningly and darting frightened looks from side to side. When they were almost within striking range Albert suddenly called, "Hey Jack, let Alfie go! I'll pay him out on the two-to-one."

The men stopped and looked at the game's sponsor. It was a custom in ghetto gambling to let a cheater buy his way out of trouble by forfeiting his earnings and paying double that amount to the aggrieved players. The obviously terrified Alfie would have already made the offer if he had the money.

One-Eyed Jack turned to Albert, a sombre, brooding look on his dark, intelligent face. "That's the second time we caught a switch artist and you wan'a buy 'im out," he said quietly. "Why you so soft on these cheaters, Goldboy?"

Albert searched hastily for an answer, found none, and finally told the truth. "I jus' don' want to see somebody killed over a few dollars."

"That job you got mus' pay better 'an most," the big Amerindian said quietly. He seemed more thoughtful than angry. Albert glanced at the waiting men and saw no anger anywhere. They were ready to advance on the knife, and if one of them was badly cut they would undoubtedly beat Alfie to death, but they would do it without passion. Within their own pattern these were law-abiding men, and they would enforce the ghetto rules with no more personal hate than a black-robed judge dispensing law in the technocrat society that had excluded them.

"Hey now, I don' really care!" One-Eyed Jack went on, his voice more jovial. "You wanna buy 'im out, it's al'right wi' me. Let's 'ave the cheat-fine."

Albert dug into his pocket and started pulling out bills. Alfie had bet five on each of his passes, and there were nine players to pay off . . . he saw that he had barely twice the needed sum. "Throw your money down, Alfie," he called to the Appalachian.

The cheater hastily emptied both pockets and tossed the money on the floor. The players did not even glance at it. Alfie moved to the nearest wall and sidled along it, knife at the ready. The nearest man backed away a few steps to give him room. Alfie edged past him and walked slowly to the stairs, trying to watch everyone in the group. As he went out the door the cheater threw a searching, troubled look over his shoulder at Albert, a look the younger man recognized. Alfie's conscience wasn't bothering him; he was simply unable to understand why the young blond giant had intruded and saved his neck.

As the Appalachian disappeared One-Eyed Jack bent to pick up the forfeited money and then held out a hand to Albert. When he had it all he counted the pile and started dividing the total into eight parts, excluding Albert. When each man had his due the game immediately started again, but Albert glanced at Carlotta and led the way to the stairs. Ten minutes later they were heading out of Harlem on their way to the Catskills.

They were well away from New York, and the traffic had eased to the few drivers able to afford black-market gasoline, when Carlotta unfastened her seat harness and then calmly undid Albert's. She pushed them out of the way and snuggled comfortably against his shoulder, curled up little-girl fashion with both feet tucked beneath her on the seat.

Albert freed his right arm, placed it around her shoulders to shift them to a more comfortable position for him, and then quite calmly dropped his big hand to her right breast, cupped it, and gave a gentle squeeze.

Carlotta gasped, jerked erect, and pulled violently away. Albert let her go, and kept his eyes on the road as she angrily demanded, "Why did you do that Albert? Of all the rude, coarse . . .why?"

"Easy with the adult tone," he said soothingly. "If you're going to play little teenager and snuggle up to teenage boy to get this seduction off to a good start you've got to stay young."

"Albert, you! . . ." the tone was angry, and she stopped. After a pause she asked quietly, "Why do you think I was trying to seduce you?"

Albert smiled in the darkness. At the training team's last meeting in the bugged room Ed Martin had suggested that it was past time their ward lost his virginity, pointing out that a woman who became his mistress while he was comparatively young and impressionable could acquire a tremendous influence over Albert. He had proposed hiring a professional prostitute, ostensibly as a maid, and letting her seduce their young charge. After a firm relationship was established they could, working through her, attempt to change Albert's strongly anti-social attitudes and behaviour. His justification was that none of their present tools were working too well. Anita Savez had voiced strong opposition to the idea, and no one else had supported it. The meeting had broken up without a decision.

Albert knew that Carlotta, like the other team members, was almost fanatically devoted to the idea of developing him to his full potential. He had had a strong suspicion, after he recovered from the initial surprise of finding her in the car, that his sexual education was the ultimate aim of the night's adventure. Apparently she had accepted Ed Martin's premise but carried it one step further and decided to acquire the needed influence herself. To test his theory Albert had deliberately behaved in an unacceptable manner at the first sign of intimacy. Despite her psychological training and supposed objectivity Carlotta had reacted as would any young matron to an abrupt and direct violation of her person. But if he was right she would not let his crudeness dissuade her.

Albert knew Carlotta's husband slightly, as he did most of the team members' families. Like many other men engaged in highly complex work Anscombe Jones was a tense, abstracted, somewhat neurotic worker, interested only in the demands of his job. He was very possessive of Carlotta in public, but Albert knew from overheard conversations in the conference room that he paid little attention to her at home.

"I don't think you turned from mother to sex-box just to play teener games," he finally answered her. "I don't know *why* you've decided to make me, but it seems obvious you have. Now take off your sweater and bra and move back up here."

The frozen silence that followed his order made him wonder if he had gone too far. He also realized that he was being unnecessarily cruel. Sometimes he had to remind himself that these people had only his welfare at heart, regardless of how mistaken they were in their efforts. And he had no way of knowing how much of Carlotta's motivation was traceable to unhappiness with an unresponsive husband and her own sexual needs, as well as affection for her pupil. She had been with the team only a few years, and had no memory of mothering him as a small child.

After a moment Carlotta asked, "Is that crudeness necessary, Albert? Even if you're right . . . must you behave so abominably?"

He felt a quick surge of joy at the pleasure he now knew was his, a joy marred only slightly by the knowledge she was still acting primarily as a teacher. "I'd rather skip the drawn-out preliminaries, if you don't mind," he said, keeping his voice gentle. "If you're here to complete my education then be honest about it."

There was a rustle of cloth as Carlotta leaned forward

and yanked the blue sweater off over her head. She reached behind her back and undid the bra, tossed it after the sweater, and resumed her position against his shoulder. Albert immediately cupped the same breast again, and this time she did not pull away.

"What are you grinning about?" Carlotta asked crossly.

Albert let the grin grow into a chuckle. "Nothing important," he lied cheerfully. "I was just wondering if this decision to take on my sexual education was your own idea or Ed Martin's. And I'm glad I at least managed to get away from your spying eyes long enough to lose my virginity in private!"

"Yes, and probably in a dirty bed with some filthy whore with every disease in the book!" Carlotta said savagely. She stopped, apparently as surprised as he by her vehemence, then went on, "A young man's first sexual experiences *are* important, Albert; traumatic ones can mar him for life. I wanted you to have yours under the best possible conditions."

"Such as?"

"Well, preferably with an older woman, someone who could guide you, make it as easy as possible. And no, Ed Martin doesn't know I decided to do this. All of us are as devoted to your welfare as he is, believe it or not."

Albert sighed wearily. "I *do* believe it! It isn't your devotion to me or your dedication to your task that falls short of my needs."

"That's an odd statement," Carlotta's voice abruptly changed from the sultry tone she had been using to that of the professional inquirer. "Would you mind explaining it?"

"Yes I would mind!"

There was another long period of silence, and then Carlotta said sleepily, "Next turn on your right."

Minutes later they were parked behind an enormous rock, well hidden from the highway only a few hundred feet away. "I get a distinct impression you knew how to find this spot," Albert said mockingly.

Instead of answering Carlotta turned until she was facing him, threw both arms around his neck, and raised her mouth for a kiss. He obliged, and when their lips parted she started undoing the buttons of his shirt. Now that she was no longer having to pretend reluctance Carlotta seemed as willing as Albert to forego the slow preliminaries. Within five minutes they were climbing into the back seat for the extra room. Within ten they were relaxing, breathing heavily, and Albert had learned what an inadequate excuse for sharing sex his experience with Littlebit had actually been.

An hour later Carlotta sat erect, reached across the front seat for her purse, and lit a marijuana cigarette. After the first deep puff she asked, "Sure you don't want a drag?"

"No, thanks. And if you're one of the people for whom it inhibits sexual desire, take it easy yourself."

"Don't be too ambitious. Three times is enough for a beginning," Carlotta said lazily, relaxing against him and running a hand across his almost hairless chest. "I didn't plan this as a one-time affair, and if you think I'm acting solely out of a sense of duty, you're wrong. I actually *like* you, damn it! The whole team does."

"I don't think your husband would like me if he knew about this."

"No, of course not. He simply wouldn't understand. If you want to share sex with me you'll have to keep this strictly between us."

Albert reached for the cigarette, took it from between her lips and tossed it out the open window. "Okay, it's just our little secret," he murmured, and pulled her over him, bringing her face down to his for a long kiss. When their lips parted he said, "But you made one mistake."

"What?" she asked huskily, her warm breath blowing softly on his cheek.

"When you said three times was enough for a beginning," he answered, heaving himself erect and gently but forcefully pulling her to the centre of the seat.

"So maybe I'm not perfect," she whispered in his ear, her arms stealing around his neck as his hands sought her hips.

Gold turned off the playback and pulled himself away from the familiar memory, opening his eyes to the thousand bits of information waiting in mechanical patience on his console. That night had been the start of the only period of real happiness he had ever known. The coolly efficient teacher had proved to be a warm and wonderfully giving lover. Their affair had lasted eight months, with Carlotta arranging to meet him at least once each week and often two or three times. For him the physical attraction had grown within a month into a stronger and more demanding relationship that he had no better word for than love. It had taken twice that long before Carlotta, during the course of a long night when her husband was away and she could spend the entire time in Albert's apartment, had shyly confessed that she loved him and would leave her husband if they could be together.

Albert had let his guard down with Carlotta to an extent not practised since he was a baby. If she took advantage of her new knowledge in any way he had never become aware of it. He had a difficult time concealing his feelings from the other team members, and there was no way to hide his vastly improved disposition and the general new attitude he acquired toward life. In a sense Carlotta had succeeded as a psychologist by her choice of therapy, pulling their young charge out of the withdrawal into which he had been steadily sinking. But Carlotta was no longer practising her profession after the first two months. She was in love.

Carlotta Jones was not a beauty. Physically she could not compete with the least of the 365 young women Gold had attempted to impregnate during his year on Wall Street. She was short, a little on the heavy side, with a noticeable potbelly and heavy buttocks. Her breasts were also heavy, and sagged badly when not supported by a brassière. She dyed her hair to hide the fact it was rapidly turning grey. The affair with young Albert had been her first in seven years of marriage, and she had accepted only a few lovers before meeting Anscombe Jones. In a burst of confidence one night she admitted their marital sex consisted of sharing about once a month, seldom more than twice during a session. Albert had had difficulty concealing his jealousy of the fact she still shared with her husband at all.

A few months before Albert's seventeenth birthday Anscombe Jones committed suicide. He did it noisily, messily, with a large calibre pistol that spattered his brains over their apartment wall. And he left a message saying he knew of his wife's affair with the young mutant, and could not live with the knowledge that she had betrayed their marriage. Fortunately Carlotta found the note first, and no one saw it except herself and Albert; at least they were spared the ugliness of a major scandal.

Carlotta resigned from the Institute as soon as her husband was buried; Albert Golderson had not seen her since. That same intensity which she brought to her work, and to her love for Albert, worked against her when she accepted the responsibility for Anscombe Jones' suicide. She did not even attempt to reassure her young charge of his own lack of guilt; not that it would have mattered. Albert had told himself that Anscombe Jones had felt he owned his wife, not loved her, that a divorce was inevitable anyway, that if the man had had the slightest regard for Carlotta he would not have left a note that could scar her for life or send her after him into suicide. None of these changed the cold hard fact that Jones would have been alive if Albert Golderson had not become his wife's lover.

After he had completed his year on Wall Street, and found himself impotent when he finally had to accept the fact that he was a mule, as sterile as Petrovna, Gold had hired a detective agency to locate Carlotta. He had some faint hope that she would again draw him back into the real world, give him a reason to want to live. But when the detective returned with photographs Gold saw that the woman he had loved no longer existed. Carlotta had moved to Miami, married a high school teacher, and was busy raising his four children by a previous marriage. She had stopped dyeing her hair, which had grown entirely grey, and let her figure degenerate. The sexily wide hips he had so admired were covered with a roll of loose fat. The small potbelly he had caressed a thousand times, and learned to love for the very imperfection it represented, had swollen into an unsightly paunch. In the space of a few years she had become a middle-aged woman, and not a very attractive one. She no longer practised psychology in any form.

Gold had not sent for Carlotta. It was obvious she could not help him a second time. Instead he had retreated to the mountains and started devoting his days to the grave question of whether or not it was worthwhile to go on living. Petrovna had been wrong when he had asserted Gold could not deny that he wished to go on living himself.

Without a sense of conscious transition Gold found that he was leaning forward on his console, head cradled in his arms. He slept.

Gold was awakened by a gentle shaking of the host's upper body, and sat erect to see Leet-A kneeling in front of her husband. She rose and urged the resting body to its feet. Gold almost mechanically operated his controls, glancing over his shoulder at Marina, visible to him as long as he kept the eye centred on its socket. The small woman had recovered from her earlier fatigue. She was awake and responding to the body's demand for energy by increasing the heartbeat; his own indicators registered the faster rate. They got the host to its feet and followed behind Leet-A.

Gold, finally awake, saw that the giant woman was evidently a horticulturist or plant chemist. She had made a series of grafts to the stalks in the field's hedge. Bonding them in place with three different coloured solutions. There were similarly treated sections further down the row, where new hybrid plants were already growing.

Evidently several hours had passed. The huge yellow sun that seemed to fill half the sky had moved closer to the zenith, and Gold felt cramped. When they reached the house the children were again seated in front of the black central cube, apparently absorbed by some form of entertainment; no notes were being taken. Leet-A led the host to a part of the house Gold had not yet examined, seated him in a chair, and in a few easy gestures removed her tunic and stood totally nude. As Gold had suspected, there was not a single hair on her body. She stepped into a small depression in the floor, closed her eyes, touched a switch with her toe, and abruptly the air around her became cloudy and murky. She raised her arms and moved her feet apart as though exposing all skin surfaces. After a moment she touched the switch again, the cloudiness vanished, and she stood frowning at Soam-A-Tane. Gold suddenly realized that though the men on the starship had looked after Soam-A-Tane's health with meticulous care they had at no time cleansed the great body.

Gold's allowance for the size differential between *Hilt-Sil* and human was becoming an automatic function. As Leet-A approached him she seemed less a giantess almost three-hundred feet tall than simply a nude woman, though the large feet, bald head, and comparative shortness and heaviness of form made her a strange one. Her hips were unusually wide, but so were the shoulders. There was a certain indefinable femininity about the eyes and lips, but the physical characteristics that distinguished her from the male were those shared with human women, a pair of large breasts and the curving edge of her pudenda, emphasized by the lack of hair on the prominent mons veneris. She was far more muscular than most Earthwomen, but no more so than professional weight-lifters.

When Leet-A reached him Gold found his eyes at the level of her stomach, a smooth expanse of brown flesh barely swelled by a slight abdominal bulge. He noted that there was no sign of the stretch marks so common to mothers on Earth. She helped the host to its feet and stripped off the coveralls. Looking directly into Soam-A-Tane's face, so that she seemed to be staring into Gold's eyes as well, she said slowly, "You are grimed, my husband. We must cleanse your exterior."

Gold turned the knob that pulled the huge lips into their imitation of a smile, the only response he could manage. Leet-A smiled gravely in return. Abruptly she bent and reached for Soam-A-Tane's genitals, holding and examining them carefully for a moment. Gold felt a sudden consciousness of sexual stimulation. This was the first time he had experienced that particular sensation through the sensory cap. And then he realized that a faint but persistent awareness of sexual interest had been nagging at his mind since Leet-A first stripped. He had accepted it as his own awareness of Leet-A as a woman, but now was not sure. If it was sexual stimuli caused by her image on the one good eye of the host, transmitted to him through the cap, then he was receiving sensations that had not been directly wired into the system. He was unable to see the host's pubic area without bending the head, but had a strong suspicion that Leet-A had examined the genitals of her mate because the penis had become partially erect.

The interactions between the host's body and the installed console were complex and almost impossible of final definition. Even Petrovna could not have known precisely what he had accomplished, not when external sensors could still arouse internal physiological responses. In a sense the Russian had built even better than he knew, since the intent had been to provide control with a minimum interference of normal bodily functions. But if the higher level of activity since they had assumed charge of the body was causing the drugged left half of the brain to revive, trouble awaited them in the future.

Leet-A led Soam-A-Tane to the depression and placed firm fingers on both eyes. Gold took the hint and locked them closed. She waited a moment to be certain, and then Gold felt the relayed sensation of ten thousand tiny needles barely penetrating the edge of his skin. The bath was evidently some form of sonic vibrator that removed all loose particles from the skin, and could be damaging to the surfaces of the eye. After a moment he felt Leet-A step in with him, spread the host's arms and legs, and begin vigorously rubbing him down. The sensation was one of mild pleasure. She covered the body from head to toe, but did not touch the genitals again.

When Leet-A was satisfied she led her mate to a cabinet and produced a tunic similar to her own. She dressed him efficiently, and then led him to an unused side of the central cube. Soam-A-Tane was seated in a chair similar to those used by the children, with a pad and stylus near the slack hand. Leet-A stepped to the cube face and activated it; a printed list appeared. She rapidly touched a series of very small buttons and a new and larger list replaced the first. She repeated the process once more, then made her final selection and turned two dials. A programme began, and Gold saw that it dealt with the *Hilt-Sil* language. Evidently Leet-A was continuing Ru-A-Lin's efforts to re-educate him.

Gold picked up the stylus and started to work. He saw that he was ready for a slightly higher level course, but Leet-A would soon discover that. Evidently his guesses as to the best responses for Soam-A-Tane had been good ones. In rehabilitating the damaged brain the *Hilt-Sil* were unwittingly helping Gold fulfil the major purpose of their mission, the gathering of information. The next problem would be getting it back to Earth . . . and he found himself wondering why this was the first time the thought of returning to Earth had occurred to him.

Gold worked diligently for several hours. When the shadows lengthened outside Leet-A fed her family again—evidently they ate twice a day—and busied herself in the laboratory section of the house for an hour afterward. When darkness fell both adults and children were again in front of the cube, where they evidently spent a great deal of time. Gold caught another nap in his chair as the giant family watched what was obviously a historical recreation of the first explorations in their own solar system. When the programme ended Leet-A led the host to a relatively open area and touched one of the many hidden buttons she was constantly operating. A large section of the floor lowered several feet, separated in the centre, and the two halves slid back to reveal what was evidently a bed.

Leet-A stepped downward on to the springy surface, leading her husband by the hand. With her toe she touched another button under the edge of the floor and abruptly they were surrounded by dark, smoky walls, filled with curling flames that provided only a dim illumination. Gold realized that the children's voices, which he had been hearing in the background, had abruptly vanished. He looked closer and saw that the walls were actually misty surfaces of some form of controlled light, with the odd additional property of sound absorption.

Leet-A tugged gently on Soam-A-Tane's arm and Gold

carefully seated the host, avoiding the wall until he saw the woman's elbow enter it and emerge without harm. Leet-A claimed one of several scattered pillows and curled up to sleep, eyes on her husband. Gold followed suit, noting that a narrow strip of firm material in the centre actually divided the yielding pad into two beds. When he had the host horizontal, with two pillows under the head to elevate it for the comfort of himself and Marina, Leet-A touched still another button at the end of the separating strip and a wall of smoky blackness shot up from the firm surface. Gold saw that even the light from the wire network overhead had faded out.

A moment later a giant hand came stealing through the misty darkness, fumbled a moment, and then clasped that of Soam-A-Tane high on the forearm. Gold extended the host's arm until the hand disappeared in the blackness and the forearm was in contact with Leet-A's. And then he leaned back in the console chair and wondered if he had the strength to unstrap and drag himself to his own angled cot. He had never been so tired in his life.

chapter 10

THE NEXT THREE thirty-two hour days were long and arduous ones for Gold. He made rapid progress in understanding both the written and spoken forms of the *Hilt-Sil* language, and increased his writing skill. He had adapted to the giants' work-rest cycle by sleeping twelve hours a night, and found that he was able to work continuously for eighteen or twenty. Marina became exhausted the first day and had to have a nap in the afternoon; it revived her so well that she made it part of her daily routine. By the end of that third day they had realized that the home of Soam-A-Tane and Leet-A was a disciplined, highly organized unit, where each activity occurred in its time and place. A quarter of the daylight hours were spent in the fields with the plants, which were apparently grown solely for family consumption and experiment verification. The children worked outside two hours a day and spent four in front of the black cube, obtaining the *Hilt-Sil* equivalent of a formal education. The long evenings were for relaxation, and bedtime seldom varied. There was no need for the constant vigilance Gold and Marina had maintained on the ship, and they both slept routinely at night.

The routine was broken late on the fourth afternoon, when Leet-A sat down in front of a face of the cube Gold had not seen operated. She had donned her long wig and put on a more decorative tunic, similar to the one worn to the spaceport to greet him. Gold could neither hear nor see her programme, but did see an angry, frustrated look on her face after she had watched for a few minutes. Intrigued, he raised the host to its feet, picked up his chair, and moved it around the room until he could sit by the giantess.

Leet-A gave her husband a startled glance—he seldom moved without her guidance—but turned back to the cube without comment. Gold saw that she was looking down the length of a short table, into the face of an elderly giant at its end. A square of the same jet black material as the screen hung suspended above his head, showing the life-size head and shoulders of another *Hilt-Sil* male. Four adults were seated on each side of the table, five men and three women; all females wore the long wigs. Gold felt a small start of recognition when he saw that one of the men was Ru-A-Lin.

The giant on the screen stopped speaking and his image faded. The elderly man folded his hands and looked down the table at what was obviously the camera through which Leet-A and probably many others were watching. "Will you tell us what progress has been made in the treatment of Soam-A-Tane, Ru-A-Lin?" he asked.

The medic briefly described the work he had performed with Gold on the return trip, including his opinion that the damaged brain was slowly but definitely reviving. The chairman nodded, and called for Leet-A to continue the report. She had arisen, obviously expecting the summons, and stepped close to the cube, pressing the control on the right corner. Gold could see past her to the cube face, and watched her head and shoulders appear in the screen above the chairman. She gave a brief report on Soam-A-Tane's progress since arriving home, expressing satisfaction with the rate of recovery. Another touch of the button removed her from the conference and she resumed her seat.

The people around the table seemed pleased. A new face appeared in the overhead screen and asked if Soam-A-Tane had learned anything of value during his long exile near

Earth. Ru-A-Lin informed him he did not propose to question his patient until he was far more recovered.

Gold had no way of knowing how many people were participating in this conference, but had a strong hunch the number would be large. Evidently the communication cubes, about which the lives of the *Hilt-Sil* seemed to centre, made gathering in person unnecessary.

"Let us defer further discussion of Soam-A-Tane's condition until Ru-A-Lin and Leet-A have completed their work," the chairman said firmly. "Will the Eradicator Group present their report?"

There was no English equivalent for many of the terms these people used, but Gold found that translation was no longer necessary; he was thinking in *Hilt-Sil.* He had to record and store several words and phrases for later study, but by and large had little trouble understanding the speakers.

One of the three women at the table spoke for the Eradicator Group, reporting that an analysis of all data gathered by the last ship as it passed by Earth indicated the previous biological mechanism had been as ineffective as its predecessors. Due to the unscheduled landing on Mars the data accumulation time had been greatly extended, and the cultural analysis was not yet complete. Preliminary indications were that the "small vicious vermin" were in no danger of degenerating back into quarrelling national states, unable to work together effectively.

Ru-A-Lin took the floor to point out that the microbes used in the last attempt were similar to the previous ones and would probably be equally ineffective. He advocated developing a radically new mechanism for the next attack.

"Your suggestion is more easily made than implemented, Ru-A-Lin," the woman answered the implied criticism. "Remember that the planet's ecology cannot be unduly disturbed. Any major change in approach requires intensive new studies. We have only thirty-seven more revolutions before our emigration must begin. And the task was recently complicated by the death of our last four experimental subjects. We put the final two males and females together in hopes they would breed. Instead they found a way to commit mass suicide, evidently in hopes of hampering our research. They have partially succeeded, though our accumulation of physiological data will enable us to continue with our theoretical studies."

One of the miscellaneous facts Gold had acquired during

his three days of intense study was that Bragair, the *Hilt-Sil* name of their planet, revolved around its giant yellow star in approximately nineteen Earth months. That meant they planned to migrate to Earth in the relatively brief time of fifty-nine years.

Gold filed the new information away for the moment and concentrated on the meeting. The next report was from the *Hilt-Sil* equivalent of a political committee. The woman sitting on Ru-A-Lin's right, an elderly female whose wrinkled face clashed oddly with her bright red wig, faced the camera and said, "The Negatives continue to oppose us with a determination that grows stronger each day. They seem thoroughly convinced that within the next nine revolutions they will gain enough converts to overturn our majority, and the *Hilt-Sil* will choose to stay here and die rather than survive by eliminating another intelligent species. The latest analysis of opinion trends indicates they may well be right. As a result of the new study they have requested that we Affirmatives suspend our eradication attempts. If we agree, another vote will be scheduled in nine revolutions and they will end all opposition if it goes against them. If we do not, they plan to press for a referendum within a revolution and try our strength thereafter as often as the law allows."

The chairman started slowly tapping the table with one finger, the only nervous mannerism Gold had seen exhibited by any giant. "To be rid of their constant, unjustified criticism it would almost be worthwhile to grant the suspension," he said thoughtfully. "Regretfully, we cannot spare the nine revolutions. Ru-A-Lin is reasonably certain the present attack will fail. I have three reports on derivations made from attempt number five, our most successful, and am reasonably certain that one of these can completely eliminate the vermin. Unfortunately, the one with the highest probability of success needs performance data from the first two. And if even it should fail, there would be inadequate time in which to develop a new eradicator. The attacks will proceed as scheduled."

There was a sudden chorus of voices. The elderly chairman raised a hand in sharp dissent, apparently looking down the table directly at the watching camera. "Reserve comments and criticism until the end of the formal reports, please. Jelk-A-Bin, the latest report on the sun, if you please."

The man sitting on the chairman's right faced the camera, where the unseen majority watched, and said, "Our calculations indicate the rate of contraction is progressing geometrically, as expected according to the calculations of Ken-A-Beal. The temperature of the photosphere is rising precisely as predicted. The number of prominences has decreased as anticipated, and the number of independent magnetic fields increased, though not at the anticipated rate. This is considered a minor error on our part and no change in the basic calculations is required. Our original estimate of one hundred and eight revolutions before the first pulsation still stands. The minimum safety factor allowable for error remains at forty-eight revolutions. We recommend that the evacuation begin on schedule, if our friends the *Buraruckarcs* provide the transportation at the agreed time."

There was another clamour as several people demanded recognition. The chairman waited patiently until the noise died, then named someone. A woman's image appeared on the overhead screen and she asked, "Is the abnormal hydrogen-to-helium conversion rate still rising? And does your group have even a tentative theory to explain the acceleration of the ageing process?"

"Our research team in the *Similsacul* library reports no success. You will recall that our small friends inhabit a triple star system, and have the largest body of data on solar behaviour of any known species. They have performed the only successful extension of the sun's life, by slowing one of the inner gas giants in their system until it was drawn into the largest star. Their knowledge is so great, their calculations so precise, that the temporary increase in solar energy arriving at their planet at the time of collision was known within two degrees. But all their accumulated knowledge is of no help to us; our problem is unique."

Ru-A-Lin gained the floor and asked, "Are the calculations on the expected size of the first pulsation complete, and has the frequency been determined?"

Jelk-A-Bin raised an electrostatic pad and touched the retrieval control. After a moment he said, "The diameter will increase by eight per cent, or three million miles. The pulses will occur on a four-day cycle. All unprotected life on the surface of Bragair will be dead within three cycles; nothing has changed."

There was another short clamour. When it ended a strong male voice was saying, ". . . no change, but the *possibility* of change still exists! Since the rapid hydrogen-to-helium conversion is unprecedented we might possibly reverse the process if we knew its cause!"

Jelk-A-Bin hesitated, looking troubled. His voice was very

slow and distinct when he said, "I gravely doubt there is anything whatever we could do even if we achieved an understanding of the unusual ageing rate. We have no tools with which to work. Even the *Similsaculs* concede helplessness and recommend that we abandon our planet."

"We will proceed as planned," the chairman said briskly. "I suggest we remember what we have learned about the rising strength of the Negatives and attempt to convert all doubtful associates to our cause before the next World Council Night. File individual dissenting notes with me through Kilk-A-Dan's Key. Remember: Where Vrull-A-Lin walked, triumph and tragedy met in the cold!"

There were appreciative murmurs around the table and most attendees pushed back their chairs to rise. The chairman moved around the room, speaking to one or another of the departing council members. He reached the camera that connected the room to an unknown number of participants and casually thrust his arm across the screen to touch a control. The cube before Gold and Leet-A faded to blackness.

Gold felt a strong grip on the host's left arm and turned the great head. Leet-A was staring earnestly into her husband's face. "You seem to understand so much, my mate," she said softly. "But do you truly grasp what you hear, or do old memories stir through your poor damaged brain, blindly following well-worn trails?"

Gold forced the host's lips into the mechanical lift that was the closest he could come to a smile. Leet-A abruptly turned away, hiding a rush of tears. After a moment she moved back to the cube and activated another face. She moved her chair into the new hearing area, and Gold followed. Leet-A had selected a programme of recorded music, and sat in apparent absorption . . . but slow tears continued trickling down her brown cheeks.

Nothing would be expected of Soam-A-Tane for some time, and Gold placed most of the controls in neutral and removed the sensor helmet. *Hilt-Sil* music was to him more cacophony than ordered sound. He turned the console chair around and spoke directly to Marina. "We can go home now. I have the information we need."

Marina carefully checked her console, then unstrapped herself and walked to Gold. "I saw enough to realize that must be an important meeting," she said soberly. "Please bring me up to date."

Several of the language lessons Gold had mastered during

the last three long days had been in the form of historical narratives, and the meeting had filled in enough holes to give him a comprehensive grasp of the *Hilt-Sil* predicament. He summarized what he had learned for Marina, concluding with, "We were sent to find out why they are attacking Earth, and now we know. Their planet will soon be uninhabitable and they want ours. End of mission."

"Is that all you know?" Marina asked coldly.

"Not quite. Here's one item we might be able to exploit. It seems there are two schools of thought regarding eliminating the 'small vicious vermin'—that's us—and migrating to their planet. The opposition party feels the *Hilt-Sil* should stay here and burn rather than destroy another intelligent species. They are violating a premise of their own morality by killing us. But these people operate on a basically democratic system of majority rule, and the minority Negatives have had to go along with the Affirmatives, of which that council seemed to be the leaders. The strength of the Negatives is rising, and in some future election they may win a majority and stop the extermination programme. If this happens our large friends will be left with no alternative but to die gracefully."

Marina looked thoughtful. "Can you determine our chances of influencing these coming elections?"

Gold grinned. "With our host unable to speak and known to be suffering from severe brain damage, I doubt he'd be listened to."

"There's simply no way to provide a speaking capability," Marina replied, her mind elsewhere. "Gold, do you know why they picked Earth? Aren't there suitable planets closer to here?"

"There are eight inhabitable worlds within colonization distance. One or more intelligent species live on all of them. Seven out of the eight civilizations are highly advanced, including interstellar travel and trade. The eighth is primitive and savage, and the single intelligent species on the planet has no protective agreements with the rest of the interstellar community. That's us, of course, and the only reason we've survived this long is that no one needed our real estate."

Marina looked slightly shocked. "I don't understand. I would think any intelligent species would necessarily be concerned with any other intelligent beings they encounter. Why has no one contacted us before?"

"You're projecting your own cultural norms on to other and very different beings; the interstellar policy is to leave savage species alone. But you're partly right; one of our norms they share is the ability to form opposed views on any important question. The Affirmatives are going against a very strong ethical system, incidentally. It's based on ancestor worship, or at least admiration, with a written body of legend and tradition embodying moral precepts and behavioural codes. These are preserved in the form of stories, and young people have them drummed into their heads from babyhood on. The basic meaning is always condensed into a short key sentence, and the speaker quotes it when he wants to emphasize a point. I also think they start and end meetings with appropriate quotes. I've heard these several times, but passed over them because I didn't have the associated references and they were completely beyond my understanding."

"You can tell me about their culture later. I'm more interested in trying to save our own."

"Are you?" Gold tilted back in his chair until he was looking up into her cold face. "What makes you think ours is the one worth saving?"

Marina visibly stiffened. "I've been wanting to speak to you about your prolonged contact with the host, Gold. I think you spend too much time under the helmet, live too much by using the host's senses rather than your own. I wonder if you realize how much it's influencing you."

"Yes. Not at all."

"You're in no position to judge. I realize a close integration between your brain and the nervous system of the host is necessary, but I'm wondering if the symbiosis hasn't gone too far. Petrovna was unable to predict how strongly the sensor helmet would project. I think it's working entirely too well!"

"How would sensory impression influence my brain or behaviour?"

"I'm not certain you're receiving only sensory impressions. Perhaps you're getting more thought than you realize from the left cerebrum."

"That's utter nonsense!" Gold said angrily, turning back to his console. He sensed Marina standing behind him for a moment, and then she turned and walked to her own chair. When Gold glanced back she had a front panel off her console and was busy with some delicate adjustment on the interior.

Gold donned his sensory helmet again and started listening to the *Hilt-Sil* music. It seemed more melodious than before, and vaguely soothing. He relaxed, not trying to understand it, and his time-sense stretched, slowing the tempo. The music became far more pleasing. When he realized he was actually beginning to like it he felt a wry pleasure in thinking that perhaps Marina was at least partly right.

Next morning, to Gold's surprise, Leet-A deposited Soam-A-Tane in front of the cube and went to the fields alone. Evidently she had decided he was capable of looking after himself and needed more time at his lessons. The children were also outside, and Gold took advantage of the opportunity to see if he understood the cube's control system and its almost unlimited access to *Hilt-Sil* knowledge.

Gold had little difficulty cancelling the material Leet-A had programmed and calling up the first level of the reference system. Some of the words were difficult, but he managed to trace his way downward through three increasingly detailed lists. He was finally referred to a summary on the topic he wanted, the unexplained rapid contraction and expected pulsation of the *Hilt-Sil* system sun. After that he read the full article, though it was so technical as to be beyond his grasp and he gained little more than was afforded by the summary. He was able to confirm the overall picture he had grasped the night before. The one really outstanding characteristic of the contraction, the figure to which the puzzled researchers returned again and again, was the abrupt acceleration in their sun's hydrogen-to-helium conversion rate. It was unexplainable in terms of any scientific knowledge possessed by any species with which they had contact, and the interstellar community was large.

The *Hilt-Sil* reference system was quite similar to Earth's. Gold traced his way through the article's associated references to a longer work that dealt with pulsating stars, an area in which his knowledge was scanty. He found that they were statistically rare but not actually uncommon in a galaxy of billions. For such stars, which were always supergiants in Earthly terms, the expected three-million mile expansion and contraction was not uncommon. And he had been correct in the impression he had formed of the *Hilt-Sil* sun when they first arrived. It was a red giant almost forty million miles in diameter, and Bragair's orbit was over two-hundred million miles from the star's centre.

Gold also learned that no known pulsating star had a planet circling it. Evidently the great gravitic variations resulting from the pulsations broke up planets and sent them to a fiery death in the parent star. This was expected to eventually happen on Bragair and the other four uninhabited planets in the *Hilt-Sil* solar system.

Just before Leet-A was due back Gold returned the cube to the last of the programmes she had selected and let it play through. He doubted she would check his file of notes in the cube—the slates always transmitted to the nearest receiver, and the all-purpose cube had its own temporary storage system—and realize he had copied less material than usual.

After dinner that evening Ru-A-Lin called on the communications channel and told Leet-A that he had been asked to prepare a report on the psychological strains caused by ethical conflict in the members of the eradication teams. He would not be available to resume the training of Soam-A-Tane for approximately eighteen more rotations. (The *Hilt-Sil* used the more precise terms of rotation and revolution rather than day and year.) He inquired after Soam-A-Tane's progress.

Leet-A glanced in a troubled way at her husband, whom Gold had taken to stand within hearing distance, and told Ru-A-Lin that Soam-A-Tane was making excellent progress except for the inability to speak, and she saw no reason why she could not continue re-educating him alone.

Next morning, when Leet-A and the children went to their outside work on the family's unvarying schedule, Gold immediately turned the cube back to the material he had located on unusual solar activities. He was becoming proficient at finding his way through the complex reference systems. Gold located and scanned several more of the articles mentioned in the one he had read on the red giant's unexplained contraction rate, then decided he was weak in basic knowledge and looked for a good beginner's text. He absorbed the entire item by flashing each section on the screen and locking it in his short-term memory for later digestion and permanent filing.

Gold went from the basic text to a more advanced one, absorbing each section at the maximum speed his still developing grasp of the *Hilt-Sil* language permitted. He acquired considerable surface knowledge as he went along, although the real gain would come later, when his mental digestive system correlated all the bits of data and made its own subconscious connections and explanations. This was a process Gold did not understand himself, but he had learned early to use it to maximum advantage, while hiding the ability from the research team attempting to develop his enlarged brain. He was reasonably certain that it was only an intensification of the normal human ability to solve problems at the subconscious level, but was unwilling to let Ed Martin and his team pry into his mind and attempt to pinpoint it.

The surface knowledge Gold was accumulating followed a pattern he had found common in the physical sciences. The basic concepts were much easier to grasp than the detailed explanations that attempted to prove their truth. The *Hilt-Sil* had maintained a watch and study programme on their sun for many generations. They possessed a great deal of knowledge obtained by trade with the *Similsaculs,* in the normal exchanges that had occurred prior to the current emergency. Although they were comparative amateurs in astronomy the *Hilt-Sil* possessed complex instruments and enough knowledge to predict the first pulsation with reasonable accuracy.

By the time Leet-A returned Gold had the cube back to the planned programming, and discovered with pleasure that he could absorb the comparatively simple material she was feeding him while flashing the memorized sections of the astronomy texts before his inner eye and assimilating them. This was an advance over his known ability to study material being transferred from short-term memory to permament storage while performing physical actions, such as playing memorized piano pieces. Petrovna had been right; this task was going to challenge his full capacity as *Homo superior*.

Gold settled into the new routine, studying astronomy in the morning and the *Hilt-Sil* in the afternoon. The "rotations" passed in slow but steady order, while his knowledge in both areas grew by geometric leaps. At the end of sixteen Bragair rotations, when Ru-A-Lin was due in two days, Gold felt that he was probably the foremost astronomer on the planet, and certainly the most advanced ever produced on Earth.

Gold had moved from the textbooks to the more recent articles that had not yet been incorporated in permanent form, noting that, as on Earth, the percentage of theory and admitted speculation rose sharply when the investigators approached a new problem. Gold had for several days been suffering from mental indigestion, but could not identify the cause. As with the language books he had absorbed from their own computer, something in the vast amount of knowledge he had taken in was proving a mental poison and his system wanted to be rid of it. Unlike the bad book, he had been unable to identify the unacceptable material and discard it.

On the day Ru-A-Lin was due Gold found some information that jarred him out of his normal recording routine. Mechanically he scanned the rest of the material and sat back without calling for a new article. The nagging thought in the back of his mind had been jarred to the forefront, finally recognizable. It was not the material itself his subconscious mind refused to accept as fact; a conclusion had been struggling upward which was not justified by the accumulation of data that had preceded it.

The article had reported the arrival into the solar system, eleven-hundred revolutions back, of nine clouds of hydrogen gas. These had disappeared into the sun without attracting much attention or a field trip by *Hilt-Sil* astronomers, despite several oddities. Ground-based instruments indicated an increase in temperature inside each cloud's interior. The exact heat at the centre was not known, since the clouds were all several thousand miles in diameter and the instruments penetrated only the outer edges.

The clouds were denser than any previously reported, holding their shape unusually well. And shortly after their plunge into the sun there had been a small increase in the number of long-lived solar flares, an increase that had persisted to the present. Clouds that had travelled through space for millennia should have attained a uniform temperature; there had to be some explanation for their unusual density; and finally, their mass was so inconsequential their absorption could not possibly have affected the sun, and yet the increase in solar flares had occurred shortly afterward.

The article concluded that it had been a mistake not to take an instrumented ship into the clouds while they were in transit to the sun, as the author had suggested at the time. He also asked if it were not possible that the still unexplained phenomena had some relation to the contraction of their sun, which had started some seven-hundred revolutions later.

The article was followed by three refuting opinions by leading astronomers, all of whom pointed out that it consisted of rank speculation and that no known law of physics could relate the change in their sun to the absorption of a miniscule amount of hydrogen gas.

There was a basic premise underlying all the material

Gold had read on the superstar's rapid ageing, and it was this premise his subconscious mind had been trying to reject. All investigators had presumed the process was explainable in terms of natural phenomena. It was not. The star was undergoing change at the instigation of a living entity.

The notion was almost inconceivable, and certainly too illogical to have occurred to the *Hilt-Sil*. Yet it could explain a great deal that was presently beyond comprehension.

The implications were stunning. Even assuming Gold was correct—a broad assumption at this point—the questions of how and why loomed ahead. What entity was so advanced it could manipulate the internal processes of a sun? The *Hilt-Sil* knew of none, and they were acquainted with every form of life in their area of the galaxy. Such control was far beyond the known ability of the *Similsaculs*, and it would have been literally impossible for them to hide such knowledge from the *Hilt-Sil* research team now digging its way through the smaller species' data stores. The sheer enormity of the task of tampering with a superstar, causing the untold billions upon billions of tons of hydrogen that converted into helium each second to do so at an even faster rate, staggered the imagination. The tremendous accumulation of excess energy in the star, which would start to dissipate when that first pulsation appeared, could only be expressed in terms of high maths and meant nothing to the sense perceptions of man. And even if these questions could be answered a larger one remained. Who . . . and why? Was some malevolent intelligence attempting to destroy the *Hilt-Sil* planet? If not, if the change in the function of the star was the primary intent and the destruction of the planets only an effect, then what did the manipulating entity gain from changing the star?

Gold was accustomed to thinking in large concepts, but the enormity of the questions he was posing bothered even him. It was almost with relief that he saw Leet-A enter the door, and had to don the sensory cap again and assume control of the host long enough to turn off the cube. His case of mental indigestion had been relieved, only to be replaced by a known but even larger puzzle.

At the moment Gold could see no way of determining whether his flash of insight was true or false. Even if he were right the *Hilt-Sil* were still going to abandon their planet and the small vicious vermin still had to be eradicated.

Which brought Gold to a disturbing confrontation. Was he willing to stop the *Hilt-Sil*, if he could. During his studies of the past weeks he had decided they were a far more admirable species than *Homo sapiens*. But then he realized he was making a value judgement, and he was a creature of the same culture he was condemning as inferior, even though he did not think of himself as a member of the same species. He was damning humans by their own cultural values as they had been instilled in him!

It was unlikely he would ever be troubled by the necessity to decide between *Hilt-Sil* and human, but Gold could not repress a small feeling of pleasure at the thought that he might conceivably be the instrument that would decide whether *Homo saps* lived or died.

chapter 11

GOLD'S STUDY OF the *Hilt-Sil*, which Leet-A aided by programming more advanced material when she realized he was progressing well, proved far more interesting than astronomy. A *Hilt-Sil*, despite the many times larger brain, was only a measurable jump above *Homo sapiens* in intelligence and possessed less learning capacity than Gold. The individual brain cells were much larger than those of a human and a far higher percentage was required to manage the enormous body, leaving proportionally fewer in the higher thought centres. In that sense they were analogous to the whale on Earth, though Gold had no time to delve into the physiological questions involved.

The *Hilt-Sil* life style was slow and deliberate in the extreme, but they lived in excess of two-thousand Earth years. The giants had been an intelligent, logical, scientifically-oriented species for almost eight hundred thousand years. Their highly advanced techniques were apparently derived more from time and experience than superior intelligence. And one of the major ways in which they had accumulated their vast store of knowledge was interstellar trade.

The giants had complex and fascinating trading arrangements with their neighbours in nearby star systems. The only commodity normally exchanged in great quantities was the one most easily transported—information. The *Hilt-Sil* had long ago stopped performing original research in most of the physical sciences, supporting their highly technological society with knowledge gained in trade. They used their control of the physical world as a base on which to fashion a life-style of apparent pastoral innocence, one that did indeed keep them in close contact with nature. The city phase in their history was three-hundred thousand years in the past. The park-like exterior of Bragair had remained unchanged since the last office building fell. And the great cubes had eliminated mass meetings, or large gatherings of almost any type.

Each household planted and raised its own crops for its own consumption. The giants were vegetarians, and the foods they raised matured in sizes only a little bigger than the common fruits and grains on Earth. Caring for the huge crops required to feed a giant provided everyone with the daily exercise needed for good health. But in addition to the home chores each individual was proficient in a chosen profession, which he learned by serving a long apprenticeship with an established practitioner. A young adult usually left his family and was adopted by the established professional with whom he trained, giving everyone two sets of parents. Most adults worked only with their trainees or in small groups, but husband and wife teams were not uncommon if the two shared a compatible interest. Soam-A-Tane and Leet-A had been a botany team, working to improve the taste of some of the common plant foods.

Occasionally several professionals met in small groups for major projects, but the only ones who consistently worked together in large numbers were in the entertainment media. Those persons producing new works could not possibly provide them fast enough to satisfy the voracious appetites of the *Hilt-Sil,* but there was a tremendous accumulated backlog of great drama, poetry, song and music. The *Hilt-Sil* taste in entertainment changed slowly if at all, and stories written a half-million revolutions ago were still enjoyed in the present.

Gold had wondered about the manufacturing facilities needed to supply the technical devices that blended unobtrusively with the rural landscape. He learned there were many small factories on Bragair, but they were almost completely automatic in operation and produced only a few components each. Unlike Earth manufacturing processes, the

Hilt-Sil technology was designed around a finite number of components which could be utilized in almost unlimited combinations. Each factory was tended by a family and required only a few days' service during a revolution. The giants had a rather informal transportation system, which involved moving goods from the factories to central distribution points by anyone whose present business took him along that route. Despite this apparent casualness a distribution centre was seldom without every component produced by all factories on Bragair.

Any *Hilt-Sil* adult drew whatever items he needed from the common stores. When a couple underwent the Earthly equivalent of marriage and established a home, they had almost unlimited resources available if they provided the labour of assembly. If a new house was needed the couple could usually draw on the skills and physical help of the two sets of parents each possessed, at least until the basic frame was completed.

As Gold delved deeper into the ways of the giants he had become more and more impressed with the complexities underlying apparent simplicity. Medics like Ru-A-Lin devoted their half-day of professional work to visiting ill people in their homes. In case of emergency or delay everyone had a standard drug in the house that would slow the bodily processes almost to a state of suspended animation. Like everyone else a medic travelled in one of the flying boxes. They looked clumsy to an eye accustomed to streamlining, but were fast enough to carry a *Hilt-Sil* to any place on a planet almost twice the diameter of Earth in a matter of hours. The vehicles drew on the planet's magnetic field for power and moved by means of a beam—its operation was beyond Gold's present understanding of *Hilt-Sil* physics—which created a vacuum ahead of and above the craft. Air pressure at the rear pushed the box forward, and with no wind resistance to overcome they were capable of moving at tremendous speeds. They were braked by a similar beam at the rear.

In return for the physical science knowledge obtained from their stellar neighbours the *Hilt-Sil* offered the most advanced principles in social relationships available in the known galaxy. They had proven techniques that ensured peace between individuals, societies, races, and even species, worked out during their own war-filled past. They could help other intelligent beings avoid the pitfalls that retarded ordered progress, and their systems could be adapted to almost any civilization at any development level. In return they accepted the benefits of technology and adopted what they needed to provide lives that conformed to their own ideas of comfort and happiness.

The remark Gold had heard in the conference regarding the willingness of the *Buraruckarcs* to transport the entire *Hilt-Sil* population to Earth was a case in point. That species had failed to develop a proper balance between the physical and social sciences, resulting in a civilization that could build far better weapons of destruction than viable organizations—reminding Gold of *Homo sapiens*. The *Hilt-Sil* had provided knowledge that enabled the *Buraruckarcs* to halt terribly destructive race wars on their home planet, conflicts so severe they had threatened to destroy their civilization. At the time there had been little they could do for the *Hilt-Sil* in return and the debt remained unpaid. But the *Buraruckarcs'* interest in technology remained strong and they had eventually developed far beyond the humanoid giants in that area. Now they had enormous manufacturing facilities, so great they could produce enough interstellar ships to transport almost a million *Hilt-Sil* to Earth. The size of the logistics involved staggered Gold, until he learned that the *Buraruckarcs* lived on a planet the size of Jupiter and were far larger physically than even the *Hilt-Sil,* themselves a large species.

Both the interstellar scouts the *Hilt-Sil* presently used and the landing shuttles had been supplied by another species. The only vehicles they manufactured were their flying boxes. That explained why they seemed less than expert spacemen, and why their ground-based facilities had a temporary look. The *Hilt-Sil* did not normally travel in space. Nor would they keep the vessels being built by their larger friends, who had been preparing them for over a hundred Earthly years and expected the last to be ready shortly. The *Buraruckarcs* would serve as pilots, then use the massive ships to increase the trade of luxury goods between star systems.

Gold had found little time to talk to his companion during the period of concentrated study, but had condensed and passed on the most pertinent facts. Marina, with a good deal of time on her hands, had asked Gold if there was any way he could transpose knowledge stored in the *Hilt-Sil* files directly to their own computer, where it could be printed out in English or Russian. Gold had investigated the idea and discovered that machine translation was not possible with their available resources. The evening before the day Ru-A-Lin was due he decided to experiment with a translation, choosing one of the ancient moral stories the *Hilt-Sil* often referred to in the key sentence form. The easiest method he could devise was to hold the text in his mind's eye and translate into English while recording into their computer. He chose a simple form of transcribing that eliminated the most complex *Hilt-Sil* speech patterns, emerging with a style that seemed odd, but was easily understandable.

After he finished dictating, which was a rather slow process, Gold left his chair long enough to walk to the computer and order a print-out. He returned to his console to read it, and was amazed to see how poorly he had expressed himself in English. He cancelled the entire story off the memory banks and tried again, this time drawing heavily on his limited knowledge of literary form. Decent creative writing was a more complex task than he had realized.

It was time for the giants to retire when Gold finished. He manoeuvred the body into the hidden bed and placed his controls in neutral. Marina, who seemed more tired than usual, was still at her console. The afternoon naps had become almost mandatory for her, or she was unable to function effectively throughout the long evenings. She still performed a few housekeeping chores required in their unique quarters, seeing to their creature comfort as well as the limited facilities permitted. Her manner was as cool and remote as at the beginning of their enforced intimacy—even her hands seemed withdrawn when she shaved his head every other Bragair rotation—but apparently she had conceded to Gold the leadership of their mission and made few suggestions.

Gold handed the completed manuscript to Marina. She nodded and said, "I heard bits of it while you were dictating into the computer. This took you far longer than seems justified for my benefit. I suggest you not waste time on other translations unless you think they are absolutely essential."

"I hadn't planned to," said Gold.

Marina nodded again and read the title aloud. Gold had used the key sentence that the speaker quoted to make his point: "WHERE VRULL-A-LIN WALKED, TRIUMPH AND TRAGEDY MET IN THE COLD." She looked up at Gold and smiled slightly. "Picturesque, at any rate." She read on.

In the days when the world was young, when the *Hilt-Sil* soul was filled with pride, when knowledge was new, there lived a mighty youth called Vrull-A-Lin, renowned for his great strength and skill in sports, and filled to overflowing with a joy of life. Now Vrull-A-Lin was a good man, a worthy man, a valiant man, but he took overweening pride in his skill and strength, a pride that drove him to compete with all who would try him in games and sports. He won far more contests than he lost, and his pride increased as his ability grew great, and while still a very young man he was acknowledged the best athlete among the *Hilt-Sil.* Now Vrull-A-Lin wanted to devote himself to his games, but his parents, wise people, deterred him from spending his life in what was play to others, pointing out that as he grew older the certain decline of physical strength would cause him to need a life-work of a more enduring nature. And Vrull-A-Lin heeded their words and became a glaciologist, because it was an uncrowded field where the work kept him constantly in the open air that he loved, in the warm tension of effort that could fulfil a man's days. And when Vrull-A-Lin was ready he went searching and found his life's companion, and her name was Sond-E.

Now Sond-E too was an outdoor lover, an exertion of muscle, sweat of accomplishment woman. She wished to be a biologist, to work with living animals, and took no delight in snow or icy winds that chilled the bones. But after meeting Vrull-A-Lin she began specializing in small creatures that lived in the cold, knowing that one day they would work together in the frozen lands. And so it came to be.

In the year of the great cold, when the sunlight first weakened, Vrull-A-Lin and Sond-E were in a small shelter at the edge of the polar cap, looking across the cold sea to the great ice sheet that covers tall mountains at the Northern pole. No animals lived in all that high expanse of ice and snow across the narrow sea, but where they worked many small creatures thrived on the low land or in the cold water. And Vrull-A-Lin had instruments with which he measured the progress of the several glaciers that rolled down the icy carapace on top of the world, and cameras that recorded their birth pangs when they calved, and sensors that told him what effect they had on the sea. And Sond-E had her animals to study, and one of them was the *sifid,* which had a fire in its belly.

Now the *sifid* was a peculiar creature, one that lived in the water but was not a fish, and came ashore to breed and bear its young. The *sifid* lived well in the icy sea, for somehow, in the years before the *Hilt-Sil* spread over the land, it had developed a unique defence against the cold. Inside its digestive system was a strange organ, one that broke the strong bonds of water molecules and turned them back to gases, releasing much heat in the process. And none of the hydrogen and only a little of the oxygen was absorbed by the *sifid*, and the extra gases were expelled through the same channel which removed other bodily wastes, emerging in a strong and continuous stream. And the *sifid* sank.

The *sifid* was fat and clumsy on land, but in the sea it was an able creature, and its unique organ kept it alive and warm, while the forced expulsion of gases moved it easily through the water, with little expenditure of energy. But there were large fish in the sea that did not mind the *sifid's* smell, and its noisy propulsion system made it easy to find and kept it from any great speed. And the *sifids* were eaten as much as any other, and did not grow too numerous.

In those days when the world was young the *Hilt-Sil* did not know that their solar system, in its great sweep around the galactic wheel, was entering a region of much free hydrogen gas, and only when the sun dimmed in the sky did they understand their danger. Then the gas cloud was noted and measured, and they knew several revolutions must pass before Bragair and its sister worlds would again receive their full measure of heat from the sun. And then someone realized that the unique organ possessed by the lowly *sifid* might be of use if its function was understood. Huge glass houses had to be built and heated to grow food, and they needed to know how to break down water and produce both heat and oxygen as the *sifid* did. And so to Vrull-A-Lin and Sond-E a message was sent, and it was this: learn what makes the fire burn in a *sifid's* belly, bring us the answer, and you will have served your people well in a time of trouble.

And so Vrull-A-Lin went looking for the small creatures that pushed their way through the water by expelling gas from the rectum. And though he captured a few they died when confined, no matter the size of the pool or cage, and Sond-E told him there were none in captivity because they failed quickly out of the water. Once death took them the fabulous organ collapsed into a mass of spongy tissue that could not be understood, and was of use to no one. And so Vrull-A-Lin, with much labour, built a barricade that fenced off a narrow bay where the *sifid* came to breed, and began closing a gate behind them when they entered, and was able to furnish Sond-E with some of the creatures. But even in the large bay they died all too quickly, and luring more inside was a sore task, and Vrull-A-Lin was a busy and frustrated man. And his task was easy compared to Sond-E's.

Now the *sifid* died swiftly under the touch of the biologist's hand, and Sond-E was working with inadequate equipment at an assignment that should have gone to an older and more experienced person. But she was there and the task had been given to her, and Vrull-A-Lin stopped his own work with glaciers entirely and became her assistant. And so they worked hard at trying to solve the puzzle, and their days were busy ones that passed quickly and were forgotten.

Now this was in the days before the *Hilt-Sil* flew by removing air from in front, when the craft had wings and moved slowly as birds, and many days were needed to get from one place to another. Vrull-A-Lin and Sond-E had no aircraft, for they were scarce in those days and their need was not great. But it chanced that in the time they had lived and loved in the cold Northland Sond-E had come to be with child, and they arranged for a flyer to come after her several rotations before the birth, that she might be with family and friends in the warm Southland at the time of trial. And thus they worked to solve the secret of the *sifids* under a double compulsion, knowing that they could not spare time for the birthing and the secret must be known before departure. And this was more strain on Sond-E than Vrull-A-Lin, for hers was the major responsibility and hers the body weakened by nature's demands for the growing child.

And so, not many rotations before the plane was due, when the baby in her womb was kicking lustily and dreaming of freedom, Sond-E turned from her lab bench one day with a glad cry. Checks and computations on the crude machines they used in those days confirmed her findings, and she went running outside crying for Vrull-A-Lin, to share her joy. And she found her husband and led him toward the bench, and as the strong man closed the door she had left open in excitement Sond-E bent forward, the happiness and joy changing into a look of pain, and clutched at the child in her womb. She had just felt the first pangs of labour, and their baby had chosen to be born early.

And when the pain died away, and Sond-E stood erect again, smiling with pleasure, she asked her husband was it not wonderful that they should finish their assigned task and welcome their first child on the same glorious day?

But Vrull-A-Lin was more surprised than happy, more alarmed than pleased, and certainly more worried than expectant. He had planned to be back among their people at the time of birth, where experienced help would be available, for though medical knowledge was well advanced many women still died in childbirth, which never comes easily to a *Hilt-Sil* woman. For while this was in the ancient days the *Hilt-Sil* were far changed from their animal kin, and some of the abilities of the animals were already gone, and one of them was the natural dilation of the cervix for the birth of a child. A drug had to be administered to accomplish this function, and it was possible that as unskilled as he was in medicine and childbirth, Vrull-A-Lin's aid might not be sufficient for an easy birth. It was even possible that Sond-E or the baby might die. Vrull-A-Lin saw little at which to rejoice.

And so the young athlete went to the radio, which he had not used in many days, to call for the plane that flew like a bird, for it was in his mind to give Sond-E another medicine in their kit, one that would stop the work of labour and hold back the birth for a time. And Vrull-A-Lin turned on the radio, and it failed to function properly, and sweat appeared on his brow while he said impatient words and searched for the trouble. And the problem was a defective semi-conducting crystal, and he went to the kit which held the spare parts for all their major items of equipment, and looked, and there was no crystal. And then he remembered.

On the last day before leaving the Southland, when Vrull-A-Lin had been packing the emergency spare parts kit, one of Sond-E's brothers had challenged him to a final foot race. He had accepted with joy, and left the work inside a smothering building to breathe fresh air and demonstrate his prowess one last time, and returned to finish his labour minutes later, after beating the brother soundly. He was hot and covered with good sweat and happy in the joy of his own body, and he had hurried through the remaining items as rapidly as he could, yearning to be through with the dull chore and back with his beloved young wife, where she waited at his parents' home. And he had been careless, and had omitted the parts for the radio. And after a moment of frantic searching through their medical supplies he saw that he had omitted the drug that dilated the cervix as well, though the one that could retard the birth was there. He had let pride in his strength betray him into playing at a time when he should have been carefully working.

And Vrull-A-Lin felt deep despair, and the faltering of hope.

But then the man of strong muscles and joy in his body remembered they were not totally alone at the top of the world, and hope revived and lived once more. Less than a rotation's walk away, on the same icy shore, another young couple were living and working, two honeymooners whose interest was in those creatures that lived in the tidal flats. They had talked to this second couple several times on the radio, but each pair of lovers was complete in itself and neither had made the long walk to visit the other. But this other couple would have the drug that expanded the cervix, for it was standard equipment, and Sond-E's baby might be delivered safely there.

Pride in his strength had got Vrull-A-Lin into this great trouble, but possibly that same strength might yet save his beloved. He paused, and pondered all alternatives, and could see no other way, knowing well the schedule of the few people who visited the young couples in their isolation. And in the end there was only one answer, and he told her what they must do.

Vrull-A-Lin helped Sond-E dress in her warmest clothing, and gave her the medicine that would delay birth. He wrapped her in their heaviest blankets, then lifted her in his arms and walked into the cold air of midday. Vrull-A-Lin was dressed only lightly, for walking would keep him warm. He took a container in which to melt snow but no food, and a hand light that would let them move safely through the rough country after dark, and more of the drug that delayed birth as long as nature permitted such delay. He took with him also his greatest resource, the strength of his body, but he left behind that which had got them into this trouble, undue pride in that strength.

Sond-E was not a heavy burden to a man like Vrull-A-Lin, and the cold that gripped the flat land facing the icy carapace on top of the world was a still cold. But they had not gone far before he realized the strength in his arms would not last until dark, much less through the long night. And Vrull-A-Lin thought, and then paused long enough to tie the four corners of the outer blanket together, throwing one fold over his shoulder, leaving Sond-E still snuggled against his chest but with most of her weight shifted to his back. And he struggled onward.

Now when Sond-E first understood her husband's intention she had pleaded that they remain in the cabin for the birthing, and when those words fell on deaf ears she had suggested that Vrull-A-Lin go quickly through the cold alone and return with aid, while she held back the baby with the medicine. After they started she asked at intervals that she be allowed to walk, and so relieve his mighty back of her heavy burden. And then she stopped pleading and relaxed into the blanket with a feeling of despair, afraid all three were destined to die in this frozen wasteland, yet with her love for Vrull-A-Lin unshaken and no blame for him in her heart.

The strong man walked steadily across a barren landscape, one that stretched endlessly as far as the eye could see, without a single tree and no bush that grew higher than his knee. And it was cold, very cold, but his labour warmed him, and his warmth reached through the layers of cloth to keep Sond-E comfortable. And Vrull-A-Lin felt hope return, hope that grew into promise, for the medicine to hold back birth was working well, he was using his strength again and taking joy in his body, and he had faith in his endurance. The life of his wife and coming child rested on his mighty back and strong legs, and he would not fail them.

On he marched, over a monotonous emptiness of frozen deadness, stumbling sometimes over rough ground or snowdrifts, but never falling with his precious burden. His back started aching from the constant strain and his eyes stung from long exposure to the cold, but he did not falter. When darkness crept over the edge of the world Vrull-A-Lin knew from a long headland extending far into the sea on their left that they had covered almost a third of the way, and before the sun rose on the morrow they would see the welcoming lights of the other couple's home, beckoning them to safety.

They paused a moment in the last light, and Sond-E slipped out of the blanket and stood on her feet, to stretch and take more of the inhibitor, for her pains were strong again. Vrull-A-Lin rested also, though he was not fatigued save for the ache in his back, and melted snow for water. When the darkness grew deeper he lifted Sond-E and set off once more, though this time she faced away from his broad chest and held their light, that he might see his path in the bluish glare. And on walked Vrull-A-Lin.

But a small wind sprang up, and the voice of a greater

one sighed in the distance, as though a giant were waking. Moments later a stronger puff drove bits of snow into Vrull-A-Lin's face. For when the sun faded the gathering cold drove a mighty wind down off the icy top of the world, to howl along the flat land. And this was a wind with icy teeth, one that tore at frail warm bodies and robbed them of their heat.

When the wind started blowing in earnest Vrull-A-Lin lost his contact with the shoreline, which he had followed by listening to the angry waves attacking the shore. He had to move closer to the pounding surf. As the wind increased fresh snow began falling, and the driven sleet cut into his exposed face like frozen knives. He could see only a short distance at best, and the light that Sond-E held showed only his next few steps. When the wind grew stronger yet he had to move still closer to the sea, and the shoreline was crooked and moved in and out in long headlands, lengthening his journey. But Vrull-A-Lin walked on.

The hours of the night passed slow and hard, but the man of strength plodded on. From deep in his heart Vrull-A-Lin had drawn on a reservoir of power he had not known was there, and it poured into his body in an endless stream of warmth. Once they paused behind a large rock, out of the driving wind, to give Sond-E more medicine and rest his straining back, but the cold soon drove him on. There was no hiding from it, for even out of the wind the lower temperature that had come with the darkness bit and tore at their exposed skin, numbed their feet and hands, sucked the heat from their bodies and scattered it over the land. To stop was to die.

Vrull-A-Lin picked up his beloved and resumed their journey, leaving the despair that had again come to plague him behind the cold rock. For he was strong, the mightiest man among a mighty people, and he was using that strength to save the woman without whom life would not be worth living, and the child in her womb that was a part of them both. And Vrull-A-Lin walked on.

Slowly, painfully, the hours dragged past. After a time the man's back became a rigid cord of muscle, frozen into stiffness, and the muscles in his legs worked automatically, numbed but determined to move their heavy burden forward, and he had long ago lost contact with his feet. And Sond-E, though huddled against his chest, yielded the battle of warmth to the driving wind and clinging snow. She grew cold, and not even his body heat and the blankets could save her. She did not tell Vrull-A-Lin when she lost all feeling in her feet, or when the hands holding the small light grew numb and she had to hold it steady by pressing it against the blanket with her palms. She did not tell him when the cold finally stopped hurting and was gradually replaced by total numbness, a feeling that was almost pleasant in its lack of pain. She did not tell him she was slowly freezing to death, for there would have been nothing he could do. And Vrull-A-Lin walked on.

He finally stumbled once and fell, but managed to fling an arm ahead and twist to the side, to cushion his precious burden with his own body. The extended hand sank through soft snow to hard rock, and when the strong man rose and staggered on the hand was numb for a time. When feeling returned, it brought pain, sharp and enduring, and he knew he had damaged his hand, perhaps past repair. But his feet were still moving, his legs still strong. And Vrull-A-Lin walked on.

Through the long, long night the mighty Vrull-A-Lin plodded endlessly into the darkness, not stopping again, moving slowly but with the dogged certainty of one followed by the skeletal hounds of death, yielding neither to the deadly cold nor the growing fatigue that sucked the strength from his body. He put one sodden foot ahead of the other with remorseless, relentless determination. Sond-E huddled passively against his chest, holding the light with her numbed hands, its flickering beam and the sound of the sea their only guidance.

The wind died away just before dawn, when Vrull-A-Lin knew they would have already found shelter if he had not been forced to follow the curving shoreline. As the first frail rays of light peeked over the edge of the sea he saw the small house he was seeking in the distance, on a small headland that, like their own, rose high above the waters of the always angry sea. And there was help available at last.

It was still a great distance to shelter, but with the goal in sight his strength revived, and as the weak dawn light brightened he walked faster, able to see well ahead and careless of the rough ground. He looked down into the face of his beloved, snuggled against his chest now that the hand light was not needed, and saw that she seemed peacefully asleep, her breath shallow but regular. And Vrull-A-Lin walked on.

The other couple were still in bed when a pounding at

their door told them help was needed. And luck was with the cold travellers at last, for the wife of the two was a medic, and not only had all the drugs required for delivery but the instruments and other medical aids. And it was well that this was so, for the inhibiting medicine had delayed the birth as long as it could, and when Vrull-A-Lin placed his beloved in a still-warm bed the time of delivery was near. Sond-E was awakened to the knowledge they were safe at last by the return of the labour pains, this time so strong they could not be denied.

The woman placed Vrull-A-Lin in a corner, with instructions to let his numb limbs warm slowly while she and her husband delivered the baby. The strong man lay still as he had been instructed, watching them with eyes that seemed to see from a great distance, knowing the matter was out of his hands and he could rest at last. He saw the woman administer the dilation medicine, though it should have been used much earlier, for the baby was pushing hard against its prison. He saw her working with desperate speed over the form of his wife, saw the massive shot of dilation medicine she administered in an effort to ease the birth, and knew she had partially succeeded minutes later when his son was born, his delicate large head emerging from the birth canal unhurt by the pressure that could have crushed it. He heard the baby cry when it was whirled into life, and saw the woman clip and tie the cord. In numbness of mind as well as body he saw the afterbirth delivered and laid aside, and then his senses sharpened as he saw the woman resume her frantic work on the form of Sond-E. She massaged arms and legs, attempting to restore warmth that had been too long absent, and at last, in obvious desperation, she gave Sond-E two shots of a drug whose purpose he did not understand. He saw all this, and wondered, and at last rose and staggered to the bed, walking on fiery needles of pain from returning sensation, to see his beloved's face was white as the cloth on which she lay, and hear her breathing lightly, faintly, as though with much labour . . . and slowly, much too slowly. He saw that the bed was covered with blood where the baby had emerged, and that Sond-E was still bleeding. But she opened her eyes, and there was no longer any real pain, and she smiled weakly at her husband and made a feeble attempt to hold out her arms. And when he hastily knelt and gathered her close, barely noticing the jolts of pain in his broken hand, she looked into his eyes and whispered, I have given you a son.

And the woman doctor stepped back, leaving the two alone, for there was nothing more she could do. And, still gazing into her loved one's eyes, held in the strong arms that had cradled her through the long cold night, Sond-E died.

Vrull-A-Lin the Strong held his dead wife in his arms, and he was no longer strong.

After what seemed a long long time, an hour of silent sorrow, there was a small stirring in the room behind him, and then the wailing cry of a baby brought Vrull-A-Lin back to life. He eased the form of Sond-E to the bed, and turned to see the woman cleaning the baby. It was her ministering action that had started the infant crying again.

Slowly Vrull-A-Lin rose, walked to the baby and took it in his arms, gently cradling the large head and fragile neck. The medic stared at him in wondering surprise. After a moment he handed the baby back to her and walked toward the door, not even glancing at his clothes discarded in the corner, and his step quickened as he neared the waiting cold. But the woman understood and spoke to her husband, and that perceptive man moved quickly and blocked the door, standing between the strong one and the death he desired. And Vrull-A-Lin, somewhat recovered now, raised his mighty fist to break this weak barrier, attain his desire . . . and the much smaller man waited, watchful but not afraid. After a moment Vrull-A-Lin lowered his arm and turned away. He walked to his corner and sat on the floor with his back to the others, to grieve alone. Indulging his pride-in-strength had cost him Sond-E. He would never lift a hand in competition or anger again.

And so Vrull-A-Lin lived, and after a time returned to the warmer lands with his son and the secret of how the *sifid* turned water into oxygen and heat. And the years of the Great Cold were not the terror they might have been, and Sond-E had not died in vain.

Vrull-A-Lin, formerly the Strong, devoted the years of his young manhood to raising the child that was all he had of Sond-E, and not until the baby had grown into manhood did the hurt and despair in his heart ease, so that he was again able to find love. And the son of Vrull-A-Lin and Sond-E was named Whit-A-Lon, he who formulated the Four Basic Points of Agreement Between Intelligences, and so provided the *Hilt-Sil* with their first item of value to trade with their neighbours among the stars. And from that day to this the contribution of the *Hilt-Sil* has been knowledge of the proper order of relationships between intelligent beings.

WHERE VRULL-A-LIN WALKED, TRIUMPH AND TRAGEDY MET IN THE COLD!

chapter 12

Gold saw Marina look up from the manuscript. "Well, what do you think of it?"

She studied him a moment before saying, "I hope you never have to earn your keep as a writer. May I ask why you used no dialogue when it was so obviously called for in many places? In one spot—here where Sond-E is smiling as she dies—you even quote her. A lot of your exposition is overdramatic, and the whole piece seems badly written. That bit of Vrull-A-Lin plodding on and on grew tiresome toward the end, too. But literary criticism aside, what is the meaning of the story?"

Gold could not brush her comments aside that easily, but he hid his chagrin and explained, "The story can be used in at least three different contexts. In one it means don't play when you should be devoting yourself to careful work. Vrull-A-Lin did, and it cost Sond-E her life. With another background it can be interpreted to say that pressing on regardless of obstacles is the best way to succeed, since the strong man who never gave up did at least save the baby. On an abstract level it can mean that a species progresses by the sacrifices of the individual members for the common good. Sond-E's solution of the *sifid*'s heating trick was a nice contribution to the group welfare during a bad time, but the real value came from the baby whose life was saved. Whit-A-Lon grew up to become a very famous man, the originator of the first principles of behaviour that apply to any group of intelligent beings. His discovery laid the ground work for the *Hilt-Sil*'s eventual specialization as advanced behavioural scientists, the position they hold in the interstellar community."

"I'm impressed by their moral ethos," Marina admitted. "On Earth it would resemble sheer anarchy of thought, but obviously it works here."

"We like our platitudes wrapped up in simple, easily opened packages. I'd say their moral code is analogous to their social co-operation. To us their methods seem loose and disorganized, but they work quite effectively. I think it's because each *Hilt-Sil* adult has a better understanding of what constitutes the common welfare than *Homo saps*, and works toward shared goals from conviction rather than some form of compulsion."

"The more we learn about these people the more admirable they seem," Marina said thoughtfully. "But nothing can change the fact they deliberately set out to destroy an intelligent species that had done nothing whatever to them. I couldn't forgive them for that even if we were not the intended victims."

Marina had already placed the host in the low metabolic activity rate that now served as sleep. She ended the conversation by rising and climbing down the sharply slanted floor to the living quarters. Gold followed, and saw her short form disappear into the equipment room. He could not see the toilet, but after a moment heard it operate. Marina returned, dimmed the light above her bed, and retired. The bunk was level by gravity but tilted in relation to the floor, at the usual odd angle it assumed with the host's head propped up to sleep. She was lying with her back to Gold, the zippered cover hiding her shape except for the womanly rise of hip.

Gold was tired but not sleepy; the work of translation had stimulated him, and he felt restless. He turned and went back to his console. When he donned the sensory helmet he immediately became aware of an odd sensation, one he could not identify. It was a strong but diffused feeling, and he received the distinct impression it was not from the body's sense organs.

Gold heard a sound on his audio input from the exterior and hastily opened the host's eyes. He was looking upward into the great brooding face of Leet-A, only a few feet away. The dark barrier that normally separated the large bed into silent halves had been turned off. As he stared, wondering at this deviation from the night's usual routine, the huge face swooped toward him, stopping with one giant closed eye so near he could have opened the cornea and touched it. And he felt the odd sensation again, and this time identified it. Leet-A was kissing the host on the lips . . . and Gold was getting what seemed to be a secondary feedback from the living half of the brain!

For a moment Gold was paralysed by indecision. When the pressure Leet-A was applying increased he decided any response was better than the yielding slackness she was getting now, and pulled the lips upward into the mechanical grimace that served as a smile. There was a sudden sharp intake of breath when the giantess felt the lips beneath hers move. After a moment she broke the contact and drew back with a low cry of happiness. Gold saw that she was smiling now, though it seemed tremulous and uncertain, and there were tears gathering in the corners of the huge brown eyes. Her expression was tender and there was a yearning readiness, a sexual softness beneath it, that Gold had seen many times on the face of Carlotta when she initiated the play that led inevitably to sharing sex.

Leet-A shifted again, and Gold felt her hand as it moved across Soam-A-Tane's abdomen. The sensation died away but one of mounting excitement followed, a sensation that again seemed to be coming from the opposite half of the brain rather than the sense organs. The genitals were not connected to the sensory cap. Somehow he was receiving backfeed from the sexual awareness the autonomic system was generating in the sleeping half of the brain.

Gold felt himself mildly aroused through the backdoor contact, but swiftly became aware that he was sharing far stronger sensations of strain and physical weakness. And then he realized the body's heartbeat, respiration, and other automatic functions had not speeded up in response to the demand for sexual energy.

Gold felt slightly alarmed. He turned and called for Marina, and when she did not answer, called again. A moment later she appeared and hurried to her console, wearing only her tight-fitting undergarment and rubbing sleep from her eyes. She saw the signs of strain at once, and her quick small hands moved to rheostat and switch. Almost immediately Gold felt the heartbeat accelerate, and a moment later the general feeling of strain eased. And as the body's strength increased, the sensation of sexual excitement he was receiving as secondary feedback grew stronger.

Gold looked back at Leet-A and saw that she was smiling broadly, the shining eyes glistening rather than wet. The great bald head lowered for another kiss, and this time Gold responded immediately with the smile control.

After a moment Leet-A broke the lip contact, though she moved back only a few feet. The huge mouth opened, and the sounds that emerged were a singing chant of which he caught only a few words, and they were of love and need. Gold, still wondering what had brought on this unusual display of physical affection, finally lifted the host's arms and clasped Leet-A around the shoulders, pulling her down on the great chest. That seemed to be the signal she had been awaiting. The ready tears suddenly spilled over, but the sob that choked off the singing seemed more a sound of joy than sorrow.

A moment later Leet-A eased herself over Soam-A-Tane. Gold felt the sliding contact of skin on skin, and shifted the arms to her waist. There was a feeling of pressure as she lay almost full-length on the host, but the lightness of the burden indicated she was partially supporting herself on elbows and knees.

Marina's voice on the helmet phone circuit was alarmed when she asked, "What is happening, Gold? Blood pressure is abnormally high, there's a general bodily strain, and several stimulants I didn't release are in the blood stream."

"We have an emergency," Gold answered briefly. "Keep the activity rate high."

Gold knew from the strength of the secondary feedback he was getting that the body was deeply aroused sexually, though the full impact was lost on him because of the lack of sensory contact with the genital area. Despite the diffused nature of the stimulation Gold realized that his own body, which had become difficult to separate from that of the host, was also in a state of tumescence.

Leet-A continued to sob quietly while caressing her husband, and Gold felt himself more and more a part of Soam-A-Tane. He could almost share the faster beating of the heart, feel the added blood pouring through the huge arteries, taste the air moving rapidly in and out of the heaving lungs.

Leet-A stopped for a moment, as though gathering her resources. Gold, deeply immersed in a well of sensation, waited breathlessly. He was still getting generalized instead of specific sensations from the genital area. After a moment he felt his hands move downward several yards as Leet-A lowered her hips; the length of her warm body rested solidly against his.

Leet-A paused, and then began the almost automatic movement of sexual conjunction. Gold heard her heavy breathing, interrupted by many small gasps, as she performed the more active role. After several minutes her arms locked around his neck, in a frantic need to cling and hold.

Her body went into small shuddering convulsions that Gold felt throughout the length of the skin contact. And abruptly Gold felt a new flood of sensation sweep irresistibly through his mind, wiping out the last vestige of his individual consciousness. He was one with the host, a unity, and the unity itself was lost in a flood of pleasurable sensation as the body finally reached climax. Gold willingly surrendered to the tide, letting it wash over and through him, absorbing him completely.

It seemed like hours, but could only have been minutes, before Gold felt full consciousness returning. He was being drawn back by a new disturbing sensation, a wetness on his face. After a moment he identified the source; Leet-A was crying. A flood of warm tears was dripping steadily on to the host's cheeks.

Gold felt the pressure of his hands on her waist relaxing, realized that his own fingers on the console were turning knobs as the arms fell limply to the bed. He was back in his own body. Soam-A-Tane was still breathing heavily, though his physical exertion had been small. After a moment Leet-A realized her weight was a burden. She rolled to the side, back to her own bed, and lay with one hand clasping the host's arm. She was crying openly now, though not loudly, and Gold could not tell if it was from relief or sorrow. He was certain it was not from joy. As he listened the sound slowly died away, trailing off into occasional sobs. She lay holding the arm she had grasped until Gold knew from the regularity of her breathing that she had fallen asleep.

The body had calmed rapidly after the climax, but Gold realized his own was still filled with a pervading sense of sexual excitement. He unstrapped the sensory helmet and spun around in his chair, to see Marina adjusting her console controls to the lessened demand. She spoke into her mike, and when he did not answer turned around and addressed him directly. "Is the emergency over? Can I put him back to sleep?"

"Go ahead," he called, and then undid his seat belt and clambered down the incline toward her. Marina worked over her console a moment, made one final visual check, and then unbuckled her belt and rose. She had not heard Gold and was surprised to see him standing there, but headed down the sloping floor to the living quarters without comment. Gold followed her closely, and was just behind when she went immediately to her bed and sat down.

Marina turned and glanced up at him questioningly when

she realized Gold had accompanied her. Instead of speaking he sat by her, causing the unbalanced bed to tilt, and calmly reached for her shoulders. The surprise on her face changed to shock as he pulled her toward him, and for a moment she did not even resist. He drew her to his chest and lowered his head to kiss her. Their lips had barely touched when she placed both hands against his heavy chin and shoved hard; he lost his balance and almost fell off the bed as it shifted with their movements.

"Gold! What is wrong with you?" A sudden awareness crossed Marina's face. "That midnight activity! The demand on the heart and the stimulants! That was some sort of sexual activity you took the body through with Leet-A, wasn't it?" She studied him narrowly as he sat erect again. "And now you're excited from contact through the sensory helmet and suddenly I look very good to you as a woman! Gold, please calm yourself. We are not here to indulge your lusts."

Gold hesitated. His body was still throbbing with need, but Marina's lack of response and cold words stopped him. And then he realized that for the first time since the last attempt to impregnate a woman more than two years ago he was physically potent; he knew with an inner certainty that he could complete the act of sexual sharing. He was fully in command of himself and could do as she asked . . . but to do so might plunge him back into the agony of frustration and withdrawal that had been leading him steadily toward suicide.

Gold grasped Marina's shoulders again and pushed her back on the bed, getting to his knees as it tilted once more. He held her pinned with one hand while the other darted to the zipper at the throat of her single-piece garment. He had it almost to her waist before she caught his wrist. "*Gold!*" the anger in her voice was the strongest he had heard. "Gold, I demand that you stop this! I will not have you indulging yourself with my body! I am a scientist here to perform a job, not one of your paid mistresses. Now let me go!"

Instead of answering Gold caught both her hands, locked one to the bed with a knee, and held the other while he drew the zipper to the bottom. Marina struggled vainly for a moment, then managed to pull the hand from beneath his knee and caught him with a hard slap across the face. Gold ignored it. Moving both hands to the top of the suit he quickly eased it backward off her shoulders, impeding her upper arms. As the material slipped downward he saw that she wore only a brassière above the waist. Marina was almost helpless for the moment, but Gold could not pull the suit any lower. Abruptly he heaved her over on one side, shifted his hands to the material around her hips, and yanked so hard it had to move or tear.

The garment slid over Marina's wide hips easily enough. The sleeves came with it, freeing her arms, and she immediately twisted erect and jabbed stiffened fingers hard at Gold's eyes. He jerked his head down and took them on the forehead, then caught the hand and yanked her hard toward him, pulling her off balance. As she sprawled face down Gold swung one thigh over her shoulders, holding her immobile by sheer weight, and tugged the suit off the kicking legs. He released her and Marina again struggled to a sitting position, tears of rage in her dark eyes. She wore opaque, functional panties in addition to the bra. She swung at his face very quickly and he took the slap as he reached for her legs, catching her beneath both knees and pulling them over a forearm. He rose to a kneeling position, lifting her legs high, and Marina was thrown on her back, twisting and clawing as she tried to pull herself forward and reach his eyes. With his free hand Gold seized the elastic in the upper edge of the panties and yanked hard. They pulled apart across one leg and he shifted to the other side, yanked again, and tossed the torn garment away.

Marina abruptly went limp. Gold lowered her legs to the bed. She lay quietly staring at him, suddenly completely calm, her face a cold passionless mask; both anger and fear had vanished. Gold ignored her coldness and slipped both hands under her back to the bra snaps, unhooked them, and pulled it forward off her arms. Marina continued to stare at him with brooding intensity. Gold hesitated, still holding the bra, and she said, "I suppose I am physically unable to stop you from this rape. But would you mind explaining why you have suddenly reverted to savagery?"

Gold felt the awareness of sexual readiness he had been nursing start to wither under the scorn in her eyes. But then a saving anger came with the thought that this was what she intended; she had realized her resistance was only stimulating him. "Yes I do mind!" he snapped, and reached for her feet, pulling them apart and into the position of sexual surrender. Quickly, before his potency should fail, he stripped off his suit, shed the shorts which were his only undergarment, and mounted Marina. When she saw her last effort had failed she did not resume the physical battle, but neither did she help him. Her body was not ready for intercourse, and entering her was difficult and painful for Gold and probably more so for her. But he persisted, and after several hard lunges finally managed a deep penetration.

Gold paused with their bodies joined, feeling a fierce, exultant joy. For the first time in two years he knew he could perform as a man, enjoy the body of a woman. He started the movements of the sexual act and Marina lay still, totally slack, staring at his face in cold disdain. Their forced sharing lasted only a minute. Gold felt the first faint tremors of release in electric tension from the base of his spine, knew once more a vibrant sense of potency and power, and then the flood-gates opened and the dammed energy poured out of his body in surging jolts. He collapsed on top of Marina, his head hitting the bed above hers, breathing in great gasps of relief; he felt that he would never be impotent again.

There was a moment of quiet, and then Gold's weight pressed on Marina's chest so hard she had to turn partially on her side to breathe. Gold reluctantly lifted his upper body off hers, but not his hips. She lay passive, her gaze fixed steadily to the side, waiting in obvious patience for him to unjoin and release her. When she realized he was not going to move she turned her head and stared into his face. Gold smiled, in a contentment not even her indifference to their bodies could break, and she turned and looked away again, though this time her expression seemed faintly troubled. The silent tableau endured for several minutes, and she finally asked, low-voiced, "Will you please let me go?"

Gold shifted to his knees and flopped over on his back. Marina quickly scrambled out of the side, turning to face him once she was standing on the tilted floor. Her hair was dishevelled and she was sweaty on thighs and stomach where their skins had been long together. There was a cold, controlled anger on her small face, and no awareness that she was still nude in front of Gold. *"You selfish, primitive brute!"* she said, speaking slowly and distinctly. "You think of yourself as superior to ordinary men and in fact you aren't a man at all! How could any civilized human being treat a woman as you have just treated me?"

Gold lay and watched the hurt and angry woman without attempting to defend himself. His eyes roved over her body, and he realized she had the same short legs, somewhat heavy form and noticeable bulge of stomach as Carlotta, though her breasts were smaller. The faint scar of an old operation ran in a vertical line along the swelling roundness of stomach. Old memories of the happiest days of his life stirred strongly, and for an instant it seemed to him Carlotta was indeed standing there, mature and strong in her own dark loveliness, confronting him not in anger but with a challenge of sexual love.

"Well!" demanded Marina, the tone still icily cold but edged by a hot underlying rage.

Gold lifted his gaze to her face and all resemblance to Carlotta vanished. Marina's sense of outrage had overcome her usual rigid control, and now that the physical rape she could not prevent was over she was trying again to assert her rights as a person; only her physical resistance had failed.

Instead of answering Gold lowered his gaze again to the gently protruding stomach and the faint but distinct scar. He saw two other lines of barely visible scar patterns, interlocked rings over an inch wide that began just above the wide hip bones and curved downward and in to meet and vanish in the scant pubic hair, like the sides of a woven basket enclosing the small mound of stomach. And then Gold recognized them. He was staring at the stretch marks caused by a large baby carried to near full term. The operation scar could only be the betraying mark of a Caesarian delivery.

"You've had a baby," said Gold.

The anger fled from Marina's face. In startled confusion she glanced down at her stomach, realized the marks had betrayed her, and with a need to hide that was not from modesty, turned her back.

Gold lay on the narrow bed, mind racing. He knew enough about Marina's history to be certain she had never married, had claimed no true life of her own since she had become Petrovna's assistant. Yet the evidence that she had had a baby was unmistakable. But having a child out of wedlock was hardly sufficient to account for this strong guilt reaction. The answer, when it dawned, made him wonder how he could be so blind. He sat up and said one word aloud. "*Petrovna!*"

Marina whirled around, tears spilling from both eyes. She scrambled toward him across the tilted floor, retrieved her undersuit, and started pulling it on. Gold waited, suddenly embarrassed by a secret he had no right to share, while the implications whirled through his mind in a dizzying stream. If Petrovna was capable of fathering a child, why not himself? The American and Russian genetic manipulators had been working with almost identical sets of data. And why had the Russians claimed Petrovna was sterile?

Marina, dressed again, turned and faced Gold, still sitting nude on the edge of the bed. Angrily she wiped the tears from her eyes and snapped, "Yes! Petrovna! And is that any concern of yours?"

Gold looked away and reached for his own suit. When he had zipped it up and turned to face her he said, "Of course it's my concern. You know Petrovna and I were supposed to be virtually identical, and no one was surprised when I proved sterile because you had already admitted this about your older genius. I'd like to know why you lied and what happened to the baby. And how many others are there?"

"Nobody lied. Our baby was born deformed, in both brain and body." The anger in Marina's voice could not hide an old hurt. "And there are no others. Ours had limbs identical to Petrovna's and a nonfunctioning brain. It died within an hour, its heart kept beating that long only by machines. Does that satisfy you?"

Gold took two steps across the sloping floor, filled with a sudden tenderness that made him want to hold and comfort the small woman. Marina immediately backed away, angry grief replaced by a cold rejection. Gold stopped as if she had erected a glass wall. "I'm sorry," he said after a moment. "I knew that you loved Petrovna of course, but I never realized . . ."

Marina stared at him in stony silence. "Well, you're the one who claims to love the human species so damn much!" Gold went on more harshly. "Why did you conceal news so important to the whole world?"

"What was important about giving birth to a monster?" Marina demanded. "It happened over a decade ago, in the second year after I joined Petrovna. It's well enough known in Russia, I assure you. His seed was planted in literally thousands of fertile women, and like you he tried the direct route except that it was with some of the most respected young women in the Soviet Union. Nothing worked. For several years just before I became his assistant he had been living celibate, pouring all his energy into work. When I learned to love him so much I would have died to bring a little happiness into his life, he came to care for me as a woman. In the end we went to bed because I wanted it far more than he, but I brought him comfort and some joy during the months we were together. Neither of us could believe it when I became pregnant. Petrovna was examined again and they found his sperm count had increased slightly and the activity level was higher, though still less than that of a normal man. But I was definitely pregnant by him, so we waited with great hope and expectation, not telling the world Petrovna's seed had finally been transmitted. I was delivered by Caesarian to protect that precious head, and they swiftly discovered they needn't have bothered. The brain was only a mass of undeveloped tissue."

Marina had lowered her gaze as she spoke. There was a long moment of silence. She finally lifted her eyes, the anger gone from her face, and quite calmly asked, "Why, after these months of living together, did you suddenly attack me? Did the stimulation you received through the sensory helmet affect you that strongly? And for that matter, why did Leet-A and the body have intercourse after all these nights without?"

Gold hesitated, then slowly told her the simple truth, that he had committed rape because he felt certain it would cure his impotency. "As for Leet-A, these people lead fairly active sex lives, and she had been continent for over two of our years while Soam-A-Tane was away. I think sleeping with the husband again night after night finally overcame her scruples about sharing sex with a mental cripple, and she yielded and used her husband's body as best she could. Which was good enough to give her the *Hilt-Sil* equivalent of orgasm, incidentally."

Marina listened quietly and nodded. "Leet-A at least I can understand. Petrovna wouldn't share sex with me after the birth of our monster, and I found adjusting to continence again very difficult. But as for you . . . you honestly think that success in raping a helpless woman will cure your psychological impotency?"

Gold smiled slightly, glad to see the anger of outrage yielding to Marina's usual cool rationality. "You were far from helpless; in fact you almost stopped me when you went from fighting to tongue-lashing. And yes, basically that's correct. I enjoyed the experience tremendously—though you were a little dry—and I'm positive I can perform normally again if we get back to Earth."

Marina nodded thoughtfully. "Yes, that attitude fits your

demonstrated proclivities toward self-indulgence and pleasure-seeking. So basically you were using my body as a catharsis, to cure yourself of a severe mental problem."

Gold found himself unable to look away from her small, intent face. She seemed determined to worry the problem until the last facet of a complexly cut stone emerged into the light. He had not expected her condemnation to take this turn, since he had not considered her a desirable female and been unaware she thought of herself as a woman as well as a scientist. Evidently even Marina had her feminine vanity.

"I don't know whether I hate you more or less now," she went on musingly. "I've often wondered why you seemed to have no interest in me. On the other hand I despise you, and wouldn't want your love or even your desire."

"I apologize for violating your personal dignity," Gold said slowly, moving until he was looking down into her upturned, unafraid face. "Physically I don't think I did you any real harm."

Marina's lips curled in disgust. "I had rather one of the hundreds of women you've bought had the honour of restoring your so terribly important potency, Gold. And now if you don't plan any further attacks on me I'd like to get to bed. I'm very tired."

She walked past him to the equipment room and the toilet. When Marina returned she went directly to the floating bed, crawled inside and zipped up the cover, and within two minutes was fast asleep. Gold watched her in brooding silence, but finally cleaned himself and prepared for bed also. Unlike Marina he was a long time getting to sleep.

Next day the normal routine in the house of Soam-A-Tane and Leet-A resumed as if the dramatic events of the night before had never occurred. Another *Hilt-Sil* woman engaged in taste research dropped by early in the morning, in one of the few personal visits they had received from adults, but left after a detailed examination of Leet-A's current experimental plants. Ru-A-Lin arrived that afternoon, and dispelled a nagging worry that had been at the back of Gold's mind—that he would bring machines to physically probe Soam-A-Tane's damaged brain. Instead the medic almost immediately started a more intensive therapy course. Evidently he was satisfied with the rate of progress, and willing to accept the changes from the old Soam-A-Tane as permanent alterations in personality.

Ru-A-Lin moved in with the family, and Gold discovered there were several more concealed beds under areas of open floor. He also learned that Ru-A-Lin was that comparatively rare *Hilt-Sil*, a person who normally lived alone. His wife had been killed many revolutions back, in one of the occasional accidents that took a *Hilt-Sil* life. The giant medic had decided to devote his full time to Soam-A-Tane and turned his normal practice over to others.

Ru-A-Lin's arrival complicated Gold's astronomical researches. After two days of therapy he had finished digesting all previously absorbed material and needed more. He had no sure way of predicting Ru-A-Lin's reaction, but took a chance and operated the cube controls himself on the third morning, cancelling an assigned lesson in favour of an advanced article on the sun. Leet-A, who was just going out of the door, paused and watched in mild astonishment. Ru-A-Lin also stared, but when Soam-A-Tane indicated the medic should seat himself and study the material he did so at once. Gold had Soam-A-Tane resume his seat, and then started printing the new material on his temporary memory in the usual way, occasionally taking notes in *Hilt-Sil* to maintain the charade. There was little new in the chosen article and he went to the next, stepping up the replay speed; he advanced it again, to what he felt was the fastest Ru-A-Lin could absorb, on the third. The giant, his face troubled, studied the articles intently, taking copious notes. By the end of the morning session he appeared to have become as interested in the material as Gold.

That afternoon Gold immediately returned to his planned course of study, and Ru-A-Lin followed his lead without demur. Since the giant seemed genuinely interested Gold settled for a leisurely pace and used his remaining attention to replay and record the relevant facts from the morning's work.

At the end of two more days Gold had absorbed all the important data the *Hilt-Sil* files contained on their red superstar, and was suffering from mental indigestion again. As before, the cause was unknown. And he had decided it was time to tell Ru-A-Lin of his theory that the change in the sun's conversion rate was due to outside instigation, and the hydrogen clouds of eleven-hundred revolutions before were the weapons used.

Ru-A-Lin read Gold's hastily scribbled explanation with close attention, but it was difficult to tell if he was being convinced or simply polite. When Gold finished he asked a few intelligent questions, and after the answers were quickly but carefully written out, several complex ones. Ru-A-Lin knew more advanced solar physics than Gold had expected. These took time but were eventually answered to Ru-A-Lin's satisfaction.

The medic sat back in his chair, appearing somewhat baffled. "I do not understand, Soam-A-Tane. In many ways you still appear to be suffering from the effects of oxygen starvation, and yet you have mastered a complex subject in which you previously showed no interest. In our distant past we have had recorded cases of 'idiot savants,' people who were mentally defective except for one skill that was developed to an extreme, but there have been none like them now for many generations. Still, you are also the first person on record who has suffered severe oxygen deprivation and then lived in isolation for over a revolution. You are certainly unique, and I do not think your theory should be ignored. I will speak to Jelk-A-Bin."

Ru-A-Lin activated the communications side of the cube and contacted the chairman of the group watching the sun. The *Hilt-Sil* astronomer listened to the idea in obvious astonishment, questioned Ru-A-Lin about Soam-A-Tane's condition, and then politely but decisively dismissed the idea as beyond the bounds of possibility. It was inconceivable that any known intelligence could or would tamper with their sun. It was equally impossible for nine comparatively small clouds of hydrogen gas to have any effect on a superstar. Jelk-A-Bin did not voice his thoughts, but it was obvious he felt the preposterous idea had arisen in a brain still far from recovered.

When the conversation ended Ru-A-Lin turned to Soam-A-Tane, his face troubled, "My friend, our foremost astronomer considers your theory untenable. Does this lessen your own belief in the idea?"

Gold wrote that it did not, and added a suggestion he had not previously considered himself . . . that they check his theory by a personal investigation of the sun's surface, including a close examination of those long-term flares that had started appearing after the clouds were absorbed.

"You are thinking of using the Sunwatchers' research craft?" Ru-A-Lin asked. This was a vessel the *Similsaculs* had built for their giant friends early in their trading history, a unique vehicle capable of penetrating well into the sun's interior. When Gold nodded Ru-A-Lin shook his head in bafflement. "Why is this mission so important to you?" he asked.

The question jarred Gold; he did not know himself why he wanted to venture to the red giant's surface. There was no logical reason whatever why Soam-A-Tane should have become interested in studying the sun, much less want to visit it. Then an illogical reason that might suffice occurred to him, and he hastily wrote, //Because I am apparently never going to recover my full faculties, and I wish to know that I am at least strong in the area where I have become an "idiot savant." If I can master only one subject I will be content. And can we afford to neglect the chance that I am right?//

"No, it seems not," Ru-A-Lin said after a moment's thought. "But even if you were proved correct, how would we find the intelligences responsible and what could we do to reverse their work?"

Gold had no answer to those questions either, but he did have a sudden awareness that it had been the unacceptable knowledge lurking deep in his subconscious that had made him propose visiting the sun. Hidden information was struggling toward the light, and until it emerged he would have to act on whatever hints he received.

//I do not know// Gold wrote //but if I am proven right surely the *Hilt-Sil* and their friends can find a way.//

Ru-A-Lin smiled slightly and said, "I have no future plans except working with you, and that we can continue during the trip. The Sunwatchers are no longer using their vessel and it should be available, but it is a slow vehicle and the trip will take many rotations. Is your wife agreeable?"

Leet-A had varied the afternoon routine by a trip to a distribution centre. While they were waiting for her, Ru-A-Lin called several *Hilt-Sil* leaders and discussed the proposed trip. He received some reasoned arguments that conclusively proved the expedition a waste of time, but no one denied their right to the unused research vessel. When Leet-A returned Gold presented the idea to her as something Soam-A-Tane wished to do to prove himself at least partially recovered. In her grave way the giantess agreed that if the two men felt the trip would be good for Soam-A-Tane, she would not object.

The decision had been made, and before dark they were on their way to the flying solar observatory. In less than half a Bragair rotation, so quickly and easily Gold would not have believed it possible among a people so informally organized, the supplies they needed had been located and sent to the ship, two astronomers who were operating experts had agreed to check it out for them, and they had gathered a few personal possessions they needed. Gold, somewhat dazed by the speed, realized this high efficiency resulted from a lack of procedures and authorizations. Among the *Hilt-Sil* each individual was responsible for his own actions, even those that might affect many others. On Earth such decision-making at the bottom would have resulted in utter chaos. Among the giants it worked unbelievably well.

Jelk-A-Bin and the chairman of the Affirmatives were the last two officials notified. Both accepted the trip with good grace and both made it clear they considered it a waste of time, except for the possible therapeutic effect on Soam-A-Tane. Here Gold caught a glimpse of a few fragile safeguards in the *Hilt-Sil* system. If either chairman had registered strong opposition to the expedition Ru-A-Lin's own sense of co-operation would have forced him to cancel it.

There was a certain element of danger in this mission, but Ru-A-Lin was a comparatively skilled pilot and the protective mechanisms on the ship were automatic in operation. The *Similsaculs* built well; in Earth time the vessel was three hundred thousand years old, and it had not cost a single *Hilt-Sil* his life.

Soam-A-Tane's parting with the children had been a sad one for Gold. Both the boy and girl, neither of whom he felt he had come to know, were apathetic and listless in saying good-bye. Gold received a distinct impression that they had somehow accepted what Leet-A could not, that the consciousness in the body of Soam-A-Tane was not that of their father. After the first joyful welcome the children had grown steadily away from Soam-A-Tane, finally virtually ignoring him.

The solar observatory was in the rear of a hangar somewhat smaller than the one Gold had seen on arrival. Leet-A landed the flying box near its front door and walked in with them. The vehicle was a doughnut-shaped craft almost as large as the interstellar scouts. The two giants checking it out were just finishing. Ru-A-Lin talked briefly with them and sat in the pilot's chair for the final operational checks. When they proved satisfactory he thanked the two men for their work and they left without even waiting to see the departure. The *Hilt-Sil* way of life required a minimum of ceremony.

It was time to go, and Gold noted with wry amusement that Leet-A's farewell to Ru-A-Lin was almost as affectionate as the one she accorded her husband. During the few days Ru-A-Lin had shared their household she and the medic had become close friends. He had a strong feeling that if Soam-A-Tane were not in the way the friendship between the widower and the woman who was a widow in all but name might ripen into a strong relationship.

When the door closed behind Leet-A, Ru-A-Lin seated himself in the pilot's chair and activated the propulsion systems. Gold strapped the host into the only other chair and waited for the lift-off.

chapter 13

GOLD'S INTEREST IN particle physics had never been strong enough to take him deeply into the subject, but he knew the basic reason for the observatory's doughnut shape. The gravitational pull at the surface of the superstar had to be nullified or the ship would be crushed into a thin plate. The exterior ring around the central hull was actually a magnetically charged torus in which protons were whirled at speeds approaching those of light. By a control system that was far beyond his understanding more and more protons could be added, until their combined mass in motion produced an artificial gravity. The ship was designed so that the gravitational field was aligned with the short axis and positive to the roof.

On Bragair only a comparatively small number of protons were required to neutralize the gravitational pull, and a few more produced a negative gravity that opposed that of the planet. The vessel's primary propulsion was by nuclear rocket, but the torus provided additional lift. Near the great superstar it had been designed to investigate, the observatory needed the full capacity of the torus, and travelled with only the power of its rockets. By utilizing the pull of the sun the ship could reach its surface in eight weeks, but opposing that tremendous force caused the return trip to last more than six months.

The small living area in the protected centre of the vehicle had been designed for only two *Hilt-Sil.* It was crammed with equipment for solar research work, most of it incomprehensible to Gold. Soam-A-Tane was sitting in the co-pilot's chair, before a console equipped with a television screen; the craft had no windows. The camera was focused on the building's roof, which was slowly tilting ahead. When the way was clear Ru-A-Lin touched a control and the vehicle gently lifted. There was almost no sense of acceleration. It picked up speed rapidly, and within five minutes was almost out of the atmosphere. Their course had already been programmed into the ship's equivalent of a computer, and no operator was needed except to monitor the craft's performance.

The timing of their departure had compelled Marina to work through her usual napping period, and she was almost exhausted. Gold noticed her slumping over her console and wrote to Ru-A-Lin that he felt tired and wished to rest. The medic nodded sympathetically, and Gold lowered one of the two folded hammocks available and strapped the host in. Once the body was comfortable, with the head propped as high as he could arrange it, he brought her up to date. She accepted his decision to visit the sun without question and left for her nap.

The body was in the relaxed mode that passed for sleep, but Gold decided not to leave his console. He compromised by closing both the host's eyes and his own, and leaning back in his chair to relax. To his surprise he awakened several minutes later to realize he had dozed off. He opened the host's eyes briefly and saw Ru-A-Lin busy familiarizing himself with some of the complex equipment aboard, including methodically rechecking a few against the records he had received from the two helpful astronomers. Gold had heard them telling the medic about several items that had failed to reach optimum performance.

Ru-A-Lin was something of a puzzle to Gold. He knew that the giant and Soam-A-Tane had not been personal friends prior to their meeting on Mars. The only reasonable explanation for Ru-A-Lin's strong interest in him was that psychologically the giant had adopted the Soam-A-Tane/Gold personality. The host had behaved very much like an infant during the relearning process. Ru-A-Lin, with no children of his own and for some revolutions now no wife, had come to think of the slowly recovering brain of Soam-A-Tane as his child. Which made for a rather ironic situation. Soam-A-Tane was a father in fact but did not behave like it. Ru-A-Lin was not a father but did.

Marina was another puzzle. Gold closed the host's eyes and thought about his short partner. Since the night of the rape, five rotations back, she had gradually mellowed from the attitude of cold aloofness to her normally neutral self. There was an air of watchfulness about her, as though she could never trust him again, but she spoke without hesitation when it was necessary in the course of their work. He had several times caught her staring at him with a thoughtful look on her usually impassive features, without the expected anger or hate. He had also noticed that she paid no more attention than before to the conventions of modesty. She ignored him when he saw her sitting on the toilet, and said nothing if he was present when she stripped down to the functional opaque panties and bra in order to repair her one-piece suit. She still shaved his head every other Bragair rotation and apparently touched him without hesitation. She continued doing their household chores and bringing him food at his console.

Gold had been surprised to find that his brief re-exposure to sex had not revived his dormant appetite, so strong during his long affair with Carlotta and the succession of women who had flowed through his bed after he left the Institute. The especially chosen beautiful girls he had tried to impregnate during his year on Wall Street had been a great joy. Each had been promised a million dollars tax paid if she conceived, and guarded for a month before and two months after their night with him. They had ranged from women very much like Marina to tall Scandinavians like himself, from Negritos to Amerindians. The intent had been to try every possible racial type since, like Petrovna, his sperm had been only a little below the minimum necessary count and activity level. But he had enjoyed sharing sex with such a diversity of women as well.

At the end of that year he had reached his goal of a billion dollars and accepted as proven fact the scientific judgement that he would never father a child. He had also abandoned Wall Street and moved to the country, with no strong idea of what he wanted to do except the certainty that it would not be unselfish devotion to the good of mankind. He had stopped the flow of women for the week it took to complete the move, and ordered it resumed with the intention of keeping each woman a full week. He intended to share sex for pleasure, not progeny, and he had learned that the physical act alone provided much less fun than a mutual sharing of body and personality.

Tall blonde Nordics were Gold's favourites, and the first woman to arrive for a week was of this type It had been an unnerving shock to reach for her in bed that first night and discover that he was completely impotent. The memory of that long night of terrible frustration still rankled. She had left next morning laughing at him, and Gold had immediately sent for a highly experienced New York prostitute. All her skill at mental and physical stimulation had been useless, but she had at least left his bed sympathetic and regretful that she had been unable to help.

Refusing to acknowledge impotency Gold had sent for several more professionals, including several with exotic techniques who guaranteed success. For all realistic purposes they had been equally useless, and he had had to face the fact the trouble lay deep in his mind . . . an uncharted territory where no one, including himself, knew the paths. The simple, obvious explanation was that he had become traumatized by the knowledge he was sterile. He could not accept such an easy answer; it linked him too closely with ordinary *Homo sapiens.*

Gold fell into a light reverie. One of the hotly debated points among physiological experts and psychologists had been the actual amount of difference between the world's two enlarged brains and ordinary men. The American physiologists' efforts to have Gold officially classified as *Homo superior* had failed, primarily because the psychologists had insisted their intensive transactional training would have produced a superior being anyway. In their view it was impossible to determine how much of the enlarged brain's demonstrated superiority was due to genetic change alone. And it was certainly true that transactional psychology had been used on Albert Aaron Golderson to its maximum known effectiveness. Like most adults Gold could recall few events in his life prior to the age of two, but unlike most babies careful and detailed records had been made of virtually his every action. There was seldom an awake moment, from the age of one day through two years, when a camera was not continuously focused on him.

Albert had sneaked into the file room at the age of fifteen and run some of the films showing his babyhood transactions with a carefully controlled environment. His crib had always had eye-stimulating designs, photographs and objects built into its walls. Very early he was given a three-toned rattle that shifted from one sound to another according to the manner in which it was shaken. As soon as he could produce three tones at will it had been replaced with a more complex one equipped with five sounds and three taste dispensers. Sweet and sour were permanent, and the third flavour was constantly changed. When he grew bored with his fourth rattle it was replaced by one designed to develop his vision, a device with inset buttons controlling lights which could flash, change colour or burn steadily, according to the order in which the buttons were pressed. The twelfth and last rattle was an elaborate creation deliberately made so that no baby could possibly master all its functions. As expected, he tired of rattles as a class and was ready for more complex toys.

Albert had been amazed to learn how much care and attention had been lavished on that one baby. The money to train him during the first two critical years had already been appropriated, and it had been spent; there was an abrupt diminution of funds for the third year. But during those first twenty-four months someone had guarded his special cradle day and night. Every physical item with which he came in contact had been selected in advance. His varied diet was probably the most carefully chosen in the world. Though he had no specific mother figure every member of the team played with Albert, held him, talked with him, and became as familiar as the multi-parents common in primitive societies. His enriched milk was taken from a bottle, but he was always held next to a woman's bare breast to simulate the tactile contact enjoyed by a baby while suckling. The "play" in which his foster parents continually indulged challenged the baby to exercise his tiny muscles. Virtually every factor in his environment had been designed to develop either his body or mind. Albert could think in symbols by the age of two. By three he had mastered all the simpler mathematical theorems, and at four his education was equivalent to that of a twelve-year-old and his rate of development far faster.

The trainers had been good in their field. Subtly, ingeniously, in a web of intricate patterns of which the child saw only those edges immediately around him, they had constantly stimulated both brain and body. He was always striving toward new and more difficult goals, mastering more and more of the complex systems of information that constituted a formal education. And the behavioural scientists in the group had not neglected the boy's emotional development, though they had not known until his adolescent years how badly they had failed. The physical hurt inflicted on the baby in the womb during the wreck, the traumatic birth, the death of his mother, had all somehow combined to damage Albert's emotional equilibrium beyond repair. The psychologists and psychiatrists had admitted to each other in secret records that the young genius would never attain the emotional stability they desired. The combination of increased brain size and intensive transactional stimulation from birth had produced a mind and personality beyond their understanding. A measure of their failure was the fact Albert had suffered an extremely distressing experience, the encounter with the janitor, and successfully hidden it from them.

Gold aroused the host long enough to feed it when Ru-A-Lin prepared a simple spaceman's meal, and gladly agreed to retire early when the medic stated that he also was tired. Next day, with both himself and Marina feeling more energetic, Gold began manipulating Soam-A-Tane through some of the complicated functions needed to operate the observatory and its complex equipment. His performance was so slow that Ru-A-Lin eventually suggested he should do most of the routine work. Gold somewhat reluctantly agreed, and returned to his studies of the sun. His co-pilot's console screen could command the *Hilt-Sil* central files in the same manner as the household cubes, and he branched out from studies of the expected pulsation to more general astronomical knowledge. There was little to do but eat, sleep and study, and Gold quickly became bored. It must have been far worse for Marina, but she never complained. Gold spent part of his time attempting to dig into his own subconscious and learn the reason for this trip, but the effort was fruitless. When he made a decision on the non-reasoning level he was no more capable of understanding it than *Homo sapiens.* He did avoid the mistake of producing a rationalization and repeating it until he believed it himself, a common human failing.

The observatory entered the outer edge of the active corona in the seventh week out, and Gold's astronomical studies ended in a burst of static; they had lost contact with Bragair. The ship had been losing speed for some time, the nuclear rockets firing steadily while the mass of protons in the torus ring grew particle by particle. The observatory had already passed the point where it could supply sufficient power for the torus' magnetic field, and was drawing on energy from the sun. The physics involved were again beyond Gold's grasp, but he learned that the ship converted the energy of heat into an electromagnetic force and fed it into the torus ring. The conversion both cooled the physical body of the observatory and supplied the tremendous power needed to hold the protons in orbit within their comparatively small circle. When operating near the sun more heat energy was absorbed than needed for the torus, and the excess was discarded in the form of discreet magnetic fields left in the wake of the ship. These were eventually broken up by the natural processes of the sun, which created and destroyed independent magnetic fields in a similar fashion.

As they drew closer to the great flaming disc Gold found that he did not miss the studies that had absorbed him so intensively for the past several months. The ship had a large screen mounted overhead in front of the consoles, displaying a view of the sun's surface derived from an analysis of the entire range of electromagnetic energy emitted, rather than the comparatively narrow frequencies of visible light. It showed the photosphere as a light cream colour, with cool areas such as sunspots appearing dark and hotter ones like the flares they were seeking a sharp, bright shade of white. Gold had seen many similar views during his intensive studies, but the living reality made all reproductions seem puny and artificial. Brilliant spicule streams rose out of the homogeneous lower layers of the chromosphere in exploding jets of plasma that fell back or dissipated into the solar sky, tremendous igloo-shaped fiery structures more than a million miles in diameter, some of which would endure for months. Sunspots moved slowly across the surface in dark, irregular blotches, their black centres surrounded by the lighter shades of penumbras. And occasionally the phenomena they had come to study, the hot white beauty of a solar flare, appeared below and drifted across the surface of the lower chromosphere, or dissipated into the constantly rising and falling streams of plasma.

When the screen was restricted to the visible surface of the photosphere it disclosed the rice-grain structure of the parent body, a teeming sea of jets, mounds and other irregularities. Each grain was actually a rising column of gas that transferred heat from the interior to the surface, where the top broke and fell back. The cooler falling gases registered as small darker circles around the top of each column.

The varied and complex activities in the boiling sea of motion, most of which Gold understood reasonably well, formed an ever-changing panorama which could absorb the eye and brain indefinitely.

On Earth's sun Gold knew that flares were a short-lived phenomena that usually appeared in the region of sunspots, drifting upward from below the photosphere and dissipating like the granular gas columns. On the red superstar they appeared anywhere, were capable of holding their shape for a time after reaching the surface, and usually drifting horizontally through the chromosphere before apparently sinking back and breaking up in the denser material below the photosphere. The red star flares were basically round in shape, while those on the smaller sun were as irregular as sunspots. Another major difference was that the ones they had come to observe appeared and vanished in a regular pattern, while those that threatened the lives of space travellers on Earth could erupt from deep in the sun at any time.

As they drew near the upper edges of the chromosphere Gold had Soam-A-Tane urge Ru-A-Lin to halt the observatory above the area where the next flare was expected. According to a chart the *Hilt-Sil* astronomers maintained they had arrived only two hours before it was due, and Gold wanted to hover and observe it at close range. He was no nearer than before to understanding the compulsion that had driven him to the sun, but the flares were the only solar phenomenon that had undergone a change after the nine hydrogen clouds were absorbed; he wanted to study one as closely as possible.

Gold had never had a mental indigestion problem that clung so stubbornly to the unseen fringes of his mind. Always before he had devoted himself to the subject for the next few days or weeks, absorbing new material that eventually jelled with the old on the subconscious level to produce an answer. Here the inputs were either insufficient or so much on the wrong track that he was obtaining little of what he needed. To date he did not feel capable of even defining the problem, much less solving it.

Gold was happy to note that Ru-A-Lin seemed to have become absorbed in their project, as in the studies followed on Bragair, without worrying over the fact he did not understand their overall purpose. The giant medic appeared to be enjoying a typical *Hilt-Sil* pleasure, the gathering of knowledge. The fact that it would have little practical application after the red superstar's first pulsation did not bother him. The giants drew on their accumulated data when a need arose, but there was far more stored in their banks than could ever be applied, with new material being continuously added. They seemed to think of information as Earthmen thought of money; something to be gained, stored, and used throughout one's life. If an individual was unable to make practical use of all that was available it was left to the next generation. The *Hilt-Sil* lived an orderly, controlled existence, and changes that occurred in a single generation on Earth might occupy ten-thousand Bragair revolutions. They had long ago passed the point where the acquisition of new technology could affect the life-style they had perfected for themselves.

Ru-A-Lin stopped the observatory deep within the chromosphere. They were still more than a hundred-thousand miles above the surface, but the torus ring was fighting gravity and heat at near full capacity. Gold knew that the thin gas surrounding them was actually higher in electron temperature than the upper regions of the star, but it was too diffused to impart its full heat to a solid object. He also knew that the red giant was cool on the surface compared to his native sun, averaging less than a thousand degrees Fahrenheit. Neither factor would save them from instant death if the torus failed. Gold remembered that they were riding in a vessel over three hundred thousand years old, and realized how much of a *Hilt-Sil* he had become in his thinking when the memory failed to bother him.

Near the end of the first hour of hovering a tremendous horseshoe of white flame appeared below the observatory. It was a solar prominence erupting, a burst of fiery beauty standing out against the slightly less bright background of chromosphere and photosphere. As the centre climbed steadily toward them Gold was able to observe one of the interesting facts he had learned in his studies, that the visible eruption was an illusion. The gigantic loop was formed by an increase of temperature in the material raining down out of the corona, not rising from the sun. The peculiar disturbance that constituted the prominence moved upward through the falling rain of hot gas, the top of the arch passing them and dying out shortly afterward in the corona. The rain down the existing arms of the horseshoe continued for several minutes, until they too gradually faded away.

As Gold watched the screen there was a noticeable change in the area directly underneath. The surface was growing whiter, the individual spicules fading as they made way for a more cohesive body. He glanced at their magnetic strength indicators. The coded lights which the *Hilt-Sil* used instead of drawn figures were blinking rapidly, already past three thousand gauss on an Earthly scale and rising toward four. The flare was forming exactly on time.

Ru-A-Lin had the observatory's equipment focused on the developing hot spot. Two instruments were continuously taking and recording spectrograms in the extreme ultraviolet range, and two more were recording X-ray emissions below the 60 angstrom length. A fifth measured both the energy and direction of the cosmic ray emission; the relatively unimportant lower energy frequencies were ignored. This type of data had been obtained on flares before, but not since the hydrogen clouds had entered the superstar. Gold planned to run comparison checks and search for changes in the flares' life cycle.

Ru-A-Lin was watching the indicators and gauges that were visually displaying the high energy wavelengths translated into mathematical terms, as well as others showing the discreet magnetic fields and area temperatures. After a moment he said, "Our instruments show little of flare formation that has not been recorded before, Soam-A-Tane."

Gold nodded Soam-A-Tane's head. He had noticed a slow upwelling effect, as though a coherent body of gas had been hovering beneath the photosphere and had risen to displace the surface granules and higher chromospheric spicules. The mass of the flare was now clearly visible below, a rough disc almost 200,000 miles in diameter. The gases of which it was composed appeared to flow in circular horizontal patterns, unlike the up-and-down motion of the granules and spicules. Though the instruments could not penetrate very deeply Gold received a distinct impression the bottom of the thick disc was resting on the breaking tops of the photosphere granules, while the bulk of the structure towered into the thinner chromosphere. He made a suggestion to Ru-A-Lin, who obligingly shifted the screen's viewpoint. At the edge of the flare there was a distinct line between the outermost swirl of horizontally moving gas and the vertical granular flow.

The flare hovered quietly on the surface, while the circling gases seemed to pick up tempo as they moved in gigantic whirls around an apparently steady core. Ru-A-Lin brought the focus back to the centre, and Gold caught a new movement. A great mass of chromospheric gas was moving inward from all sides and flowing downward, to vanish in the central core.

So far the flare appeared very much like any other of which they had record. Gold checked the temperature scanning device and saw that the flare was considerably hotter on top near the core than at the outer edges, moving up from barely warmer than the thousand Fahrenheit degrees of the photosphere to over fourteen hundred degrees at the centre. And the heat sensor penetrated far enough into the core to indicate that the temperature rose steeply deeper in the disc. The total formed a picture of a central hot interior; if the flare had taken the shape of a sphere instead of a disc it would have had a uniform outside temperature.

While the observatory was busily recording data the whirling streams of hot gas below seemed to reach a final speed and maintain it. After a few minutes of consolidation the entire flare began moving slowly across the star's surface. This too matched the reported behaviour of previous flares. It was also one of the major differences between those on the superstar and the ones observed on Earth's sun; the ones reported by humans had remained in one spot until they dissipated.

Ru-A-Lin returned to the flight control part of his console and the observatory moved with the flare, holding its position above the centre. Gold felt a gnawing sense of unease. He turned and glanced at Marina, to see that she had swung around in her chair and was watching him. Her expression was reserved as usual, but there was a definite air of expectation about her, similar to that shown toward Petrovna when she had handed him a problem and was waiting for the solution. Gold had been able to share only his own strong sense of unease about the flares with Marina; there was nothing definite to tell her. He had also explained what he knew of the internal workings of his own mind when he had insufficient data. She had nodded thoughtfully and confirmed something Gold should have suspected; it had been the same with Petrovna. But, with the highly disciplined scientists, training and application had given him a more reliable control of his ability, and he could work at a problem consistently until it was solved. Gold had to blunder along aimlessly until a plan of attack became apparent.

Gold reached for Soam-A-Tane's writing pad and asked Ru-A-Lin to lower the observatory toward the flare. He had no clear idea of what he wished to do, but wanted to be closer to the vast hot gas cloud. Ru-A-Lin glanced sharply at Soam-A-Tane, but complied. Moving too swiftly would interfere with the recording instruments, and for the next three hours Gold sat and watched the fiery body draw closer and closer as the observatory sank downward at an angle that kept it above the centre. He was waiting for his mind to jell and bring to the surface a reason for being there. When they were only a few thousand miles above the core, their entire field of view now taken up by the flare, Gold realized that he still could not formulate the question that was tormenting him, much less the answer.

Gold wrote for Ru-A-Lin to drop the ship into the edge of the stable centre.

The giant medic glanced at Soam-A-Tane again, but silently obeyed. The doughnut-shaped craft sank toward the waiting surface and a test of its heatshield. The observatory had a built-in safety factor that would let it sink thousands of miles into the photosphere, until the temperature doubled that at the surface. But the flare was already 400 degrees hotter than the photosphere, and Gold felt certain the temperature would rise quickly as they penetrated toward the centre of the disc, much faster than when moving downward into the star.

Gold and Ru-A-Lin sat quietly watching the flaming cloud draw closer. After a few minutes the view blurred, grew amorphous, and then they were inside, with no sense of transition or change. But the temperature indicator climbed rapidly to 1,400 degrees, and the gauss reading had passed 4,000. There was an odd, baffling sense of electrical force in the air, as though they had entered a region of negative ions and were feeling the prickling effects of high electrical potential.

Gold glanced around at Marina; she was still watching him. He turned Soam-A-Tane's head; Ru-A-Lin was calmly waiting. He looked again at the instruments, watching the temperature gauge as the observatory sank downward at several miles an hour. Minutes passed, while the external heat rose slowly but steadily. And then they were deep in the flare's body and had reached the observatory's safety limit. Ru-A-Lin brought the craft's vertical movement to a halt. They were still flying horizontally with the flare across the surface of the star, well above its actual centre.

Slowly and hesitantly, not really aware of what he was doing, Gold turned dials and flipped switches. The hands of Soam-A-Tane rose to his console and turned on the communications screen, which had been mute for a week. Gold adjusted the individual controls, setting the transmitter to its highest frequency and power. There was nothing but a whirling brightness of static on the screen.

Gold stared at the meaningless patterns for a few seconds, and then Soam-A-Tane uttered the loudest sound of which he was capable . . . a deep, mournful groan.

There was a tense, eerie moment of silence. Gold turned the host's head and saw Ru-A-Lin staring at him in mild astonishment. He did not know himself why he had turned on the communicator and made the noise that would modulate the carrier wave. And then, in a burst of overwhelming insight, all his doubts were resolved. Both the problem and solution presented themselves clearly at last, and he knew precisely what he was doing, and why.

The screen hurled five seconds of meaningless static back at him.

The sense of electric tension in the air had grown more pronounced. Gold felt it primarily through the sensor cap, though a strong field penetrated into their hidden compartment. The air in the observatory seemed to crackle with potential, as though every atom had gained electrons it could not discharge. Gold had a strong but indefinite sense of *presence*, as though they had been surrounded by a coherent free field of electric energy. The feeling seemed to grow in intensity, and after a moment he felt vague but discernible mental fingers plucking at his mind. The feeling was something like the constant presence of the drugged half of the host's brain, impossible to separate and define but clearly there.

There was a chilling feel of alienness in the probing fingers, but Gold ignored it. The sense of external consciousness grew stronger. The primary impression Gold received was of unused strength, as though whatever it was that sought a way into his mind was having difficulty converting electrical charge into the infinitesimal currents that constituted thought. This feeling grew stronger but shifted in direction, as though the entity demanding entrance was gaining a measure of control. And then stray words, errant thoughts, whole phrases were jarred out of Gold's subconscious into the active mind and moved and filtered aimlessly about before disappearing again. The phrases were in the *Hilt-Sil* tongue, in which Gold now thought more than in English. The flow of words grew, expanded into a meaningless swarm he could not read even as nonsense, and finally died away. After them came the first clear intruding thought.

You are a small pattern of consciousness.

The creature around them—and Gold realized it was nothing less than the entire 200,000 mile wide flare—had penetrated into his mind through some subtle control of magnetism and electrical potential far beyond the knowledge of science. Like some ultra-refined and remarkably sensitive electroencephalograph working in reverse, it had created a field around his head and reached into the brain, reading the established pathways of current flow that constituted stored knowledge. The probing mechanism had stimulated and absorbed a tremendous amount of data in seconds, running it through the brain's circuitry and copying it as though taking from a computer. It was still at work. The creature had easily learned the language and was now using words to communicate with Gold, though it ignored the normal process of forming sounds and instead stimulated the auditory nerve with electrical impulses, in the same manner as the ears' hair-bearing sensory cells.

Gold hesitated, wondering how to respond, and what seemed to him a disembodied voice said, *Organize your thoughts clearly and project them; I will receive.*

Gold turned to look at Marina, and then Ru-A-Lin. Both were simply staring at him. *Are you speaking only to me?* he projected as strongly as he could.

Yes; I have drawn on the minds of the two other small creatures for information but I am communicating with you, the reply came back almost instantly. *The electrical patterns in your brain are the most complex.*

There was an air of waiting expectancy in the consciousness hovering around his mind. Gold found his thoughts racing furiously but to little purpose. Now that his subconscious was clear, the knowledge that the hydrogen clouds were actually living creatures at last in the open, he found that he had no idea what to do next.

A stray question worth asking flashed past Gold's attention, and he desperately caught it and asked, *Where are you from?*

There was a short silence, while Gold felt an intensification of the continual probing at his mind. When the data it needed had been found the voice said, *We are from the nearest group of stars from the main body you call the galaxy, in your terms a "globular cluster." The specific star is the one nearest us of the type you call "RR Lyra Variable."*

There was an odd tone of withdrawn neutrality to the chosen words, as though they were spoken by a creature totally without passion. Yet Gold could sense a type of intellectual curiosity, and when the words stopped he felt again that sense of expectancy that told him a reply was needed. He asked, *Why are you here? Why did you cross the open space from your group of stars to ours?*

This time there was a longer wait, while the searching fingers seemed to reach deeper into his brain. *Our group of stars suffers from . . . overpopulation. Each is capable of . . . supporting a number of our kind in proportion to its size and temperature. But we . . . reproduce much as you. And since we do not . . . die, our number increases steadily. My . . . family . . . the term is not fitting . . . and I crossed the great cold space. We are creatures of . . . our consciousness is a form of electrical energy interchange, maintained by shifts of potential within a magnetic field. We obtain energy from heat, but a certain minimum is necessary to stabilize the prime field or we . . . die. My family . . . volunteered . . . again the term is inadequate . . . to learn if we could hold enough heat in our centres to keep consciousness alive. We lived, though it was . . . another thousand revolutions of Bragair around its sun and we would have faded into . . . non-consciousness.*

Why are you turning this star into a RR Lyra Variable? Gold asked.

For a signal to our . . . kin. When light from the first pulsation reaches them they will know the crossing is possible and . . . follow. For each who leaves a new . . . baby? You have no equivalent . . . can be . . . created.

If you do not die naturally why do you wish to create more babies? asked Gold.

The fingers had faded from Gold's mind, as though their copywork was complete. The answer came more quickly. *The desire to propagate is apparently universal among living creatures. It exists in all I found in your mind, and in the three types of living gas of which we know.*

The sense of neutrality which Gold had noticed earlier continued to come through with the words as an easily caught side impression. It was as though the creature derived a mild enjoyment from exchanging thoughts with a being so different from itself, but had no emotional characteristics to which a human could relate. The only attribute it seemed to share with man was curiosity . . . which was perhaps another universal trait among intelligent living creatures.

You have the most complex electrical patterns in the smallest fields of which we know, the flare suddenly volunteered. *My "brain" that you call the core, or umbra, is 40,000 of your miles in diameter and 25,000 miles deep. You are also the only creatures whose patterns are formed through the chemical generation of electricity.*

Now that his mind was no longer being probed Gold found that he could think more clearly. These creatures were obviously totally beyond the reach of any possible force the *Hilt-Sil* and their friends could bring to bear. If the superstar was to be saved it would have to be by persuasion. And even then . . . Gold projected strongly, *You say you are subject to the non-consciousness of death, though you do not die after a limited passage of time. Are you aware that by turning this star into a pulsar you are condemning either my own people or almost a million giants like the one beside me to death?*

Explain! the word came back quickly, with a sense of what Gold could only think of as shock.

Hastily Gold formed and projected the thoughts that explained the battle for survival between *Hilt-Sil* and human. He finished by asking, *Must you turn this particular star into a pulsar? There are others which have no planets around them.*

There was a long silence before the voice said, almost hesitantly, *There would be a delay of . . . in your terms, eight or nine thousand years. I see the star you are thinking of in the data taken from your mind. To reach it we would have to condense ourselves again, make another long journey . . . though not as far as before, not dangerous to us. But it has been 80,000 of Bragair's revolutions since we left our home.*

Can you permit the consciousness of the billions of my own people, or the near million of my giant friend here, to die? Gold asked.

The sense of neutrality seemed stronger than ever when the flare replied, *Yes, we can permit this. But it is not pleasant to contemplate. We must weigh the cost in your lives against the inconvenience to ourselves.*

There was no arrogance in the mental voice; it was simply stating a fact. Gold fought back a rush of awe at the immensity of the forces with which he was dealing. This was no time for a loss of self-confidence. He kept his mental tone level and said, *If you respect the existence of other life you should be willing to delay your signal a little longer.*

There would be no point in leaving without first restoring this star to its original condition, which would require another eight hundred of Bragair's revolutions, the calm voice replied. *From the data in your mind I see that speeding up the conversion in the giant to which you would send would take longer than with this one. It would be another 10,000 revolutions before our signal could leave for our old home.*

We ask that you do this, said Gold, projecting slowly and strongly. *We ask that you inconvenience yourselves to spare our lives.* And he knew that he was projecting a pleading sense that was surely as obvious to the flare as its neutrality to him.

I would have to . . . obtain the consent of my family, the answer came back. *To convert a star to pulsation is a . . . pleasure. To change it back is . . . dull work. When we . . . dive deep and increase the heat we know joy. When we dive deep and decrease the heat we know . . . nothing.*

Do you always . . . dive deep and change the conversion rate in the stars you inhabit?

No; we normally live near the surface and absorb the heat we need as it rises from the centre. We are similar to but not the same as the phenomena you call flares, which exist in every star and are unorganized patterns without consciousness.

Then there is no reason why your kind and mine cannot live in the same star system, Gold projected strongly. *We inhabit only the solid bodies around the sun. Why can we not both live without harm to any consciousness, exchanging knowledge and gratifying the curiosity we both possess?*

We can, the flare replied. *My family will consent. We will restore this star and set out on our new journey. And now I must dive deep and notify my kin to reverse their labours. In your terms . . . good-bye.*

The sense of presence began to fade. Gold glanced hastily at the observatory's indicators and saw them recording the descent of the flare, the temperature falling and the strength of the magnetic field decreasing. And then the presence was gone; they had been barely within the area of consciousness.

Slowly Gold moved Soam-A-Tane's fingers to the sylus, picked up his pad, and wrote, //Let us go home.//

chapter 14

Ru-A-Lin glanced at the pad, then back to their visual data indicators. As Gold watched, the temperature abruptly fell the 400 degrees that indicated the penumbra of the sun creature's body had faded below them. After a moment the coherent mass of gas again became visible on their screen, swiftly sinking into the photosphere.

Ru-A-Lin lifted slow hands to his console and activated the main drive. When the observatory was well under way he turned to Soam-A-Tane and said, "I sensed that the fire creature was speaking only to you. Will you tell me what you learned?"

Gold resumed writing; it took him several minutes, even in the more exact *Hilt-Sil* language. When he was through the giant sighed with relief. After a moment he said, "Strange; strange indeed. Your theory that the faster conversion rate in our sun results from alien manipulation has proven true, but not in the manner you expected. Still, you saved Bragair, which was more than our foremost astronomers accomplished. And in turn you have saved the small men of Earth. When we are out of the corona we must notify Jelk-A-Bin and the other members of the Affirmatives Council."

Gold hesitated, mind racing as he considered possibilities. Then he wrote, //Should we not wait for the sun creatures to start the reversal process? If we report now we risk disbelief; they will think your brain as damaged as mine.//

Ru-A-Lin nodded thoughtfully. "True; and there is no necessity for hurry. The next eradication party will not depart for many rotations. If the energy creatures begin undoing their work immediately our sensors should be able to detect the change before the ship leaves Bragair. And there is always the possibility the other eight members of the family will disagree with the one who promised to leave."

//We do not know their familial ties. It may be that any one decides for all. Equally, it may be that the one who spoke to us is a youth, whose word will be repudiated by the elders.//

"And it may be there are no youths, each new family member being created fully grown," said Ru-A-Lin with a smile. "A fascinating species; it will be a pleasure to learn their behavioural patterns once they are established in their new star." It did not seem to occur to him that he would have been dead for many thousands of revolutions before the energy beings reached their new home, even if they chose to emigrate once more.

Gold knew that the schedule called for the next eradication party to leave Bragair within a few rotations after their tentative arrival time. He had persuaded Ru-A-Lin to wait because it had occurred to him that if he could arrange for Soam-A-Tane to be on that next ship for Earth, and if the crew could somehow be persuaded to land at the Mars station . . .

Which brought Gold up short, facing a moral dilemma of his own. Did he really want to return to Earth? He turned and glanced at Marina, at the moment bent over her console making an adjustment. She had been wrong in thinking that the sleeping left cerebrum had any real influence over him, but her suspicion that he felt more sympathy for the *Hilt-Sil* than for humans was certainly correct. If the choice as to whether the peacefully intellectual giants or the "small vicious vermin" would live had been placed in Gold's hands, he would have had a difficult time choosing between his progenitors and the far more admirable *Hilt-Sil*. But he had to consider Marina as well as himself. He could live a life of sorts through the sensory helmet, but she would be only a prisoner in the skull.

Gold decided to postpone the decision on returning home until later. He would have almost six Earth months in which to make up his mind on the trip to Bragair.

The observatory continued to accumulate data until they were high in the thin corona, which required two days at their slow rate of ascent. Ru-A-Lin placed the ship on automatic and turned off the recorders when they had risen enough for a visual sighting of Bragair. After a brief discussion Gold and the giant medic decided to reduce their tremendous accumulation of data before preparing their formal report. It was unlikely they would learn anything of major importance about the sun creatures, but they could not afford to ignore the possibility.

They started work immediately, and Gold found that through Soam-A-Tane's fingers and his own knowledge he could contribute almost as much to the reduction task as

Ru-A-Lin. Though he still could not operate the instruments with any finesse he had become enough of an astronomer to be good at the exacting mathematical analyses required.

When they were able to establish contact with Bragair Ru-A-Lin reported that they had some important information and were preparing it for formal presentation on their arrival. The chairman of the Affirmatives received the news with equanimity; he had no more faith than before in the worthiness of their mission.

Two slow months dragged by. The observatory was gradually building up speed, but the great red disc of the superstar still dominated the sky behind them. Gold and Ru-A-Lin worked patiently at their task, more to pass the dull hours than from any need for diligence. Marina spent less time than usual at her console, letting the automatic systems control the host's physiology. Once or twice when Gold walked through the living quarters during the day—he disliked the console chair's urine relief tube and seldom used it—he saw her sewing, repairing some of her garments. She sewed up a few tears in his own without comment, shaved his head every other Bragair rotation as usual, and seemed to be passing the long dull days without undue boredom.

Gold received the surprise of his life one night when he gradually awoke from a light sleep and realized he had been disturbed by a warm body snuggling close to him in the narrow bed.

There was sweat on Gold's skin in those areas where Marina's body touched his, indicating she had been there for several minutes. His companion's breathing was slow and even, but he realized immediately that she was awake. Gold discovered that he had become strongly aroused in his sleep. But after a moment, when Marina made no further overt move, he knew that if sharing was what she had in mind he was expected to take the next step.

Gladly, Gold took it. He placed his hands under both arms and gently slid her upward until he could reach the small mouth. She met his lips with warm eagerness. Gold locked her firmly against his chest, one hand moving down to press the curving buttocks. Her own arms slipped around his neck, and Gold realized this was the first time they had kissed.

When their mouths parted Gold started to speak, but a small finger quickly found his lips and pressed them gently closed. He quieted and waited passively; the finger slipped away and she returned his kiss, her mouth a firm pressure, high passion lurking close beneath. When Marina finally broke the contact and moved away Gold brought one hand from back to front and cupped a small breast. She immediately arched her chest, raising the captured soft mound higher. He lowered the hand and ran it over the rounded shape of her belly, then on down to caress the genitals. A brief exploration told him Marina was ready for sharing.

Again Gold attempted to speak, and got out the word, "Why?" before the imperious small finger returned to seal his lips. And then Marina became the aggressor, her other hand moving to clasp him directly and forcefully, with no pretension of shyness or ignorance. Gold returned the caress, and after a moment of mutual stimulation he gently rolled over on her, keeping most of his weight on elbows and knees. Marina wriggled toward the centre of the narrow bed, Gold followed, and as their lips met and their bodies moved easily into position he thrust to enter her. Marina shifted her hips to accommodate him. Gold penetrated her at once, and then their joined bodies were moving smoothly and steadily in the rhythmic joy of sharing.

It was only a few seconds before Gold felt the electric tension that heralded discharge. Marina locked her arms around his buttocks and held him deep within her as the spasms surged through his body. When it was over both lay quietly, still joined but neither kissing, caressing nor talking. Two or three minutes passed and then Marina, as though knowing almost precisely when Gold would be ready again, raised her hips. He felt a new surge of sensuality, and became tumescent almost at once. Even more slowly and gently than before they began the movements of sharing, and this time it was Marina who uttered a low cry and stopped him after only a minute, enclosing him tightly in the cradle of her arms and legs as tiny shivers ran up and down her body. Gold waited through her climax, but when she relaxed he started again, and though she was passive at first it was only a few seconds before she responded and they were once more moving in conjunction. Gold sensed the potential for climax swiftly building in her again as the longer sharing continued. The cooler part of his mind realized both were sweating profusely now, and if he could stop long enough to lower the zippered cover they would be more comfortable; but he could not stop. And then Marina reached her second orgasm, a stronger, deeper series of muscular convulsions that seemed to wrack her small form in long shuddering waves. In the midst of it Gold felt his own second ejaculation coming and gathered her close, squeezing hard while their bodies experienced the great human joy of sharing.

When the waves of sensation finally subsided Gold found the contact between their sticky, sweating skins distinctly uncomfortable. He reached with one long arm and unzipped the right side of the cover, then eased himself off Marina and did the same for the left. He flipped the cover backward and a rush of fresh air replaced the warmth they had locked in with them. Gold felt it envelop his hot body like a cooling balm.

Marina turned on her side to face him. Gold lay still, breathing deeply, his mind in a pleasant haze. And then he realized he had dozed off but was awake again. Marina's face was only inches away, and he felt her warm breath on his cheek. She was smiling tenderly, a smile shy yet revealing. "I'm pregnant, Gold," she said softly.

The words hit with the force of a blow, jarring him fully awake. Gold reared up on one elbow, staring down at her in unbelieving wonder. The smile widened into a low laugh when she saw how her news had affected him. "It's true," she insisted when the laughter faded. "I haven't had a period since the night you . . . forced me, and the third one was due yesterday."

"But how could it be?" Gold asked helplessly. "After those hundreds of women . . ."

The look of happiness faded, the objective expression of the scientist replacing the feminine softness and sexual awareness of the woman. "I think I know," Marina said quietly. "You are a late maturer, as was Petrovna. The average boy of twelve or thirteen can produce sperm sufficiently mature to impregnate a woman. In both of you the sperm appeared a year later and were very weak, as you know. I have done some careful checking through the propagation experiment records. All of the laboratory efforts to produce a viable embryo with sperm obtained from yourself or Petrovna occurred in your early twenties. Your experiment with the 365 girls of all races and types occupied part of your twenty-fifth and twenty-sixth years. I became pregnant by Petrovna when he was twenty-seven. You have just recently turned twenty-nine. If I am correct the *Homo superior* species is sterile until the age of twenty-seven, then undergoes another period of sexual maturation and becomes fully adult and able to propagate. During the first phase of this second puberty some sperm become lively enough to produce monsters, such as mine."

Gold slowly eased himself back to the bed. "Why isn't it possible that my sperm have simply become active enough to create another monster?" he asked curiously.

Marina's happy look faded. "That is a possibility. But the time sequence traces so logically to the development of normal sperm by the age of twenty-eight or nine that I couldn't accept another explanation without proof. And since all your *superior* features were designed as dominant traits, with a throwback ratio of only one in twelve, I have complete confidence that the baby I am carrying will be a normal *Homo superior.*"

Gold could only shake his head in mute wonder. Marina was by far the better geneticist, but to him it seemed equally likely that he had simply reached the same point as Petrovna, the ability to father monsters. If so, she was in for a terrible disappointment. And he was not certain he could trust her judgement; Marina seemed far too involved to be objective.

The small woman's abstracted look faded. She leaned forward and snuggled her head on Gold's shoulder, one arm creeping across his chest. He felt her lips brush across his cheek; the scientist had retreated, leaving the woman in command. Her small hand moved to caress his genitals, and Gold discovered his fatigue had vanished.

And for the third time the abstraction of words was replaced by the reality of sharing.

During the next month Gold grew to regret that the beds were attached to the levelling bars, making it impossible to move them. After that first night Marina seldom slept in her own, and his was too narrow for both of them. There were no words of love spoken but Marina's whole attitude had changed, as though the baby he had planted in her womb had flowered into love in her heart. She still fell back at times into the cool aloofness he had thought to be her normal manner, but the strong emotionalism which had always lurked beneath dominated her more and more. Gold found himself being led along a path of greater and greater communication. Though there was no discernible point of transition he knew, when he awoke one morning and saw her small face sleeping on his arm, that they had moved from sex/affection to love. This time there was no doubt of it, and as a bonus he realized at last that he had honestly loved Carlotta as well.

Gold still found Marina's serene belief that their baby would be born whole and *Homo superior* somewhat disconcerting. He could not share her confidence. But she at least was wonderfully happy, and one of the measures of her transformation was that she laughed often and frequently sang folk songs to him in Russian, of which he understood not a word. She had abandoned the strong self-possession that had been her most dominant trait, as though it was a shield she no longer needed. Gold spent some time trying to understand how a rape and unexpected pregnancy could so transform a woman but gave up the effort. It was something in feminine psychology beyond his grasp.

Gold and Ru-A-Lin had been working steadily on the data reduction, and had the mammoth task almost complete. The picture they had produced did not change the major impressions they had received while inside the gigantic alien. The basics of its structure were fairly simple—the penumbra was a mass of hot gases whirling in horizontal circles, the umbra a thicker core of varying potentials and discharges, with a temperature several thousand degrees higher than it should have been—but this told them nothing of how it maintained intelligence. Not that it mattered; the facts had been firmly established on the empirical level.

Gold also learned that the next eradication expedition would leave from the same landing field they were using. There were only two on Bragair. He had not as yet formulated a convincing reason why a brain-damaged Soam-A-Tane should accompany them.

When the remaining data reduction could be left to Gold, Ru-A-Lin started work on his report. Gold had grown tired of the monotonous labour but it did keep him busy, and for variety he had the happy internal life he was now sharing with Marina. During the third month of the return trip, when the honeymoon aspect had begun to wear off, he was caressing her swelling belly one night when he felt the tiny tremor of a heartbeat. He placed an ear against the distended skin and clearly heard the faint but steady beating.

When Gold lifted his head he saw that Marina was smiling. "I've been hearing it for weeks," she said contentedly. "Petrovna's baby had a heart action so faint and erratic it couldn't be detected without a stethoscope."

"I only hope you aren't disappointed when it comes," Gold said gravely.

"Stop worrying. I'm to be the first mother of a naturally transmitted *Homo superior*; it will be born healthy and whole," Marina replied with equal gravity. "But we may have a problem. The birth will be due about the time we reach Bragair, which is very poor planning. You will have to deliver it by Caesarean, you know. We can't risk hurting that enlarged head in the birth canal."

"I was born with no apparent damage," Gold pointed out.

"You, like Petrovna and our monster, would have been delivered by Caesarean if that accident that killed your mother hadn't happened. And according to your father's account the birth was an extremely short one. In a long labour you would probably have suffered some brain damage from the compression, in addition to the beating you took from the accident. In fact some people have felt that you *were* harmed, and could never be the equal of Petrovna."

"I'm familiar with that theory," Gold said dryly. "The other side claims that it was solely due to poor psychological training that I never matched Petrovna in science. They point out that I seem capable of doing anything I want to do."

Marina smiled. "At one time I belonged to the first school, but I know now that your capacity is as high as Petrovna's. You are more alike than you could possibly realize. But we will not take chances with our child. I am a very small woman, and both your mother and Petrovna's were large Nordics with a wide pelvic structure. You must perform the operation."

"I've read the material in the computer on Caesareans. But delivering a baby is as much a matter of experience and skill as knowledge, and I have none. I am very much afraid I would kill you. It will have to be a normal birth."

Marina shook her head. "We have no drugs to help dilate the cervix, as your young athlete had in the story. We cannot take such a chance."

"Let's worry about it when we reach Bragair," Gold said, and stopped further protests with a kiss.

The baby grew steadily. At seven months Marina's belly was larger than that of many women at term. They still shared, but Gold had to be careful to keep his weight off her, and move slowly and gently. Marina deliberately stopped having orgasm, though she had no certain knowledge the contractions would hurt the baby. Gold's sexual appetite had returned in full strength, and she insisted he continue gratifying it despite her own lack of participation. After the eighth month, when they passed the point of maximum speed and started slowing for the descent to Bragair, they stopped sex completely. Marina was so large and awkward it had become a burden on her.

The last month of travel was a dull one. All the data work they could do was complete, and Ru-A-Lin's careful report and recommendation was ready. Gold had grown to like Ru-A-Lin even more during the long journey, and felt him to be completely trustworthy within his own mores. Even so, he felt no inclination to tell the medic the truth about Soam-A-Tane's supposed recovery. Ru-A-Lin was loyal to his own people, and until they had positive evidence the sun creatures had decided in their favour it was safest to keep the giant ignorant. Their best chance of returning home lay in getting Soam-A-Tane on board that next interstellar ship for Earth.

And Gold did want to return to Earth. Marina's unexpected pregnancy had put to rest all thoughts of staying on Bragair and living as *Hilt-Sil.*

Despite her advanced pregnancy Marina, during the ninth month, started spending more time at her console. Gold heard her working one morning and turned to see the access panels open and Marina filling one of the drug dispensers. When she straightened up and saw him watching she shook the empty container and said, "That's the last of the reserpine. I didn't think our host would live long enough to use it all."

The remark sounded odd to Gold. "You mean you thought we would be killed before now?"

Marina's face sobered. "No; we had expected the body to finish dying by this time."

"Finish dying?"

"Of course, Gold. Don't you realize that all of Petrovna's work, all that I have done in these months, is only a delay of the inevitable? Our host was dying when he was brought inside Moonbase."

"I don't understand. I thought he could live indefinitely."

"That was an unwarranted assumption on your part. One we did nothing to discourage, I must admit. But this body is kept alive only by stimulants and drugs. Now that I've used the last of the imipramine and adrenalin, and am almost out of catecholamines, our host has only a few more weeks to live."

The news bothered Gold. There was at least an echo here

of the old desire by *Homo sapiens* to manipulate their superior creation, and Marina had been a part of it in the beginning. It also upset his tentative plans for reaching Earth again, which had been dependent on remaining within the body of Soam-A-Tane. After a moment's thought he asked, "Can't we obtain equivalent drugs from the *Hilt-Sil*?"

"I doubt it. From what you've told me they don't seem to use tranquillizers or stimulants. Even if you could persuade a *Hilt-Sil* chemist to produce them the body's life could only be extended by a few months. The continuous use of drugs while at a high activity level has greatly weakened it."

"Then we would have to stow away on the ship as the very small people we are," he said, troubled.

Marina only smiled, not sharing his apprehension. "You will find a way. I know now that you can do almost anything, when you must. And your child will be like its father. Have you listened to the heartbeat lately? And the size of him! I've tried to watch my diet, but I've put on over thirty pounds and all the old stretch marks on my stomach are tearing again. He is certainly going to be too big to chance letting that head come through the birth canal."

This was a return to the friendly but determined argument they had continued since the first discussion. But Gold had done more research and arrived at some definite conclusions. "Marina, I will not take a chance on my ability to cut into the womb and sew you back together. We have no assurance but what my lack of skill might harm the baby as much as the natural birth pressures. Despite your arguments, I'm not convinced the child will have a fully functioning brain. And finally, even if I'm wrong and the baby is normal but harmed at birth, let me remind you we can have others later."

Marina's face turned angry, in a manner Gold had not seen for months. Before they became lovers she would have immediately turned away, suppressing the emotion as was her habit; now she was free to express it. She said, "Gold, this is *my* child as much as yours! Do you think that because of scientific training I am not as concerned about my baby as the most ignorant peasant woman in Brazil? I want *this* child to live!"

Gold sighed in mild exasperation, and took the chance of unstrapping and walking back to Marina. He found himself wondering how much her love for him, and the previous devotion to Petrovna, was caused by the deep, driving desire to bear their children. Not that it mattered; he could no more condemn her than he could himself because his love for both Carlotta and Marina had started and grown in the joy of sharing.

Gold gently took Marina's awkward form in his arms and kissed the rosebud lips she obediently turned upward. He said, "I love you. I honestly, genuinely care for someone for the second time in my life. I can't bear the thought that you might be hurt, much less die. When we get home I'll give you a dozen children, if you want them. For now, if we must sacrifice the life of this baby in order to save yours, then I'll do it. There's no point in further argument. This is one decision that only I can implement."

Marina, who had leaned back slightly to stare up at his face, snuggled into his arms, her bulging stomach pressed against his thighs. "Since I can't compel you I can only plead," she said quietly against his chest. "But I do want our child born unharmed."

"He will be, I promise you," Gold said tenderly, patting her on the shoulders and running a hand through the coarse black hair.

When they were three rotations from touchdown Ru-A-Lin called the chairman of the eradication committee and learned that the next ship was scheduled to leave in five days. That gave them enough time to check on the sun's contraction rate with ground-based instruments and stop the expedition if the reversal process had started. Gold formulated reason after reason why the expedition should depart even if the sun had stopped contracting, but knew none were strong enough to convince the *Hilt-Sil* leaders. The truth was that in saving the sun he had greatly lessened their own chances for returning home undetected.

Marina went into labour when they were eight hours from touchdown.

chapter 15

GOLD HEARD AN involuntary gasp of pain, and swung around to see Marina pushed back from her console and doubled forward. The host was strapped in his own console chair at the moment, and Gold took the chance that no activity would be required and hurried back to her. When the spasm passed he helped Marina to her feet and led her to a bed. She sat on the edge and stared up at him out of slightly shocked eyes. "Bad timing. Very bad. If only we could have landed first . . ."

"Are you sure this isn't a false labour pain?" Gold asked as he zipped down the cover and tucked her in.

"I've already had several of those; this is different." She curled up into a tight ball of pain as a second seizure hit, and Gold realized with dismay that they must be fairly close together.

There was nothing more he could do at the moment, and Gold hurried back to his console. Fortunately, nothing had happened in the external world. He seized the writing pad and scribbled to Ru-A-Lin that he felt badly and was going to lie down, then walked the host to the hammock and eased him into it as gently as possible. With a pillow tilting the head sharply forward the floor was almost horizontal again. One advantage the slow observatory had over the interstellar scouts was that the torus ring always maintained normal Bragair gravity in the living quarters. Leaving his own controls in neutral, Gold stopped at the autonomic console and lowered the metabolic rate before hurrying to Marina. He found her stretched out on one side, looking reasonably comfortable.

She smiled wanly on seeing his concern. "Another pain just passed, no worse than the other two. I think it will be a few hours before it comes."

Gold unzipped the cover long enough to examine her. He could find no discernible change, but had no previous experience by which to compare. For all he knew, cervical dilation could be well under way.

They still had a large quantity of one of the stronger tranquillizers. Gold prepared several doses and gave her one. Marina took it with a grateful smile, and lay staring at him for a few minutes before dozing off. She was awakened by another pain that caused her legs to jerk upward as she curled into a ball. When she was at ease again Gold returned to his console for an exterior check. After assuring himself that all was well—including activating the giant head long enough to nod a slow assent when Ru-A-Lin suddenly turned and asked if he was feeling better—Gold hurried back to Marina.

She dozed for several hours, awaking just as they were

nearing Bragair. Marina was over the first dizziness and cramps, and insisted on returning to her console long enough to check the host over carefully. Gold sat in his own chair and worked with her. Ru-A-Lin was busy at the controls, guiding them to a re-entry point directly above the landing field. They abruptly passed below the edge of the horizon and plunged into darkness. Gold glanced at the co-pilot's console screen, focused on the world below, and was not surprised to see only darkness. With no large concentrations of people and little exterior lighting, the *Hilt-Sil* were invisible to visitors using only visual scanning.

There was a sudden gasp in Gold's earphones. He turned quickly, to see Marina leaning forward in what was becoming a familiar posture. She was working nude. He hurried to her and assisted her back to the bed. The pains shaking her seemed more intense, and Gold hurriedly gave her a double dose of the tranquillizer. When it started to take effect, and Marina was able to straighten her legs again, she said, "Our child will be born soon now."

They were within a half-hour of landing. Gold hesitated wondering if he should attempt to persuade Ru-A-Lin to go down slowly and hope the baby would appear before he would be required to move the host. He decided it would be easier to continue playing ill and leave the body in the hammock for a time after landing, if he must.

Gold had washed his hands in a strong antiseptic solution before examining Marina earlier, since he had no rubber gloves. He washed again, hurriedly but carefully, hoping his sensitive stomach would not betray him if there was much blood during the delivery. He inspected Marina once more, and this time was able to detect a noticeable widening of the cervical passage. While Gold was attempting to see how many fingers he could get into the external os the bag of waters broke, wetting his hand and the bed.

Marina was bearing down hard with each return of the pains, gripping the edge of the bed with both hands, keeping her legs apart and knees up. The double dose of tranquillizer had taken effect, but it was only capable of lowering the pain to a bearable level. She was fully conscious and worked hard for several minutes, her breathing heavy. When Gold was certain that the foetus must have its head in the cervical canal he gently inserted his hand and tried to find the top of the skull. He touched the baby . . . and felt a thrill of horror when he found himself clasping the front of a tiny foot!

Something in his manner alerted Marina. "What is it?" she asked, alarmed.

"The baby; it's in the wrong position!" Gold said tautly, continuing to feel around the small member. It was alone, barely protruding into the distended vagina. And it meant disaster.

Gold pushed against the miniscule toes, and the foot moved slowly backward. Encouraged, he continued shoving until it abruptly popped back out of contact. "Now," Gold muttered, knowing what he must do, and said aloud, "I've got to try to turn the baby around. Somehow it's changed position until the feet are downward and the legs are sitting across the birth canal."

A fresh spasm of pain twisted Marina's face. "Can you do it?" she whispered, and when the pain eased added, "And will it harm the head?"

"I don't know. I've read the books, but it's a lot easier described than done." He moved his hands to her abdomen and started gently trying to force the small curled-up body to move. Now that the membranes holding the protective cushion of water had burst, he could more easily feel the shape of the foetus. The head was facing him, and upright. The small body would have to be turned until the face was to the interior with that large head down, leading the way into the birth canal.

Gold used a little more pressure, trying to push the head back and the feet up; the foetus did not move. He shoved harder, and Marina gasped with new pain. There was a yielding of the tissue beneath his hands, but no real movement. Gold tried again, and then once more, hearing the grunts of pain Marina could not suppress each time he exerted pressure. He saw that a fresh cover of sweat had appeared on her forehead; he could not detect any actual movement of the foetus. His efforts seemed useless.

Gold stopped, admitting defeat. In that position only an experienced obstretrician could turn the child without harming it or the mother. There was a possible way to save Marina, but he knew he could never force himself to use it. The native Hawaiians, before the arrival of the white man, solved such problems by allowing a small leg to extend into the open and cutting it off at the joint to the trunk. The other leg was then urged into the opening and cut off, and the legless body was relatively easy to deliver. If the cutting was performed soon enough the mother usually survived.

The bloody images of what he was thinking flashed through Gold's mind and he leaned forward, almost sick at the stomach. Fortunately his ability to visualize from imagination was much weaker than replay imagery, and lacked sharpness and clarity.

Marina realized that Gold had failed to move the baby. She caught one hand and pulled him forward until his face was above hers. "Gold! Now the choice is out of our hands! You must deliver this baby by section! You must!"

"It's too late for that!" Gold said almost angrily, unable to keep the desperation out of his voice. "Everything I've read said that a Caesarean should be performed before labour starts. The contractions may tear you apart if I try to operate now. You'd both die!"

"No! The baby won't die!" Marina said harshly. "Deliver it now, before there's any damage to the head. *You must!*"

"But it may kill you!" Gold almost shouted, dumbfounded.

Marina smiled through her pain. "The books have been wrong before. I'll live. Give me another dose of tranquillizer and cut."

Gold made one more effort to turn the baby; it was as futile as the others. Fate had boxed them in, and he had no choice but to admit that Marina was right. If either child or mother were to have a chance at life he had to operate . . . if he could.

Gold raised his head until he was staring into the small, set face, certain now that she would have her way. "Marina, I . . ." he stalled, wondering how to tell her that the sight of blood sickened him, that he had always been willing to risk death with machinery but that contact with injury or personal violence turned him into a quivering mass of jelly. He could not tell her of the technots whom he had saved from beatings because he did not want to be forced to watch. She would find it incredible that he could dodge automobiles on busy streets with equanimity, but even one small dog's vicious living snarl terrified him. He had never struck another person in anger, and had received only one beating in his life . . . and his memory had locked that one away for over twenty years! "Marina . . ." he tried again, and finally got out, "I don't think I can do it. I . . . can't take up a knife and cut someone, even to operate."

Marina caught his hand again, holding it in a grip that

hurt. "Gold, you must! There's a knife in the utensil drawer, behind the rack. I sharpened it on your shoe. Now get it!"

Gold rose to his feet and stumbled to the cabinet, where he found the knife. He stood holding it, staring at the clean sharp edge, knowing he could not possibly draw that shining steel across her stomach. But when she called he turned and hurried back to the bed, knife in hand.

Another spasm wracked the small woman's body, one so deep and prolonged Gold thought she would faint despite the drug. When the pain finally eased she whispered, "*Now, Gold! Now!*"

Gold fixed his eyes on the knife, shaking wildly in a hand that could barely hold it, and said helplessly, "I can't!"

Marina released her right-hand grip on the bed and grasped his wrist, physically forcing it down until the knife quivered only an inch above her abdomen. When he still made no effort to begin she exerted all her strength, pressing the sharp blade firmly against her skin. Gold's shaking hand did the rest; the razor edge penetrated in a short gash and a flow of blood appeared.

Gold jerked away, easily overcoming her pull, and turned his head just in time. The vomit boiled into his throat, choking him; it shot out of his mouth, spattering on the floor several feet away as he went into retching convulsions. There was a brief pause, and then a second spasm followed the first. This time he bent over, letting the bitter stream pour out and on to the dirty floor. The heaving continued until his stomach was empty and he could only retch dryly, gulping air and tasting acid and partially digested food.

When his guts stopped churning Gold turned back to Marina. There was an odd look on her pain-wracked face. Lurking beneath the surface was a trace of contempt, almost lost in a far stronger sense of compassion. Above all there was an iron determination, as implacable as death itself. She abruptly reached to the floor and offered Gold a container of water he had placed there for her earlier. He took it and stumbled to the tiny kitchen disposal, rinsing his mouth and spitting out the foul liquid.

As Gold straightened there was a change in the lighting in the room, as though a door had opened to a brighter exterior. And then a great booming voice that was nevertheless whispering filled the small compartment with sound.

"GOLD! RETURN TO MARINA AND BEGIN THE OPERATION! I WILL GUIDE YOUR HAND."

Gold whirled around as the voice stopped, looking through the open entryway into the autonomic control room and on to his console. The hinged cornea above it was open. As he watched, a glass tube as thick as his body entered and moved steadily toward him. It passed through both control rooms and entered the living quarters. When it was well inside, a lens in the end swivelled and focused on Marina.

Gold could see through the remaining open space in the round doorway. An enormous brown eye was peering into the opposite end of the optical tube.

"COME, GOLD, TO WORK. THERE WILL BE TIME FOR EXPLANATIONS LATER. I HAVE PLACED US IN A HOLDING ORBIT AND INFORMED THE GROUND THAT WE WILL NOT LAND FOR TWO MORE DAYS, WHILE WE PROCESS DATA. IF WE ARE TO SAVE MARINA'S LIFE YOU MUST HURRY."

Gold almost ran to the bed, placing himself on the opposite side from the tube. Marina, at first equally startled, had recovered faster. She smiled encouragingly and grasped his wrist again, and he realized he was still gripping the knife. She was bleeding from the first cut, but only slightly. "Is he going to tell you what to do?" she asked.

"Evidently the optical tube also contained an audio pick-up; Ru-A-Lin heard her. "I HAVE DIRECTED THIS OPERATION TWICE BEFORE, AND BOTH WERE SUCCESSFUL," he boomed out in *Hilt-Sil.* Gold hastily translated for Marina; he had known Ru-A-Lin understood English, but not this thoroughly. "BOTH BABIES DIED LATER FROM OTHER CAUSES. NOW WE MUST BEGIN; EVERY MOMENT OF DELAY WEAKENS MARINA."

The giant medic directed Gold to determine the baby's exact position, and he hastily felt over the hidden form and relayed the information. Evidently the huge lens was providing Ru-A-Lin a clear picture of the operating area. He instructed Gold to make a light incision, parallel to the old one but slightly toward the centre of the abdomen, starting just beneath the baby's chin.

Gold placed the sharp edge against Marina's stomach and drew it across the taut skin in a short smooth cut. She gasped with the new pain, then clenched her jaws tightly together. His hand was unexpectedly steady, but when blood gushed from the new wound he had to pause while dry heaves wracked his body. There was no further sound from Marina.

Ru-A-Lin was watching closely. "GOOD; NOW REPEAT

THE SAME CUT UNTIL THE SKIN PARTS OVER THE MEMBRANE."

Gold positioned the knife again, this time staring at the steadily bleeding line without effect on his stomach. He drew the edge lightly down the same cut, watching a fresh wave of blood form as the blade sliced through the last of the skin. Ru-A-Lin started speaking almost constantly, guiding him every step of the way. Gold extended the incision, learning how much pressure to apply without cutting into the membrane beneath. Ru-A-Lin stopped him when he judged the planned cut long enough, and Gold returned to the area when he had felt a vacancy, just below the baby's chin. With a light pressure on the blade he penetrated into the membrane, pressed slightly harder, and found himself cutting into fluid. He drew the blade downward, carefully parting the membrane without penetrating beneath, and a flood of blood and uterine fluid poured over his hands and on to the bed. When he reached the bottom of the incision the flow eased; Gold was staring at two small knees.

Ru-A-Lin saw them also. The tiny form was incredibly slippery, but Gold managed to gently grasp each knee and move it upward until the little foot appeared at the bottom of the incision. When both were outside he held them in one hand and pulled steadily. The smooth wet form slid through the opening and suddenly the baby was free in Gold's hand, the placenta still dangling from the small belly. He saw tiny but perfect genitals; it was a boy.

Gold laid the baby by Marina's side long enough to pick up the knife again, and cut and tied the umbilical cord. Ru-A-Lin urged him to hurry. He lifted the infant by the heels with one hand and smacked it sharply on the bottom. There was no response. Ru-A-Lin told him to check the mouth. Gold forced a finger between the tiny lips and found a plug of some mucous material. He pulled it out, and some bloody water immediately ran from the nose. Gold spanked the red bottom again, and the baby gasped, shivered, and gave a thin bleating cry. More fluid ran from the nose. The infant started breathing in little gasps. Gold cradled it in his arms and the breathing deepened and grew more regular. And then the infant started crying in earnest.

"HE CAN SURVIVE NOW: WRAP HIM WARMLY AND ATTEND TO MARINA," directed Ru-A-Lin.

Gold laid the small form by Marina and covered it up

to the tiny arms with the bedclothes; it continued crying. He turned back to the small woman, now almost unconscious. The afterbirth was loose, and he lifted the slimy, bloody tube out of her body, amazed to find no more reaction in his stomach than if he had been handling a pink rubber hose. She was still bleeding, but the flow had eased.

Marina stirred and opened her eyes. "The needle and thread are in my drawer," she whispered, nodding to the anchored cabinet that contained their clothes.

Gold found the needle and hurried back. Fresh blood continued to ooze from the incisions, but this no longer bothered him. Marina had lost what seemed an enormous quantity, but he was unable to judge if this was normal in a Caesarean, or too much for her to bear. He started sewing.

Marina did not even twitch as the needle penetrated. Gold drew the edges of the membrane precisely together and tied the suture. He started another, and Ru-A-Lin asked if he were making it as close as possible to the first one. Gold worked as quickly as his large but nimble fingers permitted, keeping each stitch small. The membrane was slack in his hands, and he had no difficulty sewing it from end to end. He tucked the folds of tissue inside and started immediately on the skin.

Ru-A-Lin was watching without comment. Gold felt Marina stirring and lifted his gaze, to see that she had slipped one arm around her son. The overlarge head rested just beneath her chin. With the top of a blanket she was wiping the worst of the blood and water off its face. The infant was still whimpering slightly but no longer crying, snuggled in apparent contentment against his mother's side. Gold saw by the swelling in the parietal area and the width of the small forehead that their son had inherited the dominant *Homo superior* brain, just as Marina had predicted. And the baby appeared normal and healthy.

Gold returned to his sewing, working slowly but steadily. The bleeding had almost stopped. When he finished at last he suffered from a sudden fatigue reaction, his hands shaking uncontrollably. Ru-A-Lin suggested he give Marina another dose of tranquillizer and let her rest. When his trembling eased he brought it to her. She smiled as she drank it down, a drowsy smile of love and gratitude. Gold unzipped the cover of his bed and moved first the baby and then Marina, leaving the wet and bloody sheets on hers for later. She dozed off almost immediately, and at last there was time to pause and assess the changed situation.

As though sensing his thoughts, Ru-A-Lin withdrew the large optical tube that had served them both so well. "I BELIEVE YOU HAVE QUESTIONS TO ASK. COME TO THE DOORWAY; I WILL HEAR IF YOU SHOUT, AND IT WILL BE MUCH FASTER THAN WRITING."

Slowly Gold followed the tube, climbing outside and standing on the bony rim of the eyesocket. Ru-A-Lin was sitting on the next hammock, smiling slightly.

"AND SO AT LAST WE MEET FACE-TO-FACE, LITTLE FRIEND." He was obviously speaking as softly as he could, but the sound still seemed terribly loud to Gold. "YES, I CALL YOU FRIEND, FOR OUR SHARED TASK HAS MADE US THAT, THOUGH IT IS NOT A FRIENDSHIP DESTINED TO LAST."

"How long have you known about us?" shouted Gold. The *Hilt-Sil* words were strange and difficult for his throat, but understandable.

"SINCE THE FIRST NIGHT AFTER YOU SHARED YOUR INTEREST IN ASTRONOMY WITH ME. I COULD NOT ACCEPT A DAMAGED BRAIN HAVING RECOVERED SO WELL. BECAUSE YOU HAD ALWAYS FOUGHT A CLOSE EXAMINATION OF YOUR HEAD I ASKED LEET-A TO HELP, WAITED UNTIL YOU WERE ASLEEP THAT NIGHT, AND EXAMINED IT WITH A TISSUE PENETRATING DEVICE I HAD IN MY AIRCAR. I DID NOT TELL LEET-A WHAT I SAW, WHICH WAS THAT SOAM-A-TANE WAS TRULY DEAD. INSTEAD I PLACED A SMALL DEVICE WE MEDICS USE FOR INTERNAL SOUND AMPLIFICATION IN THE SKULL ABOVE YOUR LIVING QUARTERS. THE RECEIVER IS IN MY EAR, AND I HAVE MONITORED YOUR CONVERSATION SINCE THAT NIGHT."

"Then the next question is obvious. Why did you keep quiet and choose to help us?" called Gold.

Ru-A-Lin looked grave. "THAT IS A DIFFICULT QUESTION, LITTLE FRIEND. INITIALLY I SOUGHT A WAY TO SOFTEN THE BLOW TO LEET-A. THEN I BECAME INTERESTED IN YOUR STUDIES AND BEGAN WONDERING IF YOU COULD POSSIBLY BE DOING SIGNIFICANT WORK. FINALLY, I DECIDED TO LET THE MASQUERADE CONTINUE, BOTH TO SEE IF YOU WERE RIGHT AND TO STUDY TWO SMALL PEOPLE ACTING AS FREE AGENTS. TO MAKE THE

SUPPOSED RECOVERY PLAUSIBLE, I SUGGESTED THAT YOU HAD BECOME AN 'IDIOT SAVANT' IN ASTRONOMY."

"Why did you reveal yourself to save Marina and the baby?"

"BECAUSE I HAVE GROWN ATTACHED TO YOU BOTH; BECAUSE ALL YOUR PEOPLE WILL HAVE THE BETTER BRAIN YOU POSSESS IN A FEW GENERATIONS, AND PERHAPS IT WILL THEN BE POSSIBLE FOR YOU TO JOIN THE INTERSTELLAR COMMUNITY; BECAUSE AFTER YOUR MATURITY ARRIVES, HUMAN AND *HILT-SIL* MAY BECOME FRIENDS."

"Our descendants may benefit," Gold shouted. "But we short-lived people always have an overriding concern with our own lives, which brings us to the next question. What do you intend to do with us now?"

The giant lips curved into a smile. Ru-A-Lin asked "WHAT DO YOU WANT ME TO DO?"

Gold made a final check of the contents in his improvised pack. Some of the items were equally improvised, such as the diapers Marina had fashioned out of old clothes several weeks ago. The medicine that Ru-A-Lin had given them was stored in plastic bottles. There was a strong drug that would fortify Marina's weakened body against the strain of prolonged high acceleration. It lay against the remainder of the bottle of purple gell Gold had already spread along the incision in her belly. The material held the edges of the wound, already healing, immovably together, and could only be dissolved by a chemical catalyst in another container. There was a small amount of concentrated food, and some of the tools and kitchen implements Gold felt would be most useful while hiding aboard the interstellar ship.

Gold slipped on the pack and turned around. The baby whimpered and Marina murmured soothing words. She sat up in bed, unzipped her one-piece suit, and pushed the cloth back from one swollen breast. She no longer wore a brassière. The baby took the nipple immediately and began to suckle, making small contented noises. Marina's smile was the most beautiful expression Gold had seen on a human face.

There was a gentle bump as the observatory touched ground for the first time in almost nine months. Gold hurried to his console chair and looked out. Ru-A-Lin was deactivating the flying systems. His last action was to open the door leading to the outside. Through it Gold could see the front of the building, which was open. The first faint greyness of morning was breaking through the woods at the edge of the field. There was a familiar shape looming darkly against the lighter background of fading night. It was the shuttle, due to lift off for rendezvous with the interstellar ship shortly after dawn.

A flying box settled gently to the ground outside.

"You had better hurry," Ru-A-Lin turned and said to the host, which Gold had sitting in the co-pilot's chair.

Gold got the body to its feet and then made it kneel and lie flat on the floor, on its stomach. With the head turned hard to the left the right eye was only an easy jump above the metal deck. Marina had moved to join him, standing on what had been the side wall of the false eyeball. The baby was asleep.

Gold twisted the knob that opened the right eye to the maximum. He hesitated—this had not been discussed with Ru-A-Lin—and then climbed back to the autonomic control room and Marina's console. He reached for the knob that controlled the activity rate, unlocked the safety strap that prevented it moving into an area marked in red, and twisted it all the way off. That rheostat supplied power for a variety of functions, including the heart pacemaker. There was a shudder throughout the great form, a mild trembling that seemed to start in the chest and spread outward in convulsive waves. And then the host relaxed and grew still. Gold almost heard that last heartbeat that meant the captured body had finally surrendered its simulated life.

Gold hurried back to Marina and unfastened the latch on the transparent cornea. He attempted to push outward and felt panic when the swinging panel barely yielded; the eyelid had partially closed when the body died. He pushed harder, holding the pressure steady, and the round edge slowly moved outward, abruptly breaking free and lifting. Gold stepped through and on to the base of the eye socket, then jumped six feet to the deck. Marina came out and handed the baby down to him. Gold held it with one arm and caught Marina around the knees with the other, lowering her gently to the floor. She was still in no condition to be dropping more than her own length to unyielding metal.

A gigantic finger came down from the sky and pushed

the cornea closed. A shiny instrument with a sharp point followed, and re-latched it.

"I THINK IT BEST YOUR VISIT TO BRAGAIR REMAIN A SECRET FOR NOW, GOLD," the booming whisper said from what seemed a mile away. "WHEN OUR INSTRUMENTS VERIFY THAT OUR LARGE FRIENDS IN THE SUN HAVE STARTED THE REVERSAL PROCESS I WILL TELL THE FULL STORY. BY THEN YOU WILL BE NEARLY HOME. DESTROY THE THIRD MAGNETIC GENERATOR EXACTLY AS I HAVE INDICATED AND A MARS LANDING WILL BE REQUIRED FOR REPAIR AND REPLACEMENT. YOU CAN RADIO EARTH FOR RESCUE WHEN THE CREW HAS LEFT. AND YOU SHOULD HAVE NO DIFFICULTY RENDERING THE CURRENT BIOLOGICAL ATTACK HARMLESS, IN CASE THEY CHOOSE TO CONTINUE WITH IT AFTER THE LANDING. AND NOW I THINK YOU HAD BEST GET BEHIND THE DOOR, FOR I HEAR LEET-A COMING. MY SMALL FRIENDS . . . GOOD-BYE."

Gold heard the still deep but definitely female voice himself, and realized they had lingered too long. He scooped Marina up in his arms and ran for the door, darting behind it just as the giant female entered. She would have seen him if she had not had her gaze high, seeking Soam-A-Tane. But Leet-A saw Ru-A-Lin kneeling on the floor by her husband, uttered a strangled cry, and hurried to them.

Gold, still carrying Marina, stepped around the door and fled for the outside. The observatory had no airlock, and the first step of the wooden framework Leet-A had pushed against the door was closed. He was out to the edge in seconds, and then saw that the riser was far too high to permit a safe jump, each step having a vertical separation of over thirty feet. He ran for the edge, where both risers and flats attached to a steeply sloping side member. Gold looked down the length of wood; there were three steps and it was over a hundred feet to the ground. The angle was so severe he was not certain he could keep his footing, but there was no other way. Gingerly he walked out on the slope and started down. Behind him he heard a rising wail of anguish.

It was impossible to move swiftly. At every step gravity threatened to tear loose his weak attachment by friction, throwing all three of them into a slide that would kill when they went off the end. He heard more noises behind his back, but ignored them until he stood safely at the bottom edge. It was still a ten-foot drop to the ground, but as usual the *Hilt-Sil* had left the vegetable life alone and there was a thick clump of waist-high bush just beneath. Gold jumped, landing with his legs bent to minimize the shock to Marina. She was unhurt, but the baby awoke and began to cry.

Leet-A was also crying, and there was little danger of the child's thin wail being heard. Gold started running, lightly carrying his burden of woman and child. He had thought of Leet-A when he reached for that activity knob to kill the host. She would grieve long and hard, but it was best Soam-A-Tane finish the dying he had begun almost four Earth years before. With his imitation of life over, Leet-A and Ru-A-Lin would be free to express the affection they had obviously developed for each other.

Gold made it to the hangar door and out into the cool morning, where a scented breeze played softly across his face. Marina, a light burden, clung to his neck, and he thought of the strong young giant in the moral tale who had carried his beloved through the frozen night. His task was considerably easier; he had only to reach the shuttle a quarter-mile away. There they would hide in an equipment box with padded walls which Ru-A-Lin had told him would be carried aboard the larger ship.

The slower rotation of Bragair kept the sunrise gradual, and it was only a little less grey than when they had landed. In the distance Gold saw the lights of an approaching flyer; behind it was another. The crew of the interstellar ship was arriving, and though they would be delayed by the death of Soam-A-Tane, he had only a few minutes to get inside the shuttle.

Gold started across the open ground, running swiftly through the slowly lightening shadows, Marina cradled in his arms. He saw that she was petting and soothing the baby, who had almost stopped crying. Gold's breath was coming hard, but he held to a steady pace and after a moment got his second wind. He stepped up his speed, running lightly and easily toward the huge black ship that loomed sleek and graceful in the dimness. Gold, a man, was taking his mate and child home.